Joan Livieri, an avid reader, also enjoys golf and baseball. Writing is her passion, allowing her characters to travel wherever her imagination takes them, whether by horse or by jet. Joan also dedicates time to feeding stray animals that pass by. She travels at leisure, with no hurried plans. *The Missing Duke* is her latest published book and her aim in writing is to bring smiles to her readers through her characters' situations.

This is for Catherine living in Florida: My Sister #4 – Thank you for your encouragement.

And in Memory of Sister #1 – Sylvia
Sister #2 – Helen
Sister #3 – Irene
Sister #5 – Evelyne

From Sister #6 – We sisters did not always agree, but sisterly love prevailed.

Joan Livieri

THE RELUCTANT IMPOSTER

AUSTIN MACAULEY PUBLISHERS®

LONDON * CAMBRIDGE * NEW YORK * SHARJAH

Ordering Information
Quantity sales: Special discounts are available on quantity purchases by corporations, associations, and others. For details, contact the publisher at the address below.

Publisher's Cataloging-in-Publication data
Livieri, Joan
The Reluctant Imposter

ISBN 9798891556485 (Paperback)
ISBN 9798891556492 (ePub e-book)

Library of Congress Control Number: 2024914503

www.austinmacauley.com/us

First Published 2024
Austin Macauley Publishers LLC
40 Wall Street, 33rd Floor, Suite 3302
New York, NY 10005
USA

mail-usa@austinmacauley.com
+1 (646) 5125767

Chapter One

March 1820, London

Lady Agatha Landry and Miss Wilhelmina Thaylor, seeking a bit of privacy in Countess Benton's ballroom, weren't completely concealed behind an overly huge fern.

An auburn curl slipped, and Miss Thaylor automatically pushed it behind her ear. "My stomach is in knots, Aggie. I can't. I can't do it. It's insane!" She hurriedly added, "I know, I know I promised, but…"

Agatha gripped Wilhelmina's arm, squeezing it through their sleeved satin gloves, her mouth holding a smile while her whispering voice bemoaned, "You promised. Willie, you gave me your word. James and I are counting on you."

The crystal chandelier candles warmed the ballroom; still, Wilhelmina shivered and whispered, "There must be another way."

"There isn't!" She pressured her hold, "Grandmother and her friend, Lady Julia Barclay, made this plan a while back that I visit Seahurst, believing the Earl and I, without the hum of London, will become better acquainted, culminating into a marriage proposal. I don't remember meeting Lady Julia, and I just couldn't explain to Grandmother why it will not happen." Softly whining and now pinching Wilhelmina's glove, Agatha's tone turned spiteful. "You promised! Are you going back on your word?"

Ignoring her friend's insult, Wilhelmina tried again, "Aggie, why not go and visit with Lady Julia to please Grandmother Marlowe? And then, you can cry off. If the Earl arrives before you are able to leave, knowing neither of you have any interest in each other, you can honestly say that you must be away as you have an important obligation. Traveling with Bernice gives you solid backing as you know Bernice will do almost anything you ask of her. It will only delay you and James a week or so."

Wilhelmina heard Agatha's whine become shrill. "You promised to help us. It has to be *now*." Her fingers dug into Wilhelmina's arm. "You've got to!

Our plans are set, and we have the ship willing to take us. We need those few days you'll be at Seahurst as *me* giving us time to be far away." She dropped her hand from Wilhelmina's arm and turned toward the approaching smiling man, uttering her last plea, "Please, Willie."

"I believe this is our dance, Lady Agatha," Lord Jonathon Restin, Earl of Ventry, brazenly winked, offered a slight bow, and held out his bended arm.

Lady Agatha Landry rejoined, flashing one of her favored smiles. "Really, my lord, do you think for one minute I may have forgotten?"

"It crossed my mind," he teased.

Agatha did not want to dance. She needed Lord Restin's help without his being wise to her plan. "My lord, you haven't met my dear friend, Miss Thaylor, and leaving her alone does not seem the thing. Do you suppose Lord Barclay may keep her company? You were just with him, and he appears to be free; not dancing."

Wilhelmina needed to discourage Aggies's suggestion, as she was going to have to deal with the Earl when exposed a fraud. Taking in Lord Restin's smooth manner, his good looks, blond hair and umber gleaming eyes, she said, "Please, if you don't mind, my lord, I'd rather not." Smothering her distress at Aggie for putting her in this situation, Wilhelmina wanted to step on Aggies's toes. She turned and lightly scolded, "Your concern goes too far. I'm fine."

Lu will be furious if I tag this person on his arm. Burying a deep chuckle, Lord Restin nodded and said, "Of course; very thoughtful of you, my lady. If you will, ladies," he winged both arms, "we'll have Lord Barclay join us." He peered at Miss Thaylor, waiting for her to take his arm. *I can tell she doesn't wear bonnets. Her sun-kissed rosy outdoor look with its mass of auburn waves and those dewy green eyes is trying to appear uninterested. She's not petite and is definitely well equipped. No jewels, though her gown is good quality but void of fluff. Oh Lu, she's definitely not your style. I wonder if this is her performance to lure Lu.* Lord Restin choked back a laugh that wanted to explode. *This duty dance with Agatha is the last of the evening for me, and then Lu and I will leave. Lu will threaten to kill me, I just know it.* Lord Restin's eyes glimmered with mischief.

Jonathan was now determined, especially when Lady Agatha's friend feigning disinterest to dance with the most sought-after wealthy Earl. *It'll be interesting to see how she thinks to maneuver herself around Lu.* Smothering a grin, he said, "Nonsense. Do come along."

Rather than make a scene, narrowing her eyes, Wilhelmina barely touched Lord Restin's arm, and with no more than ten steps, was presented to the cold, unsmiling, but very handsome Earl of Grenmoor. His frown augmented the thin scar above his eyebrow, adding a daring to even approach the man. Wilhelmina could feel his dark eyes give her a quick scan and sensed bored indifference. His bearing carried a dignity rarely seen or felt—it matched his facial features. His dark eyes missed nothing. A straight nose, tightened jaws and a mouth that remained sealed. His black evening wear aligned well with his demeanor.

"Lu," grinning, Lord Restin intoned, "May I present my new acquaintance, Miss Thaylor? Of course you've met Lady Agatha. Ladies… Lord Barclay."

Agatha made her curtsy while Wilhelmina, staring at the brusque man with dark frosty eyes, made a minimal curtsy and now understood Aggies's determination to elope with the man she loved.

The Earl of Grenmoor barely nodded, no smile, his tone lofty, and said, "Ladies, good evening," and while looking at Jonathan, "And why aren't you dancing, Johnny?"

His voice sober, though his eyes twinkled, Lord Restin answered, "I knew you were without a partner, Lu, and knowing you enjoy the waltz and because Miss Thaylor has an opening on her card, I knew you would be pleased to have one last dance this evening."

Lord Lucien Barclay knew his friend was doing this to annoy him and enjoying every moment. He'd take care of him later. Without another word, no smile, no gracious words, he said, "Of course." He winged his arm, expecting Miss Thaylor to grasp it.

Jonathan and Agatha had already moved away, but Wilhelmina wasn't going to be a pigeon and dance with someone that had no wish to be her partner. Not moving but looking up into his arctic dark eyes, she said in a soft but clearly level tone, "Thank you, my lord, but as neither of us wish to dance, it would be best if you walk me to the other side of the dance floor, and I'll make my exit."

Issuing an order to me. Lord Barclay found it humorous, but no one would know. His tone not accepting a refusal, ordered, "I think not, Miss Thaylor. We shall waltz. You do know how, do you not?"

Upset with Aggie and resenting the Earl's arrogance, she purposely twisted her gloved fingers together while not looking up at him, timidly answered, "I… I think so."

Great… I'll get you for this, Johnny. Without another word, Lord Lucien Barclay, the most desired Earl of the *ton*, led untitled Miss Wilhelmina Thaylor onto the dance floor as every mother stared and wished it was her daughter on the Earl's arm.

Lucien's steps were smooth, while Wilhelmina's were light. She followed his every move. Resenting that she toyed with him, Lucien pulled her a bit closer, and they twirled around the ballroom. Wilhelmina kept in step. No matter what step or turn the Earl made, Wilhelmina was right there, not missing a beat or a step.

Lord Barclay eyed his waltzing partner's rosy coloring and intense verdant green eyes that were looking right back at him without a blink as she followed his every lead. And auburn curl loosened, and she seemed not to care. Incensed that she led him to believe she could not waltz, he moved her round and round, secretly appreciating the daring she portrayed. *No doubt she knows the waltz— why pretend? Oh, to gain my attention—this is a new unexpected ploy. Let's see how you do, Miss…* and pulled her closer, so close that he began enjoying her unidentified fragrance.

Resentment bloomed a little more as he put more force in his steps, spinning her round and bringing her back into his arms. It seemed as if the orchestra followed his determination as it increased the waltz's tempo and then slowly turned it back to smooth, rounded steps. When it ended, both the Earl and Wilhelmina were surprised as they were the only two on the ballroom dance floor.

Shaken and embarrassed, but not willing to let anyone know, she looked up at the man whose demeanor was not warm, and she knew that instant that he did not like being on display. Not smiling, though the gleam in her eyes gave her away, she looked up into his glacial expression and in her coolest voice, said, "You do waltz very well, my lord."

The Earl of Grenmoor, not liking to be on view, secretly savored their waltz—it being the best dancing for him in a long while. He took in her gibe and her audacity to mock him. Knowing they were standing alone in the middle of the ballroom, he gently clasped her arm, bent his head as if whispering something nice, and instead said, "You have a fiery character. I suggest you curb it for your future personal benefit." Anxious to be away, he escorted his dancing partner to meet with Johnny and Miss Agatha. He saw that Johnny's grin alone could have brightened the ballroom with no need for chandeliers.

The orchestra started, and though words were tossed here and there, it meant nothing to either Lord Barclay or Wilhelmina. She just wanted to be away from being under scrutiny and leave.

The Earl's arrogance at his utmost level, he issued, "Thank you for the waltz, Miss."

His haughty noticeable boredom irked Wilhelmina, and without thought, she said with a light trace of her own arrogance, "Thaylor, my lord. I'm Miss *Thaylor*." She looked up into his icy demeanor, and again, didn't blink.

Lord Barclay's tone was brisk, yet Wilhelmina didn't miss the corner of his mouth turn up as he nodded and then said, "Please accept my apology, Miss *Thaylor*." Not waiting for a response, he turned to his friend. "I'm ready to leave. Coming with me?"

Grinning, Lord Resin said, "Of course." He turned to the ladies. "It's been interesting." He bowed, winked and followed his friend.

"Oh, Willie… I couldn't believe it. You and Lord Barclay; why, you'll be the talk of the *town,* and no one will pay attention that James and I are gone. Tell me truly," her voice filled with awe, "did you like dancing with him? You both looked so determined. And then only you and Lord Barclay were waltzing; everyone stopped to watch. Oh, Willie, it was really something." She sighed, "It was beautiful."

Exasperated, Wilhelmina grabbed her friend's hand and moved so no one could overhear them. "Do you realize I've just made a fool of myself? And that arrogant man had the effrontery to lecture me!"

"Oh, you do go on, Willie; you have no idea how lucky you are. Don't you know that dancing with the Earl of Grenmoor is a wish of every lady and mothers with daughters making their come-out?"

"I don't like the Earl, Aggie. We are in serious trouble."

"You worry too much, Willie. You will cover as *me* for a day or two, and it will not be a problem that you're making it. Think, once *he* knows it's you and I'm not there, all will be forgotten." Then Aggie had the temerity to insult her friend who was doing her this disgraceful favor, adding, "Willie," she giggled, "imagine *you* as the Countess of Grenmoor?"

"Aggie, look at me." Shame ricocheted up one side and down the other side of Wilhelmina's whole being as she tried pleading again. "What about your grandmother and Lady Julia Barclay?"

"We've been over that, Willie; do not fret so. You gave me your word, and I'm holding you to it." She moved to walk away, her tone untroubled. "Let's enjoy some refreshment."

How could I have stupidly agreed? Wilhelmina Thaylor's face flushed with ire matching her red hair and her voice taut. "Aggie, I'm leaving; come with me or not."

"Oh, all right, but really, Willie, you've changed; you're only thinking of yourself."

Wilhelmina Thaylor swallowed her retort. *I gave you my word and I'll keep it… for now.*

Chapter Two

Outskirts of London, Late March

The Duchess of Northland languished upon the soft down bed without cover—her nakedness hoping to persuade the Earl of Grenmoor not to leave. She purred, "Lucien, darling, why not stay with me for the rest of the day? I promise, you shan't regret the delay."

Lord Barclay did not reply but continued to don his supremely tailored clothes. His physically fit tall frame enhanced lean strength added to the draw he surprisingly drew with the women he bedded. His good, strong facial features were offset by dark, clear icy gray eyes. His velvet black hair tied back at his nape matched his slanting eyebrows adding to the coolness of his character. He had a heart that was not exhibited, and it was believed he lacked sensitivity.

She continued, "Really, why the rush? You're rich and titled. You own a solid portion of London including Seahurst Manor—way out in nowhere land—and you can come and go as you please, so why the rush to go there?" Then she rose up on an elbow, teasing, "Oh, I know why. You're going to shop for a bride." She laughed, "In Cornwall, no less."

Silence from the Earl of Grenmoor as his brow creased, she knew she overstepped. Tension filled as she tried to lighten her words. "Well, my lord, an heir is a must. It is expected of any titled noble."

Lucien reached for his coat. He looked down at the Duchess, his tone without feeling. "You go too far, Maggie. What I do and don't do is none of your affair. However, just so you do know, marriage is not for me, so do not spread any tidbits about me shopping for a bride. I'll have the whole *ton* on me. I warn you; don't go there."

She stood quickly, not pulling the sheet for cover. She had to make amends and reached for Lord Barclay's hand.

He took a step away, but it didn't stop the Duchess from speaking as she ran her tongue over her lips, her tone cloying. "You know, you are the only man that satisfies me. I swear to you that if it were possible, I would leave that old, old man that I was forced to marry and belong only to you."

Lucien had heard enough. He knew the Duke of Northland, being infirm and disoriented from old age, was still highly regarded, and it was well known that good old Harrold denied his Duchess nothing.

"Enough, Maggie. Your charms are well-known."

She scrambled for the coverlet to cover her nakedness. Her lips thinned. "How dare you chastise me when you have just bedded a duke's wife! You are a scoundrel, Lucien. I am sorry I ever agreed to come to this inn with you. And don't you ever call me by that atrocious name, *Maggie*, again. You make me sound like a country strumpet, and I resent that."

He wanted to be away from this room, especially Maggie. Irritated with himself for accepting this rendezvous, knowing she was tenacious in wanting her way, he had to end it now with no repeats.

"Your diatribe grates on me, *Duchess*." He brushed something from his sleeve. "You know, *Maggie* is a very fitting portrayal for you. Shall we leave it at that?" He moved toward the door, turned and said, "May I remind you that I am here with you because of your audacious invitation and my overindulgence of drink?"

"How dare you!"

He returned to her bedside as she sat down. She looked up, hoping for a change of heart from the handsome wealthy lord; instead, he reached and gently raised her chin using his thumb and fore finger, his voice chilled with deceptive calm. "Your Grace, thank you for the night of pleasure. I have left two extra gold pieces." Dropping his hand, he turned to leave.

"You are insulting, Lucien," she shouted. She searched for the gold and threw them at him, but the door had already closed.

Chapter Three

Early April, Seahurst Manor, Cornwall

Lord Lucien William Barclay, the Earl of Grenmoor, entered the sitting room in the East Wing quarters belonging to his grandmother, knowing its special inviting warmth came not from the flickering gold-red flames but from the room's occupant.

He knew his Grandy would be dressed in her usual long-sleeved black dress with her favorite cameo brooch pinned near her left shoulder. Her feather-white hair would be lightly pulled back and held in place with onyx combs. And she would be sitting in her well-padded chair alongside the huge oak table laden with ledgers and papers. The fireplace in close proximity distilled the chill from the room to her exact liking.

The Earl walked directly to his grandmother. Before saying a word, he bent and kissed her creased cheek. His dark eyes vividly warmed, and a wide smile appeared. It would be rare for anyone to see the Earl's tender emotions thus exposed. He then lifted her small, veined hand and peppered it with a soft kiss. He winked and pulled a chair closer to her. "Hello, dear Grandy. Here I am," he raised his right eyebrow, a sign of agitation, "as you commanded."

Dowager Lady Julia Barclay noticed his raven hair with a few white strands, an inherited family trait. She held deep fondness for her only grandson and didn't miss the irony in his last words. Knowing well the profound feelings they held for each other, it did not cause her to be affected by his barbed tone. Regardless, she feigned resentment. "I did not order you to come, grandson. I merely had Jaggers request that you visit with me at your convenience. Cannot your valet," she stopped a minute, remembering his name, "Crooks, that is—get my message straight?"

Lucien held back a grin that wanted to leak. "Come, now; surely it is without question I observe your sway over me."

"Don't trifle with me," she scolded.

Lucien smiled, and its warmth reached his eyes. "Tsk, tsk, Grandy, tell me. What is this truly about? Do not upset yourself, whatever it will be resolved."

"Don't patronize me, Lucien." Eying him, she chided, "You have the audacity to laugh!"

Lucien's mouth, exposing his perfectly white even teeth, couldn't help but chuckle. His eyes twinkled as he took hold of her small, veined hands. "You are dearest to me and I'm very happy to be with you. Now, tell me."

Lady Julia didn't hesitate; in fact, she made it sound vital. "No doubt you've ridden Zephr and toured every spot enhancing your lifestyle and gallivanting at full pace with Jonathan at your heels. It's time you take responsibility as I need your attention here at Seahurst."

I wonder if Grandy feels neglected or is perhaps lonely. Using Johnny as a pretext isn't like her. "Come now, my lady; you know I take care of the needs of this estate and its lands." He raised his right brow, another Barclay trait. "And I am always at your beck and call. Forgive me for my neglect."

"Of course," she rejoined. "I may command, but you will do as you please, just as you always have." She couldn't help but smile. "You obey my wishes only when it suits you. Think not that I am not on to your tricks."

Lucien did not reply but walked toward the long, narrow window, staring out at the gray cloudy sky matching his unsettled temperament. He hesitated for a moment and then charged, "Grandy, if you are thinking to use my friendship with Johnny as my not being attentive, I apologize, though you know well that is preposterous. However," his tone turned caustic, "Grandy, hear me well. If we are meeting to discuss this absurd and idiotic arrangement you've made with your friend, Lady Edith Marlowe," he came and stood before her, looking down into her silver eyes, "I resent your intrusion and find it offensive. My decision if and when to marry is *mine* and off-limits to you. I forbid you to consider, think, arrange, or be party to matching me with your choice of a future Grenmoor countess."

Lady Julia recognized his stubbornness; after all, he had inherited it from her. They both abhorred falsehoods and fakery. Honor and dignity were something they never practiced—there was no need, for they lived it every day as natural as breathing. Neither could tolerate dishonesty, and it was on that basis that she versed him of her plan to aid in selecting her future granddaughter and mother of her wanted great grandchildren.

"Lucien, listen… please. Edith and I have been friends since we were small, and we trust each other implicitly. Trust me; it is in your best interest for you give consideration to really get to know her granddaughter, Lady Agatha Landry. She's a fine young lady and will be an acceptable wife and give you an heir. Is that so wrong?"

"Stop right there, Grandmother!"

The cold edge in his tone told her he was angry; especially when he called her *Grandmother*, there was no amount of reasoning with him.

Lucien Barclay, the Earl of Grenmoor, stood unmoving—the muscle in his jaw tightened from controlling his temper as he spoke slowly with inflexible firmness through gritted teeth. "If and when I decide to wed, it will be my decision and only mine. You will not, nor will anyone else select a bride for me." Without an iota of change in his demeanor, he eyed the one person he held deep affection for, but not this minute. "Grandmother, I will not be tied to a sniveling, self-centered, simple-minded female in order to provide an heir. Is that abundantly clear?" His bold, cavalier mood left no room for negotiations.

Aware of her grandson's temper and a bit apprehensive, she still would not be discouraged. Her voice soft and pleading, she said "Lucien, I am not suggesting you must marry Lady Agatha. Just spend some time with her and see if she's possibly right for you. You will see she is nothing as you described. This will be a time to get to know one another, and perhaps, it will work. An heir to the Barclay line is an inherent prerequisite, and time waits for no one."

The Earl's reply was blistering. "You think to tell me what my duty is to this family? How dare you, Grandmother!" He said not another word and went to her book table, where she kept an ornate silver tray with his favorite brandy and poured a generous amount and swallowed. Then he spoke, hostility unmistakable, "Extolling a person's virtues that you don't even know?" His laugh was unpleasant. "Madam, you amaze me."

Lady Julia leaned forward, her left arm resting on the chair's arm while she pointed her finger at Lucien. "Listen to me," her voice held mild emphasis, "I expect you to demonstrate Barclay graciousness when she arrives." Softening her tone, she added, "I know I can depend on you, Lucien."

He walked to stand before his grandmother. "Just what exactly do you mean *when she arrives?*"

Lady Julia didn't hesitate. "She's traveling this minute to visit with us."

Lucien slammed his flat hand loudly upon her stack of ledgers, "You're saying she is on her way to Seahurst?" Any apology he might have extended to his grandmother vanished. "I will not be here. I will not debate this further, Madam. The subject is closed permanently. As for your visitor, you arranged this—you welcome her to Seahurst. I wish you a most amiable holiday." He moved to sit near the fireplace facing the dowager. His voice more tolerant, he asked, "Now, is there anything regarding Seahurst that we need to discuss?"

The dowager's silver eyes darkened. "Yes, it is about Seahurst. I am getting too old to continue handling this place. It's become a bit of a burden," she fibbed.

Lucien threw back his head and laughed. "Don't give me that, Grandy. Managing this estate is what is keeping you decades young." Adding teasing sarcasm, he continued, "Besides, you are a busybody, so whatever else would you do with your time if you were not in charge of things here?"

"Don't be impertinent." She was without anger. "You are exasperating."

Lucien went over to his grandmother and knelt on one knee. "Dearest Grandy, I do appreciate your tending to matters on my behalf. After all," he winked, "women are not educated to handle the importance of estates and property. Women are just to be charming, sweet, boring and above all… biddable."

Shaking her finger at him, she said, "If you were not so grown, I would have paddled you for your cheekiness."

It was betwixt them that she was much wiser than others that had been in charge of Barclay's holdings. The present Earl of Grenmoor being exceptionally wise and proficient in all that signified. "You have done well, grandson; you were so young when the fire changed our lives. I'm proud of you."

The Earl of Grenmoor stood again at the window, silhouetted against the afternoon light. His fine tailored clothes worn comfortably snug without a single crease revealed his lean torso. He turned back to his grandmother and spoke forthrightly, "Because you have arranged for this young lady to travel all this way to Cornwall, I've decided to accept Johnny's invite to sail to France and perhaps spend some time in Italy."

He heard his grandmother gasp. "Really, Lucien, that is beneath contemptible. Surely you can spare a day or two?"

The Earl did not raise his voice, but he did raise his right brow. "Do not question my character; it is in very good stead. As for this silly-minded female that will travel for days in the hunt of a husband," he sneered, "now, I find *that* contemptible."

"So, going off with Lord Restin is the answer. He is nothing more than a two-and-thirty gallivanting rakehell."

"I suggest, Madam, that you remember, Johnny is my friend as well as an honest person. I trust him with my life. And I know that you are aware of his good qualities." He noticed his granny's hands gripping the arms of her chair; a sure sign she was agitated, but he would not give in. "Johnny does not drink all that much; that rumor has always floated about him." Lucien grinned, "And he doesn't mind in the least, but the truth is, he does like the company of ladies."

"Lucien," she lightly admonished, "must I remind you that you are a Barclay? Gallivanting! Carousing!" The old woman's knuckles whitened from her strong grip. "The two of you going off and doing who knows what."

Lucien's laughter flooded the huge room. "Why, Grandy, I do believe you are envious." He held up his hand to stop her from speaking. "Don't say nay, Grandy. You would give anything to have the freedom of coming and going and not adhere to society's guidelines." Grinning, he sympathized, "Women are curtailed with their freedom, *but* it is essential as they must not—what did you call it? Go *carousing*?"

"Oh, have it your way. I will not argue this issue with you."

"I knew it, I knew it." He went and kissed her forehead. "You have veiled desires."

Lady Julia shook her head as she buried a smile. "May I ask a favor of you?"

He raised his right brow.

"Don't be so suspicious, for heaven's sake. All I'm asking is that you not be gone too long."

"Why?"

Using her best casual tone, she said, "I'm thinking that I might decide to visit London rather than remain here during this winter. It will be necessary to set things in order."

He studied her eyes. "When did all this come about? You've always chosen to remain in Seahurst Manor and avoid London's season with all its rituals."

Her eyes were telling as they gleamed and matched the turning of the corners of her mouth. "Grandmother, I'm warning you."

"Do not threaten me for even one second. I may as well tell you that Edith and I will entertain a soiree, just a small gathering, and we would like you and Jonathan to join us, please."

He picked up one of her heavy ledgers and slammed it on the tabletop as though it was a newspaper. "Old woman, do you not listen?" Lucien's infrequent violent temper raged—bouncing off the windowpanes. "I tell you now and I will not repeat this, so hear me well and heed my words—I will not marry Lady Agatha. I have met her, and she is definitely not for me, and to have Lady Edith encouraging her granddaughter to be part of this absurdity is unconscionable. What plans you have in progress, you best cancel. As for this estate, get someone to help you. When I return, I'll relieve you of your obligations. Now, I am leaving!" There was no warm goodbye or tender kiss. He strode across the room with dispatch, not looking back and slamming the big oak door as only a powerful man could.

The waves crashed against the rocky cliffs, but Lady Julia heard only silence that permeated the room; even the logs no longer sparked. It was as if the silence patterned itself after the heavy gray mist surrounding everywhere outside—oppressive and soundless.

Still, it did not deter the white-haired woman's campaign; unruffled by her grandson's outburst, she would not give up, for she knew she was right. The Earl of Grenmoor must marry. If she must initiate a betrothal to gain an heir, so be it. For that was exactly what she would do.

Chapter Four

April, Traveling to Cornwall

The thick, silent mist hung in the afternoon air without a scintilla of breeze from the sea to move its dampness across the rough-rocky landscape. Stone houses along the way were shuttered to keep the cold from entering with smoking chimneys to ward off nature's blessing of dank gloom and chills.

The dusty black coach and four entered the orderly village of Penwyn. The coachman handled the reins with ease as the horses halted at Six Bells Inn's stoned walkway.

The corpulent hostler recognized those magnificent horses, even though no coat of arms appeared on the carriage. Still, he knew he was being graced with quality and could barely contain the avarice mounting inside of him—mentally surmising the gold that would fill his coffer.

One of the footmen sprung from his perch and immediately set the step before opening the finely crafted door.

A thin, stooped, black coated elderly man stepped out; his tall hat clamped low on his forehead. "I'm *Mister* Wiggins," he spoke in a superior-snobbish tone, "We are traveling to Seahurst Manor. We will have your best rooms and your best food to be served directly. We shall depart early on the morrow. Make haste, so we may rest without hindrance."

The next to step out and down was a small, colorless older woman, dressed completely in black with a heavy black shawl covering her head and shoulders. She squinted and looked about and then turned her attention to the interior of the coach.

Wiggins hastened forward to take the hand of the next emerging veiled woman lavishly attired in a fur-lined blue cloak and matching fur-trimmed hat with its heavy dark veil screening her face. He did not offer to help the other passenger, but the footman was quick to help her alight. Her cloak with only a fur collar, though not as resplendent, was of fine cashmere quality. Her rust-colored bonnet with its heavy veil also concealed her looks.

Anxious to escape the chill and dampness, the hostler held the door for them to enter. They were pleased to find Six Bells clean and inviting, especially after their last brief stop at an unkempt inn. The heavy odor of wood smoke pervaded the large square room, yet it was not offensive. A huge cauldron hung close in the fireplace that covered the back wall. All the cooking was conspicuously done over the fire in this main room at a long scrubbed worktable. A roasting pig was being hand-turned on a spit over coals by a scrawny boy using both his hands to do his work. He stared at the unexpected arrivals, though his mitten hands continued cranking the iron handle.

They were ushered to their rooms, and hot water was provided to wash the dust away. And soon, food was served to them. The three women ate together.

Wiggins dined alone.

Later, Mr. Wiggins stood in the hall and announced in his testy voice, "This will be the last stop before we reach Grenmoor land and arrive at Seahurst Manor. Rest well, for we will depart at dawn."

The elderly woman came to the door and nodded. "Thank you, Mr. Wiggins. All will be ready." She closed the door and listened to the two young women; unbeknownst to them, she was aware of their clandestine plan.

Wilhelmina began rubbing her arms as though chilled, and said in a disquiet voice, "Aggie, I know I agreed to be part of this charade, but it is so wrong. Please, will you let me take back my promise? I don't know what I was thinking."

"Willie," she insisted, wanting her way as usual, "you have to do this." Grabbing her friend's arm, she said, "You are our only hope. You've met Lord Barclay; surely you can't expect me to give up James for him?"

Torn, Wilhelmina argued, "But this is deceitful, and think of the hurt and scandal—its repercussions. Oh Aggie, I shouldn't have caved and given you my word."

"But you did, and you always keep your word. You can't quit on me now." Aggie shook her head, letting her blond hair fall in all directions. "Just think, Willie, I'm going to be James's wife, and we'll have you to thank." Oblivious as to the damage and hurt she would cause, Aggie went on, "And James and I will never forget you and remember, you will always have a home with us."

Knowing she'd have her way, Aggie giggled, "By the way, do you think Lord Barclay really is a philanderer?"

"This is serious." Wilhelmina Thaylor did not like herself at this moment. *Grandmother Marlowe took me into her family when my father died and gave me a wonderful life with Aggie; insisting I also call her Grandmother; giving me her love and support, and now, I'm going to hurt her and so many other people.* Panic gnawed and a knot seemed to strangle her breathing. *I can't do this.*

"Stop whispering," the older woman semi-scolded, "So you are two really going to do it?"

Both girls' mouths fell open. Finally, Wilhelmina gasped, "You know? How? I'm so sorry."

Bernice, Agatha's governess and now serving as companion, said with conviction, "I know my little Lady Agatha. She can't do anything that I don't know about, and I'll always be with her to protect her."

Wilhelmina expelled an audible breath, "You are going to go with Aggie, aren't you?"

"I must, Miss Wilhelmina. I gave Lady Marlowe my word. She's known of Lady Agatha's secret, and for reasons of her own, she would not interfere."

Raw torment gnawed in Wilhelmina. *Grandmother used me to help her granddaughter. Now it is clear why she insisted I live with her—it was to watch over Aggie. I owe Lady Marlowe this debt and will see this through. When it's finished, I will never again become a liar for anyone.* Swallowing air into her clogged throat and upset at playing a fraud, Wilhelmina reached to wrap herself in the coverlet on the end of the bed to hide her trembling.

Bernice tried to ease the guilt of Lady Marlowe's first-born granddaughter, Wilhelmina. *The child doesn't know, and I can't tell.* "This will work. I've told Wiggins you are ailing, and I will stay behind to tend you. You and Agatha will exchange clothes. In the morning, Wilhelmina, you will be dressed in Agatha's clothes and depart for Seahurst. Keeping the veil in place and your hair tightly bound, no one will suspect a thing."

Wilhelmina still felt shame on her part when pretending to be Agatha to the Dowager Countess of Grenmoor. When Lord Barclay would see her, he might remember dancing with her and mocking him just a bit; her insides knotted to match the strangled feeling that wouldn't go away.

Bernice reminded Agatha, "Wilhelmina will take your trunk and you will take hers; best you switch what you want to keep. I'll help."

Bernice held an envelope; handing it to the pretender, she gently said, "This letter is for Lady Julia Barclay from Lady Marlowe. Give it to her when you arrive. I don't know for sure, but I think it will ease your stay."

"Why?" Tears hung on Wilhelmina's long lashes. "If Grandmother knows this, why the subterfuge? Why?"

Bernice hesitated and then reached for Wilhelmina's hand as she softly admitted, "Because Agatha is with child, and they must marry and not cause a scandal. Lady Marlowe wants her granddaughter to be happy, and if this is what they want, she'll help them."

Wilhelmina's mouth gapped wide as she felt betrayed. "Aggie, are you pregnant? Why didn't you tell me?"

The blond, excited-about-getting-her-way, not-thinking-of-anyone-but-herself, tweaked, "You are so self-righteous, Willie. I'm not like you. This is mine and James's secret. How Bernice knows," she glared at her, "well, she's always nosy about whatever I do."

"Enough!" scolded Bernice. "Get ready. Wear plenty of warm clothes, child; the night air is cold and damp. We leave at midnight." Looking over at Wilhelmina, her voice softened. "As Wiggins is to see the safety of Lady Agatha Landry to Seahurst Manor, he will care not that I will stay with ailing Miss Thaylor. I have this note you are to give him in the morning, explaining he is to go on. Don't pay the old goat any mind. He thinks highly of himself and will do his duty. Just keep your veil down and make sure your hair remains hidden. He'll never know." She unexpectedly hugged Wilhelmina, "Take care as best you can. We know we can trust you. You can do this, Wilhelmina; there is deep goodness inside of you."

The chimes from the clock below stairs began to strike, and abrupt silence hung like the mist outside. There would be no turning back when they took this step. They would not see each other for a long time. No one said a word. The clock no longer chimed.

Tears rolled down Wilhelmina's cheeks as she embraced her friend and then moved to embrace the older woman. She choked, "Godspeed."

Putting their fingers to their lips, they stealthily entered the darkened hall. Wilhelmina followed, standing subdued, watching as the two women made their way soundlessly down the narrow stairwell and moved out of sight.

Returning to their room, she leaned against the glass to barely see a shadow emerge from across the way and meet her traveling companions. She saw the shadow lift the trunk being hauled by both women and then watched as they slipped away into the night.

It was now up to her. Wilhelmina sickened over her part, yet knowing she had to give Aggie the time needed to reach Channel Isle and meet James. *To have agreed to this outrageous fraud, how can I do this to good well-meant people? What am I doing?* Humiliation along with desperation infusing every part of her mind, she leaped for the chamber pot and emptied the contents in her stomach. She rinsed her mouth and went to lie down—shame being her blanket.

Chapter Five

Seahurst Manor, Early Evening

Gray skies with rain and wind assailed the coach as it crossed onto Grenmoor land, matching Wilhelmina's nerves as her gloved fingers gripped together. Looking out, she saw gloom and felt doom filling her insides, building more turmoil moving her fear to shame. *Why did I ever promise to help Aggie?*

Mr. Wiggins spoke only once, telling her that he'd be contented to have this duty completed and return to civilization, and then nodded off.

Forcing small breaths to help hide her faltering composure, her mortification doubled over her capitulation to join in with this farce. *What am I doing?* When they approached Seahurst Manor, tremors of a terror took over, and fear, as she'd never before encountered, raced through her; she gripped a hanger for support while her body faltered. Choking back sobs that clogged her throat, she didn't like herself. *Aggie, never again will I agree to go against all I believe. Not for you or anyone.* Little did Wilhelmina know what was ahead of her.

The manor's dark gray stone exterior seemed overpowering. It was as if it knew that a fraud was entering and should bolt its doors.

The reception area was cold and uninviting. The wall sconces were burning with candles almost at the end of their wicks, adding to the gloom. An aging butler greeted them in a stoical manner. "Welcome to Seahurst Manor."

Wiggins spoke with his usual air of self-importance, "Advise the Earl of Grenmoor that I have arrived. Mr. Jasper Wiggins from the office of Sir Richard Dysart. My charge, Lady Agatha Marlowe Landry, is here as requested."

The old butler looked upon the old man and in a disfavored tone, said, "Sir, I was informed there would be three persons with you."

Wiggins rudely blustered, "Never mind them; one became ill—they will be arriving in a day or two." He scowled, "Please announce my arrival."

The old butler replied, "The Earl is not presently in residence. You are to go to the dining hall for a repast and return to London directly. Fresh horses are available."

He then turned his attention to the veiled lady dressed in blue, and the butler's tone softened. "My lady, please follow Tessie. She will show you to your private rooms."

Wilhelmina nodded. "Thank you."

"My name is Jaggers, my lady. If you should need anything, just tell Tessie."

Doing her best to bury her anxiety, Wilhelmina spoke with assurance. "I have a letter for Lady Julia Barclay. Will you please see it is delivered to Her Ladyship?"

"Of course." *There is gentleness in her—she hasn't lifted her veil. I wonder why.* Taking the missive, he turned to Wiggins, "This way, please."

"Mr. Wiggins," Wilhelmina called, "thank you for seeing me safely here."

He looked back and said, "I was only following orders."

Wilhelmina would not miss him.

Wilhelmina followed Tessie up the darkened, wide, curved stairway. The young maid carried the heavy candelabra as high as she was able to, to light their way.

At the top of the landing, Tessie turned left, confronting a long, dreary corridor with Wilhelmina's footsteps echoing off the oak flooring.

An oppressive silence adding to the tension gnawed in Wilhelmina's throat, making it difficult to speak as she followed the young maid. As Tessie slowed and stopped before a sculptured arched door, Wilhelmina finally asked, "Are any of the other rooms occupied?"

Tessie, ten-and-five years, excited to be relieved from kitchen duties to look after Seahurst's guest, obediently answered, "No, my lady, not that I know. I understand that the Earl's rooms are in the other direction—he has all the other side." Suddenly worried she over spoke, she quickly added, "Begging your pardon, my lady; it is what I hear. It's Crooks, the Earl's valet that manages His Lordship's things. I have never served on this floor until now." Tessie was taught that serving the manor's nobility was a great privilege, and she wanted to be as helpful as possible. "But the Earl is not here." She stopped short as she was repeating kitchen gossip. Embarrassed over her eagerness to be helpful, she muttered, "I mean that is what I hear below stairs."

Wilhelmina nervously smiled, wanting to assure the young maid there was no upset, all the while breathing a silent sigh of relief. At least she would not have to immediately confront the Earl, and perhaps, she would be gone before his return.

Entering the room, Wilhelmina was momentarily speechless. Burning logs blazed and she walked quickly to the hearth enveloping its warmth. She dropped Addie's fur muff on a chair and removed her hat and veil.

The young maid gasped and hurriedly explained, "Oh, my lady, your hair, it is so bonny. Its color is different."

Wilhelmina smiled, "Thank you."

"Is there anything I may do for your comfort, my lady?"

"Yes, do you think I may have some bath water?"

"Oh, forgive me." Tessie rushed across the large room and opened a door that led through a dressing room and into another room that held a massive copper tub setup upon a wide platform. In one corner were other necessities needed for daily ablutions. One brightly lit sconce and a small burning fireplace lit this unusual room. A cauldron filled with water sat on the narrow hearth, ready and waiting.

Wilhelmina stood amazed as the maid told her how two other maids kept the fire going and water ready for use. "There is a side door for them to enter without going through your private rooms. Just pull this cord, and they will prepare your bath. I can do it for you if you wish."

"This is so clever!" Wilhelmina exclaimed. "Yes, thank you, Tessie. I do wish to rid this travel dirt off me."

Freshened from a warm bath, wearing Aggies's corded blue robe, Wilhelmina was wholly numbed. She moved from a small table, having eaten very little of a lavish supper. Filled with guilt over this shabby masquerade, her nerves ran the length of her body; even her toes were not spared. Her brain would not quiet; she could feel it ready to advance and pound, giving her headache it's just due.

Opening the window and staring out into the darkness, she instantly smelled cold, salty air. It invaded the room's warmth along with chilling her wet hair; she pulled the sash shut. *It seems blustery out there—just as it will be when I meet with Lady Julia Barclay, whenever that will be.*

Tessie knocked and entered to stoke the fire and remove the tray. "My lady, Jaggers said to inform you that Lady Barclay will meet with you in the morn when the clock strikes eleven."

Wilhelmina choked back a gasp. *Now the truth will come out. Oh Aggie, I hope you and James have enough time to make that boat.* "Thank you, Tessie."

"Is there anything else, my lady?"

Wilhelmina wanted to scream that she was not a lady of nobility—just a plain Miss. *I'm a fraud... a liar... and will bring distress to all connected to this charade while Aggie is safe and away. I'm ashamed, and if I'm thrown out of Seahurst, it is justly so.* She wanted to ask the maid if she knew when the Earl was expected to return, but only Jaggers would be more knowledgeable, and she'd never ask him. "I'm well, thank you, Tessie. Will I see you in the morn?"

"I believe so, my lady."

"Eight o'clock, then."

Taken by surprise at the early hour, Tessie couldn't help but ask, "But is that not too early?"

Wilhelmina laughed—her laughter coming across as cheerful. "Not at all! My favorite time of the day is dawn." She smothered a yawn. "Because of my long journey, this day, I shall rest a bit longer in the morn. I usually rise with the sun."

"I doubt if you will see the sun, my lady; lately, our days have been unusually cloudy."

"Not to worry. I'll enjoy this new venture. Tessie, if possible, I prefer coffee rather than tea in the morning."

Tessie was again surprised, because everyone knew that dark, bitter coffee was His Lordship's preferred morning drink; never tea. The maid wondered how this lady could also stand the taste; below stairs, it was tasted and voted bitter. Tessie said, "I'll see to it, my lady."

Knowing the chaos she was responsible for causing and the disgrace she agreed to perpetuate, Wilhelmina never thought she'd be able to sleep. Pulling the thick but soft cover over her, stretching on the exceptionally soft bed, she lay, worrying. *How to explain this deception? How could I have agreed to be part of it?* The warmth from the cover and glow from the coals soon lulled her into an unexpected deep sleep.

Chapter Six

The Next Morning
The Letter

Dowager Countess Julia Barclay, grasping the letter from her dear friend, Edith Marlowe, was visibly shaking; the pages wrinkled as her veined fingers squeezed the pages. A chill filled her as well as shock and then suffused into indignation.

Staring at the blazing fire yet not feeling its warmth she straightened the letter and again begin to read.

Dearest Julia,

This is a strange letter that I write. You will be stunned, and I apologize. The young lady that delivered this letter is not Agatha, my granddaughter. Agatha and her companion are on their way to meet and marry the father of the child Agatha is carrying. I have condoned her secret as I want her to be happy. Her mother did not have that option. You see, the person who is claiming to be Agatha is my first granddaughter, Wilhelmina Thaylor, otherwise known as Willie. She is the daughter of our vicar and my Karen. Henry refused to let them marry, and later, Henry married Karen off to the Duke of Rainstone. Karen bore the Duke a daughter, Agatha. Karen fell ill and died. Not having a son, the Duke had no interest in a daughter, and at my behest, gave Agatha to me to raise. Meanwhile, the vicar and his housekeeper raised his and Karen's daughter as an abandoned baby. Years later, the housekeeper died, and the vicar allowed Willie the freedom of living without a caregiver. When the vicar died, and with Henry gone, it gave me the opportunity to take Willie as my ward and insist she call me 'Grandmother', like Agatha. They are eighteen months apart in age. I must admit, she's wiser than Agatha and takes interests in everything. The vicar instructed Willie in reading, mathematics and history. She loves animals and rides as if born on a saddle. I'm smiling; Julia, as she rides astride, and I've not discouraged it as she promised to ride clandestinely on our estate. Oh Julia, she's so unlike tons of socialite daughters—she's knowledgeable, polite, yet has wit and will not be talked down to. She fought doing this favor for Agatha, but her loyalty to Agatha won out when they both concluded that the Earl of Grenmoor would not want Agatha as his bride. Forgive me for being blunt, but I'm telling you their reasoning. Willie does not know about Agatha's being pregnant, though by now, I'm sure she's been told. They do not know they are half-sisters. I could not tell them without explaining Willie's birth. So, Julia, I know not how Willie will handle her part in this, but somehow, I know that she will capture your heart as she has mine. Send Willie back to me soonest, and perhaps, in time, I can unwrap a part of my heart that has been sealed for a long time and explain the love that made her. I'm sorry our plans with your grandson won't transpire. It just wasn't meant to be. I hope you still plan on coming to London. I look forward to your visit. I miss you, dear friend.

Fondly, Edith.

Lady Barclay sat disquieted, unable to come to terms with this complicated muddle thrust upon her. Making a fist, she hit the arm of her chair. *That mendacious visitor accepting my hospitality using preposterous lies—well, we'll just see about that.* Then she thought about her friend carrying this burden for years and never letting a word slip. *Edith, I do understand your dismay and loyalty, but I will not condone what is going on.*

Sitting back in her chair, she laid the letter next to her ledgers and then leaned her head in the palm of her hand, thinking of Lucien. Gradually, as her silver eyes watched the flames and her heartbeat slowed—*all right, Grandson, Lady Agatha is out; we'll do it your way. Choose your bride, only don't take too long, or I'll have no choice but to help you.*

Looking at the ormolu clock on the mantle, she saw it was nearing eleven. *This will be interesting.* Her anger having subsided, she was now looking forward to confronting the scheming impostor. *This will be a change from the tedium of my daily tasks of caring for Seahurst. It may be amusing. This Willie person must think she is quite an actress. I'll send her on her way in due time; however, I will not go against Edith's wishes. It is well that Lucien is away.*

A knock on the door interrupted her thoughts. Jaggers opened the door, not waiting for His Ladyship's acknowledgement. Serving her these many years, they had an understanding.

Lady Julia watched the impostor walk into the room with her head high, though her eyes gave her away as they couldn't disguise fear enveloping nervous tension. Julia took in the dark blue woolen gown with fitted sleeves and a white lace collar contrasting with her auburn hair combed back and pinned. Rounded breasts filled the top of her dress, influencing an effect to her small waist. She wore only a light underskirt and moved unobtrusively with each step. Tiny silver earrings were her only decoration. She curtseyed, "Good morn, Lady Barclay."

There is a tremor in her voice she is trying to hide. I would think so. "Welcome to Seahurst Manor, Lady Agatha," she offered a thin smile, and her words lacked warmth.

"Thank you, my lady." Wilhelmina, wanting to blurt the truth but having promised Aggie to give her the needed extra day, said nothing.

"Are you comfortable? You have been served well, I'm sure."

"Oh yes, my lady. Thank you."

"Come, *Agatha*," the dowager politely voiced, "sit across from me and tell me about your journey. Too, what transpires in London. It has been long since I was there."

Wilhelmina sat on the edge of the chair, unable to relax. Her stomach clenched tight, unable to look the dowager in the eye. Her hands folded in her lap with her fingers twisted together, looked toward the window, the same window that Lord Barclay stared out of in disgust. *Oh please—I can't throw up; I shouldn't have eaten.*

Evidently, the dowager thought, *this impostor is not as good an actress as she thought.*

Tightening her fingers, Wilhelmina took a perceptible deep breath. "Traveling to Cornwall surprised me—the change from fields to rocky landscapes, and then seeing the churning sea through the mist, and then, suddenly, the sun peeked through the clouds, and the water changed color right before my eyes." Without thought, with the excitement of her experiences, a smile materialized. It wasn't a practiced one—very natural—and not missed by the dowager.

Wilhelmina continued, "The sun turned the sea blue and green, but with clouds blocking the sun through the mist, it turned gray with white crests topping the waves as they rolled in." She stopped short, feeling dismay at her part in playing this deception on this gracious lady. *I so want to confess. But I promised.* Biting her lip, she continued, "About London," the animation in her voice changed, "I suppose Cornwall is much like London with foggy days with its mist seemingly hanging in the air like a screen. One must be attentive to navigate through it." Wilhelmina turned and looked at Lady Barclay. "Forgive me; I have a habit of going on when I discover new things as I haven't traveled to many new places."

Lady Julia knew the impostor's descriptions of Cornwall were near true. *Let's see how you handle this next question.* "How is my good friend Edith, Lady Marlowe?"

Here, Wilhelmina replied without a nerve as she loved Agatha's grandmother. Her green eyes warmed into a shine, her voice turned to a gentle softness. "Lady Marlowe is well. I enjoy any amount of time I spend with her. She has a wonderful teasing humor, and it is a joy to be in her company. You probably know she's diligent about her roses and has taught me a lot about gardening, but she says that I don't have a green thumb." An unexpected giggle burst. "Lady Marlowe said it would be best if I tramp about her stable and not in her gardens."

The vivacious unpretentiousness of this impostor did not go unnoticed. Also quite noticeable was that the young woman erred as she did not refer to Edith as *Grandmother.* "Really? Would you truly prefer horses over roses?"

The auburn-haired girl beamed without knowing. "I have a great love for horses. Some say I communicate with them. That may be because I recognize not only their strength but their beauty, and that each has their own distinct personality." Realizing she may have gone on too long, she said, "Forgive me, Lady Barclay. I forget myself when talking about horses."

The devotion expressed toward her friend Edith by her unknowing granddaughter was sincere and said without thought. A twinge of envy tweaked in Lady Julia. Too, as this fraud unabashedly expressed love for those beautiful four-legged beasts that Lady Julia, too, revered, was making it impossible to dislike her entirely. *I'll delay exposing you. Let's see how far you will take this lie. I haven't forgotten that Agatha's eyes were blue as sapphires while your green eyes change in color and sparkle if what you are saying is of real interest to you.*

Lost in thought, the room was silent except for the crackling logs. Wilhelmina didn't know what to do next. She finally nerved up, "Excuse me, Lady Barclay?"

"Yes?" She stared at Wilhelmina.

"My father was the vicar in our hamlet, and he raised me to always offer to help if I could. Is there anything that I may do for you while I am visiting?"

Lady Julia realized this pretender had again given herself away. *If she were Agatha, then her father would not be a vicar. I'll let this pass for now.* "There is nothing. But thank you, Agatha. You may leave now. We will have tea later."

Shaken by the tone and instant dismissal, Wilhelmina wanted nothing more than to tell the truth, but she could not; not yet. Standing, she curtseyed and was about to leave when Lady Julia offered to call Jaggers to help her find her way.

"Would you mind if I wandered about the grounds? May I visit your stable?"

The older woman's voice tempered at the simple request. "You are welcome to do so, but April is cold and damp. If you venture out, do dress warm, and be careful not to become lost in the belt of trees that surround the manor."

Wilhelmina's warm smile did not go unnoticed by the suspicious dowager. "Thank you, my lady. I'll discover a lot about this misty weather. Exploring Seahurst is a gift I did not expect."

She continued with her voice carrying a degree of possibility, "My lady, if you could spare some time, I would like very much to hear of Seahurst history and all about Cornwall. It appears the weather is totally in control. I mean," she blushed, "I mean, traveling here, the sky was constantly busy. Sun, rain, mist and blowing wind as the elements seem to meet and collide, separate and return, demanding to be the one in charge and all within moments of each other. One wonders what will come about next," she shook her head lightly, "and Seahurst is right in its midst."

Intrigued over the portrayal of Cornwall's environments, Lady Julia asked, "You find this foreign, do you?"

"Oh yes. I am used to London and its usual surroundings. If it rains, perhaps it will be for the day, mixing in a deep fog; or if the sun shines, it goes on for days; nothing like the instant changes here. Cornwall has a lure all its own."

Unknown to Wilhelmina, Lady Julia loved talking about Cornwall's history and its people. "You are welcome to explore, but keep in mind the weather you just described. Our weather is a mixture of everything God can send us. It varies in temperature from mile to mile. In fact, at times, terrifying winds will carry the sea's salt spray upward to ten miles inland."

Totally engrossed, Wilhelmina returned to the hearth and said, "The Cornish people must be very hearty to endure the constant weather shifts."

Lady Julia, enjoying the conversation and giving this interesting pretender a pass for now, said, "I have ascertained from our family diaries that the Cornish are proud of their independence from being largely on their own and deeply rooted in their beliefs. Sometimes, they are hard to understand with their own language fashioned from past generations over centuries."

Wilhelmina, without thinking, dropped into a chair to listen to Lady Barclay, resting her elbows on her knees and her chin in her palms, anxious to hear more history.

Lady Julie noticed the unladylike position, yet the impostor seemed unfazed. Enjoying the conversation about her beloved Seahurst, she went on. "When you explore, you will see the rear of the manor has been sheltered from the fury winds and sea. It had to be built near a low hill with rows of trees surrounding it, known as the belt. That is what I referred to when I warned about getting lost. The manor faces east and southeast. Those were the unchangeable instructions laid down from the Cornish craftsmen who built the first part of Seahurst Manor. Living here for generations, they knew the weather as a foe and accustomed to its daily changes." She paused; a frown appeared. *What am I doing? I'm going on as if this were a welcoming guest.* Looking at Wilhelmina, she said, "Agatha, I must end this discussion. Join me this eve for supper."

This charade must end. I can't go on like this. I'm going to confess all tonight. And I won't fault this lovely lady when she has Jaggers toss me out into the Cornwell weather. "Thank you, Lady Barclay. I truly enjoyed hearing about Seahurst. I look forward to this evening."

"Seven o'clock, then."

Noticing the sudden change in the Lady Barclay's demeanor and knowing she was dismissed, Wilhelmina rose, curtseyed, and departed through the very same huge oak door that Lord Barclay had slammed, though when she left, she pulled it closed without a sound.

* * *

They shared an evening meal with little conversation. Lady Barclay spoke few words, and Wilhelmina answered but conversed little. Wilhelmina barely ate, the lump in her throat choking; there was no way she could enjoy roast squab with herbed vegetables and a raspberry tart drizzled with minted cream. Terrified having to confess to the plot to mislead Lady Barclay, her hands trembled. Unable to stop them except to grip the napkin on her lap, Wilhelmina carefully sipped some wine for courage. Finally, Lady Julia stood, and not saying a word, they left the dining room.

Firelight along with lighted sconces emanated a calm setting in Lady Julia's drawing room, but there was no peace in Wilhelmina.

Disgusted with this ruse, the dowager had enough. "Lady Agatha," an edge in her tone, "I am not willing to…"

Interrupting and looking directly at Lady Barclay while taking a deep breath, Wilhelmina stood straight; desperate for courage, she said, "Excuse me, my Lady. I have something I must tell you. I have wanted to explain sooner but I had given my word." Wilhelmina's fragile voice was shaky as her green eyes carried humiliation, though she never blinked, and continued to keep eye contact. "Until now, I have been unable to confess taking advantage of your goodness… you see, I am not deserving of it."

The dowager raised her right eyebrow just as Lucien often did when skepticism entered his mind. *Could it be that she is bothered by this folly she is playing? Edith is right; she is likable; however, my tolerance for this skullduggery is over. I'll see how far she goes before I expose her.* "What's troubling you, Agatha? Is it that the Earl is not here to spend time with you?"

Wilhelmina's legs wobbled, and she quickly sat on the edge of a big chair. *It's probably the Earl's,* she thought and leaned toward Lady Barclay. *Enough of being a coward, Willie,* she scolded herself, *tell the truth and face your shame.*

"Oh, no, no. In fact, I am glad the Earl is not here." Keeping her hands knotted together, she sat with her back straight, and her voice intense yet clear, she confessed, "I am not Agatha, Lady Marlowe's granddaughter. I am a fraud,

36

an impostor, and have been accepting your kindness and hospitality to fulfill a promise I stupidly agreed to without considering these wounding consequences to others. You see," she appealed, "once I gave my word, I couldn't retract it. I am so very sorry." Wilhelmina blinked as shame darkened the green in her eyes as they glistened with unshed tears.

Lady Julia said not a word, watching Wilhelmina's features playing as her jaw visibly pulled across her cheek and an auburn curl loosened while nervously gripping her fingers so that her knuckles whitened while still not allowing a tear to fall.

"I am deeply sorry, Lady Barclay." Her expression was intense as her cheeks colored, almost matching the color of her auburn hair.

I have to credit her for not looking away. She has courage.

"I regret having taken advantage of your good will, my lady. Truly, I do. I know that I will have disappointed Lady Marlowe after all the goodness she has extended to me. Still, I agreed to this pretense to help my friend." Inner torment gnawed at her. "I must explain. The real Agatha pleaded for my help to be with the man she loves, and it was difficult to say no." Wilhelmina nervously rubbed her arms. "I tried to discourage Aggie, but having given my word, she wouldn't release me from it. It was stupid, but worse than this deceit is losing trust—that my word will no longer have value. Aggie and I have involved innocent people, and it can't be undone. She is gone, and I'll take our punishment."

"All of this because of love? Does it give you the right to engage in this unconscionable hoax on innocent persons?"

Wilhelmina turned, gazing at the fire for a few seconds and then turned back to the dowager. Shaking her head no as well as answering, she said, "No, my lady, this deception has no merit, and never once did we conceive it as a funny ploy. We have hurt innocent people. I am wrong to have participated but having given my word and Aggie not willing to allow me to break it, I am here. It is not for me to say that one should choose love over an arrangement." Her eyes turned wistful in the fire's light along with her voice. "I remember when I was about seven," a tear formed but did not fall, "it was late, and I woke and found my father sitting in front of the fire with only hot coals. The room was chilly, and his head lay back with tears on his cheek. All he said was that sometimes, sadness builds and tears help sadness leave for a while. I asked him why he was sad, and he said he believed the lady left me as a gift for him, and there was no doubt it broke her heart. He wished he could have had a say in her arrangement. I didn't know exactly what he meant but as I thought about it, I think my mother wasn't able to choose love and had to give me away, and somehow, the vicar knew." Whispering as she placed her hand over her heart, "I'm glad she gave me to the vicar," her tone strengthened and she added, "Too, maybe love had no part in my being. I don't know. Still, I do believe *it* is important, and that's why I caved to help Aggie." Tears hung on her lashes as she cleared her throat, willing the lump to go away. "Lady Barclay, if you will permit me to stay one more night, I will leave in the morning. I am truly sorry. I beg your forgiveness, though I can understand your refusing me." Wilhelmina's lashes held a bank of tears, and she knew if she blinked, they would fall, and her shame with dishonor would deepen. She didn't think she could bear it.

Lady Julia Barclay's mindset altered about this hoax and this confession. *Edith is right; she does capture a part of the heart.* Trying to be curt and not wanting to let this confessor off easily, but failing to sound irate, she asked, "Tell me, who are you?"

"My name is Wilhelmina *Thaylor*. I was abandoned, and I've always assumed I am named for my adopted father, William Thaylor, Marlfordshire's vicar. But as I grew older, I think my father knew who my mother is and why she left me with him. When he died, I became the ward of Lady Edith Marlowe."

"Did the vicar never tell you what he knew or might have known?"

"So many times, I wanted to ask, but he gave me so much that I didn't want him to think I was unappreciative. We never spoke about it. Then, Lady Marlowe took me to live with her. You know Lady Agatha Landry is her granddaughter. We became very good friends, and that is how I ended giving my word to *Aggie*." She smiled, "That is how close we are. I am known as Willie around the hamlet where my father presided. The name has stuck, and even Lady Marlowe often calls me by that name."

Lady Julia had to know what this young lady knew so as to never say the wrong words. "I'm sorry for your loss. I'm sure you miss the vicar."

Wilhelmina's expression stilled—somber and just as quickly brightened. "Having William Thaylor as my father is a blessing I shall never forget. It was an amazing coincidence that we had the same eye color; in fact, he told me that his mother's hair color and mine were much alike." Lady Julia could tell she loved her father. "It would grieve him to know what I have done."

"I would say that your honesty to me would make him proud. Also to my friend, Edith."

Wilhelmina's smile reached her eyes. "Lady Marlowe asked that I call her Grandmother. I think it is because Aggie and I became so close. It is an honor, but now my deceit will be unforgiveable even when I try to explain."

"What about her granddaughter, Lady Agatha? Don't you think she also dishonored her grandmother? Especially that this marriage arrangement here at Seahurst was to be only a testing for the Earl and Lady Agatha to get to know each other. There was no permanent arrangement. Lady Agatha knew this."

"There are circumstances I am unable to reveal, my lady. But I do believe love must be the reason to marry to have any meaning in the years ahead. I believe Aggie found love, and it wasn't possible for her to consider marriage to anyone else, not even to test the situation."

The more Lady Julia listened, the more she liked Wilhelmina Thaylor. *I'm going to keep her here and see if what I'm thinking is promising.* "Tell me, do you think the Earl would regard this charade as *just* a prank?"

"Heavens, no! It's just that everyone says Lord Barclay can choose any woman he wants, and Aggie had her own plans. Aggie believed when His Lordship discovered me and not *her*, he wouldn't hesitate to send me back to Lady Marlowe, and then I could explain this entire travesty to her grandmother. Aggie would be away and married. We knew it would hurt Lady Marlowe, but Aggie was certain her grandmother would forgive her."

"So, she left you to explain."

Wilhelmina sort of shrugged. "Well, that's Aggie. Perhaps because I'm older and should know better, but Lady Barclay… now I must be direct. You see, after I met Lord Barclay, I understood why it would be an impossible match."

Lady Julia gasped. "You've met my grandson?"

"Only once. A situation came up, and he was forced to waltz with me. I doubt that Lord Barclay will remember."

"Then why," she probed, "do you think he and Lady Agatha might not have suited? Be candid," she ordered.

Wilhelmina bit the inside of her jaw. She didn't want to hurt this dear lady, and she certainly didn't want to insult the Earl, especially doing what she did here in Seahurst. She remained silent.

"Come now, *Willie*, out with it. I want to know what is said about my grandson."

"You must know that I only met Lord Barclay one time at the Benton Ball. Lord Restin set me to dance with Lord Barclay."

Of course, Jonathon would be involved. A game to him. Lady Julia continued to listen.

"Lord Barclay did not want to dance with me, and I didn't want to dance with him, but the situation occurred, and it wasn't possible for us *not* to dance." Wilhelmina laughed, "Forgive me, my lady, as I remember telling the Earl that I didn't wish to dance and that he should escort me near a door so I could exit the ballroom." A wide smile appeared as Wilhelmina continued, "Using His Lordship's autocratic manner, the Earl stated that we would waltz."

Delighted with this news, she encouraged Wilhelmina to go on. "Did he insult you?"

"Oh, no. Lord Barclay is a very proper aristocrat." She bit the inside of her jaw and said, "You see, it was his attitude." Hesitating for a few seconds, she continued, "Pardon me, my lady, but you asked for honesty. I found Lord Barclay unbending. What I mean is, he's polite with no warmth, and it's as if he will follow protocol yet resents being put upon and doesn't mind showing it. Yet, he did persevere that we waltz and then had the temerity to ask if I knew how. So, I decided to tweak his cold manner and pretend I might not know how."

"Oh, dear. That's not my grandson."

Concerned that she caused Lady Barclay upset, she offered, "Perhaps with many persons wishing to have his interest, he carries a condescending grace to keep people away."

The dowager only smiled and said, "Did you and my grandson waltz?"

"Yes." Wilhelmina suddenly brightened, "It was positively grand. The best I've ever danced. Lord Barclay can waltz, and I actually floated across the floor." Wilhelmina chuckled, "Before we danced, Lord Barclay believed I couldn't dance and that he'd have to keep me from tripping over my toes and his; but then, I started right off, matching his steps. I got the feeling he resented that I purposely bluffed. We waltzed, and I mean, truly waltzed. I believe he was irritated with my tease and that he tried to have me miss a step."

"Did you… did you misstep?"

"Not once," she bragged. "Lord Barclay is a marvelous dancer." Wilhelmina's eyes sparkled. "When the waltz ended, Lord Barclay and I were the only ones in the ballroom dancing, and there was absolute silence in that big room. I don't think either of us realized we had been on display. He didn't smile, though he leaned down and chastised me for my boldness," she grinned. "I think people thought he was saying something nice, if they only knew. Then he didn't say another word—just took my elbow and escorted me to meet with Aggie and Lord Restin."

"What happened?"

"He said good evening and left with Lord Restin."

"And you have not seen him since? You have no wish to meet again with the Earl of Grenmoor?"

"No, my lady. That's why I'm happy that he isn't in residence." She reached for the veined hand and pressed it lightly. "You've been kind, and I am sincerely sorry for this ugly game. I've no right to expect your forgiveness. I'll leave tomorrow as deliveries are made in the morning, and I'm sure I can catch a ride."

Lady Julia said not a word but studied Wilhelmina. A log fell, making a popping sound, bursting sparks. Wilhelmina could feel embarrassment budding into more humiliation and rose. "I'll get my things together, my lady."

She is just what Lucien needs for a wife—intelligent with a sense of humor. I will keep her here and see what happens. Grandson, I look forward to your return, and I'll bet my brooch that you do remember that waltz, knowing how you love to dance. "Wilhelmina—do you mind if I call you by your name?"

"No Ma'am; in fact, *Willie* is what I usually answer to."

"Then Willie it is. I live in Seahurst without a lot of company as Cornwall is not easily traveled. Will you stay as *my* guest?" She smiled, "Seeing as you offered to help me if needed, perhaps I'll take advantage of your generosity." *There, that should be reason to invite her, knowing she's a giving and doing person.*

Stunned, Wilhelmina gaped as she pushed a loose curl behind her ear. "Ma'am… Lady Julia, are you sure, especially after what I have done?"

"The fact that you told me—and I can see it bothered and embarrassed you about Lady Agatha and your plotting and not letting it continue—satisfies me. Your explanation and apology are accepted. Will you stay? Lady Marlowe expects it."

A weight lifted from Wilhelmina. "Yes, I'd love to extend my visit. There is so much to see and learn. Cornwall is very different." Her face tightened. "But what of Lord Barclay? Oh, I don't think it would be right for me to stay."

Lady Julia waved her veined hand. "My grandson will be no problem. He didn't plan on meeting with Lady Agatha; he is somewhere in France or Italy."

"Well," she cheerfully advocated with warm green eyes, "with the Earl away and knowing he'd not remember me," she paused, biting the inside of her jaw, "Lady Julia, must I confess about why I'm actually here as *your* guest?"

Relaxed and looking forward to her grandson's return, she said, "We won't divulge a word. You are *my* invited guest."

"Thank you, my lady." *No doubt, I'll be long gone before the Earl returns. I can only hope Lady Marlowe will forgive me.*

Chapter Seven

Next Day
Afternoon Tea

Wilhelmina explored Seahurst, jubilantly detailing her venture to Lady Julia. "It is sunny and bright. I couldn't believe it!" Laughing, animated, she went on, "It may be because the weather is thanking me for being truthful. Thank you, my lady, for allowing me this privilege."

Lady Julia, sipping her tea, listened to the unusual guest's voice spring forth with enthusiasm from hours of walking Seahurst's surroundings. *A reversal from yesterday eve. She is blessed with natural warmth, seemingly unaware the beauty of it. Her windblown hair does not seem to be a problem, proving she doesn't spend time before a reflection glass. I like her, and Lucien will find she is not addlebrained and chasing fripperies.*

"And I cannot wait to see the sea. I can hear it but have yet to go to the cliffs. There must be a way down to the shore, though it will be a long walk."

Lady Julia promptly cautioned, "Take care, as there are places one can get to the shore, but it can be treacherous, especially when the tide comes in and the shoreline disappears. Remember that as always, the water is cold, deep, and makes it difficult to reach safety. Never forget that you must not walk the beach if you are far from a way to getting up on the cliff."

"I'll remember." Wilhelmina, excited, went on, "Is it true about smugglers using Cornwall's long coast to hide their takings? Booty?" Her cheeks were rosy, her green eyes like fresh morning dew and her long fingers bouncing on the tabletop.

Lady Julia, caught in her guest's ecstatic joy, couldn't help but laugh. "It has been said, and I've no doubt, but no one has ever claimed it a fact. Wilhelmina, I'm so pleased you have enjoyed your outing. There is much to see—you've only started to see, and so much to learn."

Wilhelmina's charm and warm smile reached the older woman when she asked, "Please, Lady Julia, will you call me *Willie?* My father said Wilhelmina is too long a name for a little girl as well as for him and his parishioners," she grinned. "Really, everyone, even though they didn't always attend his services, knew me as Willie."

Taken by the freshness she induced, the wily dowager conspired to keep Willie with her at Seahurst. *Grandson, you have met your match.* "Then Willie it is."

"And is it all right for Seahurst's people address me as Willie, too?"

Taken aback, yet not quite surprised by the kindness she exuded, Lady Julia tilted her head to one side. "You are my guest. I have no objections, but you know that Jaggers has the say over Seahurst's household."

"Yes, Ma'am. I will not upset Jaggers. Thank you." Then Willie stood, moved around the room, and stopped on Lady Julia's left. "My father always expressed that keeping busy keeps a person reasonably happy. I have no interest in doing embroidery, and my stitching is not acceptable, but I am accomplished with reading and numbers."

"That is kind of you, Willie. I'll keep it in mind." Thinking of her friend's letter, Lady Julia thought, *you are so right—the vicar raised an extraordinary young lady.* "By the way, you mentioned that you like to ride. Seahurst has a few fine horses. Do you ride well enough for me not to be concerned that you will not injure yourself? Robbie, our stablemaster, cares for the horses, but he is rather old to have care for you."

Glowing, Willie almost exploded with joy. "Worry not, my lady," she bragged, "I am quite proficient when riding. I leaned on old *Easy Go*; he belonged to the vicarage. Then Lady Marlow introduced me to livelier horses and the equestrians' positives and negatives. Truthfully, I do not like riding side-saddle and bridal paths, as one bounces like a ball when one wants to do more than trot. That isn't real riding."

Knowing Willie liked riding astride, the dowager waited.

Willie sat again but leaned toward the dowager. "A horse should be free to travel at a good pace—to go with the wind. That is what riding is all about."

The older, experienced equestrian agreed. "You and I have a lot in common. I have ridden since I was five of age, and horses have always been my joy. You are welcome to enjoy Seahurst's stable."

"Thank you, my lady… but I have to confess, I wear breeches and ride astride." Quickly, she raised her hand and touching the dowager's arm, said, "I mean, I know it is shocking but I will only ride on your land and not embarrass you. No one will know."

Amusement flickered in Lady Julia's silver eyes. "What about my staff? And of course, there is Robbie."

"If that is a concern, my lady, I think I can sway them not to say a word, especially if it would be a negative to you in any way."

Oh, she has charm, Lucien—Lady Julia hid the smile that wanted to break—*and she didn't want to waltz with you.* "Do you have your breeches with you?"

"I do, and my riding boots. Please," she softly pleaded, "I promise not to go where I can be seen and embarrass you or Seahurst."

"You continue to amaze me, Willie. By all means, wear your breeches. We are isolated, and so, we shall abandon conventional rules. Enjoy riding in your breeches and astride."

Without thought, Willie was out of her chair and hugged Lady Julia. Her smile could have lit up the entire manor.

Chapter Eight

Last week in August—Seahurst

As weeks rapidly passed, Lady Julia intentionally came to rely on Willie, motivated by an undaunted conviction that she kept completely to herself, having decided dear Willie would make an ideal wife for her rascal grandson. And so, she connived and plotted her course. She would not be obvious as she clandestinely helped nudge human nature along.

Lady Julia Barclay calculated to make certain opportunities and events happen. Very sure of the rightness of her plan, she wrote to her friend, Edith, detailing her new strategy. With Agatha safe across the sea, there was no reason why Wilhelmina Thaylor should not become the chosen bride by the Earl of Grenmoor and, just as importantly, become her beloved granddaughter, too.

Not having forgotten her grandson's anger when discussing marriage, he would become more enraged if he believed she was interfering again. She had to act covertly.

"I'll have to return soon to London, Lady Julia, and make arrangement to sail to America. Agatha and James must be waiting to hear from me."

"I know, my dear. I do so hate to have you leave. Lady Marlowe suggested you stay and enjoy your holiday. Consider staying a while longer. I'm thinking selfishly, as you've been a great help with Seahurst's ledgers."

Willie hated to leave this kind lady who had accepted her apology and then gave her free will to do as she pleased. "I guess I can delay a while longer. I do like Cornwall, and of course, your company is exceptionally stimulating. There is much to learn, and the more I learn, the more I like the strangeness of this land and its people."

"Then it's settled, Willie." She knew she had to be careful not to expose her manipulations as Willie, being perceptive, would pick up on any innuendo she might carelessly mention. Holding silent thanks, Lady Julia marveled at

Willie's abilities to win the affection of Grenmoor's people, even the stern and proper Jaggers. *The vicar, loving his daughter, was wise in allowing her innate goodness to blossom. She does things for people without thought and can do no wrong to those who know her.* Effusive with her plotting, her heart pulsing at a steady beat, Lady Julia was beside herself. *Grandson, when are you finally going to return to Seahurst and meet your bride?*

Chapter Nine

September

Wilhelmina and Lady Julia dined early and were enjoying the warmth from a slow-burning log. A pounding wind and rain beat against the leaded glass windows, and every so often, it whistled through the chimney stirring the flames.

"It's certainly gusty tonight." With her auburn curls hung loosely down her back, Wilhelmina pushed a dangling curl behind her ear. She sat in a dreamy trance, thinking of riding Zephr across Grenmoor lands. *The horse is magnificent. It is no wonder the Earl bought the stallion and claimed it as his own.* Wilhelmina knew she was lucky that Robbie recognized her ability to handle Zephr, and thus permitted her to exercise him. Besides, Robbie saw that she and Zephr got along well together.

Lady Julia interrupted her reverie. "Willie, would you, perchance, be interested in playing cards?" She smiled and her silver eyes twinkled.

Grinning in return, Wilhemina asked, "Cribbage?"

"Let's play cribbage. I've only managed to win a couple of games. Maybe tonight, I'll be lucky."

Wilhelmina went over to Lady Julia's book table that held Lord Barclay's brandy and pulled open the drawer, removing the board and cards. "I am a fierce competitor. My father cautioned me about my passion to win. Yet, it isn't a game if you don't try your best. I never had much of a challenge with Aggie. She played but didn't care if she won or lost. There was no challenge. It wasn't fun. However, my lady, you make game playing enjoyable as you like to win, too."

The log fell with a clunk, and sparks flew, but the two ladies, intent on winning, didn't hear or notice.

Willie rode early every morn at dawn regardless of weather, except in stormy downpours.

Aware of Willie's early riding, Lady Julie continued her clandestine quest. *This will be quite interesting as Lucien is also an early morn rider.*

The wily dowager did not tell Willie that she had received word Lucien would be returning in mid-September. She had to keep Willie from leaving, as again, Willie was saying Agatha and James were waiting for her. Lady Julia wrote to Edith, and they both encouraged her to stay on.

"I've told Edith what a great help you are." Wilhelmina delayed again, but she didn't mind as she had the freedom of riding Zephr. She came to love the stallion as he gave her his heart when he galloped at great speed with the wind; many times, with mist cutting across their faces as they flew across Grenmoor land.

Lady Julia resumed her scheming, pleased with her secret ploy. She piled more work with the ledgers on Willie along with reorganizing the manor.

Having learned from the vicar, Willie pitched in and worked with everyone. She didn't mind, and the staff finally accepted that she did as she pleased and didn't mind work.

Too, Lady Julia found the once-silent manor bustling with ease. There were subdued giggles from one person to another. The dowager left to Jaggers what was to be done, and soon, even Jaggers fell under Willie's spell.

Willie suggested the windows be opened when the sun shined to freshen the rooms. She got permission to unwrap rolled rugs stored away, and soon, with dusting and polishing, the revived rugs brought warmth and harmony to the manor. Polished oak floors matched the brass fire screens; nothing was overlooked.

One big change was an unused dark room near the library. She had the unused massive desk removed and replaced with a round table to use for private dining. Regardless if it rained or the mist masked the view, but especially when the sun shined in the room, it exuded an invitation to sit back and enjoy the outdoor surroundings. The scrubbed fountain welcomed birds—they became regular visitors. Lady Julia and Willie shared their visits for afternoon tea and card playing in the comfortable atmosphere.

Remembering Seahurst's uninviting entry, Willie suggested the sconces be lighted each day with full candles. A round Aubusson rug, discovered under the stairwell, was now centered in the entry with a round marble-top table. She gathered sea-rushes, their stiff stems holding up around the base of the table, and set two huge porcelain English setters taken from the library to sit guard.

Everything gleamed from the oak floor along with the stairs and railing; nothing was overlooked.

But most taken by Seahurst's staff was the knight Willie discovered in storage. Working and polishing it herself, she named him Sir Kevin. He was towering and imposing, and she put Sir Kevin in the entry's corner to welcome visitors. Everyone acknowledged the silver knight. "Did anyone dust Sir Kevin?" It became banter for the servants, and even Jaggers straightened the knight when needed.

Lady Julia kept Willie active, also encouraging her to use Seahurst's stable, knowing she took the greatest pleasure in the freedom of riding astride.

At first, Willie shocked everyone when she appeared in men's clothing. It just wasn't done. But being Willie, she soon had them convinced she wore them as it was the only way she could safely ride Zephr. Willie could do no wrong.

Looking from her window, in a distance, Lady Julia caught sight of Willie and Zephr flying through the blowing wind. Her hair tucked tightly under a cap and jacket and jodhpurs; she didn't resemble a female. *Grandson, I can't wait.* An inner thrill filled with mischief, knowing Zephr being the Earl's joy, he let no one ride him other than Robbie for exercise. The grooms didn't care as Zephr balked having a mind of his own. Yet, Willie had captured the black beast's heart.

Speaking into the empty room, but in a cheerful mood, Lady Julia, Dowager Countess of Grenmoor, her voice melodious, said, "Hurry home, Grandson," and happily sat down to rest.

Chapter Ten

Late September

Visiting with Grenmoor tenants and learning more about Cornwall and its people, Willie lost track of time and realized she had to hurry back to Seahurst. The sky laden with black clouds challenged her to hurry before rain and wind joined forces. She knew a good blow was on its way, having become accustomed to Cornwall's weather.

Her hair wound in a knot under her wool cap, she buttoned her jacket and reached for Zephr's reins, planning to race across open land, jump the stone wall, head through the belt of trees, then out across the uncut meadow and onto the manor road—all hopefully before the cloudburst. She'd let Zephr have his way, aware a good blow would give her and Zephr a tail wind.

As she said her goodbyes, it seemed Zephr, knowing he would soon have free will to gallop, was anxiously sidestepping. No one would stand near the big horse. Willie's natural touch on the black beauty earned his quick settling response. Waving, she trotted off, and soon, Zephr went into a full gallop. The two were off as Zephr lifted his hooves with Willie riding with extreme confidence; light and smooth all the way. Zephr jumped the stone fence as if it wasn't there, and Willie lowered her head to miss the low branches as Zephr wound his way around trees—his pounding hooves silenced on wet shaded mulch covering the ground. Rider and horse sprang out from the trees as if someone were in pursuit of them: effortless and fluid as they headed across the open golden meadow toward the road leading to the stable. The wind seemed to be giving Zephr an extra push, increasing his powerful stride. Willie did not notice the curricle further back pull to the side of the road, watching the powerful stallion and its rider. Willie's elation was at its peak of pleasure when riding free with Zephr's powerful momentum with sea air and wind for company; it was untamed exultation. Leaning forward with grace, she held the reins loose, knowing the horse felt its liberty to run, giving her speed and his heart.

"I say, that lad is riding that monster as if glued to the saddle and without an ounce of fear," Lord Jonathan Restin exclaimed in disbelief. The admiration in his voice did not go unnoticed by the solemn man sitting beside him.

Lord Lucien Barclay watched, respecting the rider's control, but then his eyes flashed, and his voice hardened. "What the devil? That's Zephr! The lad will be thrown just as sure as we're sitting here. Who the devil gave him permission to take my horse from the stable? I left orders that Zephr is to be exercised. The lad's pushing him flagrantly without care."

Jonathan couldn't hold back his laugher. "I think, my friend, the lad is doing what both of them want and are enjoying their outing; they're flying and at racing speed!"

"I'll see about that!" Lord Lucien Barclay, Earl of Grenmoor, was in no mood to have his prized horse run in that fashion unless, of course, he was the rider. *I will not tolerate my orders not being obeyed.* He gave the reins a gentle snap and made haste toward the Seahurst stable.

In the meantime, Willie dismounted and handed Zephr's reins to the stablemaster. "I'm late, Robbie. Will you take care of this sweetheart for me?"

Robbie grinned. "I'll take care of the beast for you, Willie." He shook his head and added, "I don't know how you do it!"

Patting the stallion's neck, she replied, "He is pure sweetness. We had a marvelous run. Thanks, Robbie… I've got to hurry."

Robbie had just finished rubbing down Zephr and was about to walk him when the Earl wheeled in. "Logan!" he shouted.

Robbie was surprised to see the Earl. He walked over to him with Zephr. Raised at Seahurst and knowing all about horses, he still found the Earl's black stallion skittish and respected its ways, yet he didn't trust Zephr the way Willie did. Oblivious to the Earl's anger, Robbie offered a big smile, exposing his missing front tooth while gripping the halter of the exuberant horse, said, "Welcome home, mi'lord."

Though enraged, the Earl backed off at the stablemaster's warm greeting. "Yes, thank you, Logan." Eying his horse, he asked, "Tell me, who was just riding Zephr?"

Robbie broke out with a wider grin. "Oh, not to worry, mi'lordship. I know how you love this horse. It was Willie riding him." Looking at Zephr and then back at the Earl, he bragged, "They had a good run, and I'd say, Zephr enjoyed it as much as Willie."

"Who gave this Willie permission to ride Zephr?"

Robbie Logan being the fourth generation as stablemaster at Seahurst, inheriting his place from his father, wasn't shaken by the Earl's tone. Robbie thought for a minute, rubbed his gray whiskered chin, sort of shook his frizzled head and answered, "I can't bloomin' say for sure, mi'lord. Willie just came down and looked over the horses and picked Zephr." Robbie's face split into a wide grin. "That was something. Willie's got the magic touch. I'm saying, Sir, Zephr let Willie be his boss—it was right there to see." Both Lucien and Jonathan heard the awe in the old man's voice. Lucien looked over his prized horse, seeing he wasn't abused and looked exceptionally well cared for.

"Will that be all, mi'lord? Willie told me to give Zephr extra feed for their fine ride."

"Then do it," snapped Lucien. *This Willie certainly took it upon himself to give orders.* "By the way, Logan, where is this Willie?"

"Up at the manor, I guess. Said to be late and in a hurry." Robbie carefully guided Zephr into his stall, saying, "Willie usually does his rub down and feeding."

Grinning from ear to ear, Jonathan needled his friend, "You're something, Lu. Getting all worked up over a four-legged animal and letting the two-legged beauties go their merry way. Beautiful women would give anything for the kind of attention and concern you display for that black beast." Jonathan had to grip the side of the curricle as Lucien gave a good tug on the reins. Continuing to tease while eying his friend, Jonathan said, "I wonder if you're not just put out that someone can ride your horse as well as you. Seems to me this Willie can."

Lucien mellowed a little. "I'll admit, Zephr is in great shape. It will be good to ride him in the morn. Are you going to join me?"

"Me? Rise early to go riding? No thanks, Lu."

"One of these times, Johnny, I'm going to insist you rise early and see what you're missing."

"You have got to be out of your mind," he laughed. "Sorry, old friend, but riding a horse is the means of getting me from one place to another."

Lucien joined in his laughter. "No wonder my grandmother disapproves of you."

"Lady Julia has always said I'm a bad influence on you. I can't imagine how she arrived at that conclusion. Probably because I'm not into cattle as Her Ladyship is," he teased.

"Worry not, Johnny. I shall defend you to the end."

"Whatever that means!"

They were both in good humor and jovial when the Earl of Grenmoor halted the curricle at the portico. Both men rushed toward the massive carved oak door to miss the oncoming storm.

"It's good to be home." Just then, the expected heavy rain poured down, wind picking up, but the two men remained dry as Jaggers pulled opened the door.

The iron handles on the massive entry door were highly polished. Its leaded glass framing the wide entrance gleamed even with the darkened sky. Lighted sconces bounced their glow off the glass, emitting a soft shimmer in their reflection.

"Welcome home, my lord." Jaggers's stiff stature was as Lucien remembered his grandmother's aging butler. "It is good to have you home, Sir."

Lucien smiled, "Thank you, Jaggers." It was then that Lucien unexpectedly stopped short from entering the reception hall, causing Jonathan to bump into him.

Jonathan moved from behind Lucien and expressed his admiration, "You didn't tell me you had the place done over. Looks quite handsome."

Perplexed, Lucien turned to Jaggers. "What is going on?" Then speaking to Jonathan, "My grandmother must have finally decided to turn Seahurst back to its splendor. This pleases me."

Jaggers beamed. "If you mean the restoring of the hall, my lord, I do believe that Willie has been in charge, with Lady Julia's permission, of course."

Again, it was this Willie person. Lucien, vexed, didn't bother to cover his irritation. "Did you say *Willie?*"

Hearing the Earl's agitated tone, Jaggers quickly clarified, "Yes, Sir… but it was by your grandmother's leave."

Jonathan slapped his friend's shoulder, "Twice within the hour, this Willie has surprised you. I say, Lu, I haven't seen you in this mood in a long time. I have got to meet Willie before I leave."

"Enjoy yourself, for it's not going to last." Peering at Jaggers, no longer in a cordial frame of mind, Lucien ordered, "Announce me to my grandmother and see that rooms are made ready for Lord Restin. I should like to meet this Willie."

"Yes, my lord. I'll convey your message."

"Jaggers," Lord Restin called as Jaggers turned to go, "please inquire of Lady Julia if I may also dine with her."

"Johnny, you know Grandmother will welcome you without pause." Lucien looked about seeing highly polished stairs, rail, and floor. "Very impressive. I'm glad Grandmother has taken an interest in having this place brightened and livable."

Jonathan didn't reply but thought with a grin, *this kid Willie has done wonders, and to see Lu irritated is worth it.*

A cold frown settled upon Lucien's face. *Why is this kid in Cornwall, and why has Grandmother given him a freehand? Something is fishy, and it comes directly from her book room.* Leaving Johnny to follow, Lucien took the steps two at a time to get to his rooms. *Whatever you're up to, Grandy, I'll figure who, what and why...* "I'll see you later, Johnny."

Lord Restin was still grinning... *I certainly want to be there when Lu and Willie meet.* "Right," he answered.

* * *

Lady Julia sat with her grandson and Lord Restin in the huge *Seascape* drawing room. On a clear day, the sea's horizon could be viewed and its greatness awesome to the eyes, but not today.

The room's lighted candelabrums set upon several tables presented an inviting ambiance. The windows were closed because of the stormy weather, but fresh afternoon air lingered in the room with a burning fire adding to its attractive surroundings. The settees and chairs were arranged in the spacious room for easy gathering and comfort. Upon entering, one would be drawn to its hearth. This was where Lady Julia, her grandson, and his friend were renewing memories. Certain not to display a tad of eagerness, Lady Julia silently awaited her guest's arrival.

Hearing of the Earl's arrival, Wilhelmina dreaded the forthcoming evening with panic. *Lady Julia, how much have you imparted to the Earl? Am I to just go along with you? I think I can do that—at least I hope I can.* Wilhelmina wore an unadorned soft, green, light wool gown—unknowingly nearly matching her eye color and accenting her auburn hair. Having removed Agatha's favored fluffy white lace collar and cuffs because they were not to her liking, she pushed the plain, long fitted sleeves up beyond her wrists, exposing tanned arms and not giving a thought of bare skin showing. Her long auburn hair wouldn't cooperate as its curls went every which way, so she combed it back and held the long curls in place with a solitary black ribbon at the nape of her neck. She pinned on her father's gift; a sterling brooch with a single rose encircled with leaves. It could be worn as a brooch or with a silver chain as a pendant. Today, she pinned it on her shoulder, close to the gown's high neckline, which drew the eye as well as to her well-formed breasts, though she gave that nary a thought.

She could dally no longer; giving one last look in the reflection glass and seeing her tanned face, she couldn't help grinning. *Society ladies prefer milk-white skin, but I'm the vicar's daughter, and I prefer the sun. As father often said, 'Be who you are.'* Remembering those words bolstered Wilhelmina's courage. *The Earl of Grenmoor may be cold and haughty; however, I am a welcomed guest of Lady Julia, and that is what matters...* she heaved a sigh; *he won't remember our waltz with plain me.* Burying her nerves, she went to join them for the evening meal.

Jaggers opened the door for Wilhelmina, offered her one of his rare smiles and announced, as stipulated by his esteemed employer, "Miss Thaylor, my lady."

Surprised by using only her last name, Wilhelmina glanced at the aging butler, noticed his slight nod before she entered and heard the door close. Her hurried steps were graceful, carrying her across the room. Appearing to be looking at Lady Julia but stealing a side glance at the tall, handsome, temperamental Earl who was closely watching her, she couldn't miss his glowering; if possible, his eyes would spew fire. Her mind raced that he could have been Aggies's future husband. Determined not to be intimidated by him, she grasped at the reason she was here—*I saved my best friend from this tyrant.*

A warm smile from Lady Julia nurtured Wilhelmina's daring. "There you are, Miss Thaylor. You look lovely, dear. Come, I would like to introduce you to my grandson, Lord Barclay, and his friend, Lord Restin."

Lucien was standing and reached for a whiskey, its amber color and glass picking up the candlelight's reflection as he held it with his long brown fingers. Dressed in dove gray pants, black waistcoat and a crisp white linen shirt with absolutely no warmth in his eyes, he tipped his glass at her. "Grandmother, I have met Miss Thaylor as you, no doubt," his sarcasm reaching his cold eyes, "know."

Lord Restin, wearing a wide grin and bursting with humor, erupted, "She's the *no-can-waltz-lady* that you both actually drove everyone off the ballroom floor. Remember, Lu?"

"So *she* is," growled Lord Barclay.

Lady Julia smothered her smile by raising her handkerchief to her nose.

Wilhelmina, hearing Lord Barclay's nasty tone, quickly decided not to be cowed by the Earl. So standing near him, she smiled and made a minimal curtsy. "Oh yes, my lord, I remember." She let out an audible breath, "Why, it made my evening when you asked if I knew how to waltz," and purposely fanned her face with her brown hand for lack of a fan, "I was so nervous I couldn't remember if I could," and gently sparring, "lo and behold, it was magic... I remembered how to waltz."

Lord Restin couldn't hold back a broad smile and, wanting to elbow his friend, still knew he must not, remained silent.

Lord Barclay didn't crack a smile, simmering and staring at the one person he didn't forget. *She is the only person to suggest that they not dance, and she meant it, and yet, she was magnificent. I was sorry the music ended, but no one will know.* "What are you doing here?"

The Earl's direct, callous question threw Wilhelmina—she stared back at him, not willing to lie, and went halfway with the truth. Giving the Earl a minor, tentative smile, she turned toward the white-haired lady, whose silver eyes gave her daring. Wilhelmina's tone filled with warmth. "I've been remiss in explaining to you, my lady, that my having met Lord Barclay was just an unfortunate circumstance for both of us, as it didn't seem important. I had no plans to be here when the Earl returned. Being that I am present, I will direct my reply to Lord Barclay." She then returned her attention back to the Earl, and her voice mollified yet edged with an ominous quality, continued, "I am here because Lady Agatha Marlowe eloped with the man she loves. The barrister's man being *the* escort would be in need of having someone to deliver to Seahurst, so Abby contrived that I step in her place. It would aid in giving them the required time to make their escape." The room's silence enhanced the crackling of the blazing logs. Wilhelmina's chest felt its tightening as she dug deep to breathe. "I explained all to Lady Julia," Wilhelmina looked over at the unmoving dowager and then back to the Earl, "and I was invited to remain as her guest. *That* is why I am here, my lord." She didn't wait for a comment from Lord Barclay but turned toward Lady Julia. "I'm sorry, my lady, I hope I haven't distressed you overmuch. I can be away in a day or so." Then, she politely turned toward Lord Restin. "Good evening, my lord," she smiled, "I remember well it was at your insistence that I waltzed with Lord Barclay. I haven't forgotten."

Lord Jonathan teased, "I imagine that you didn't realize that dancing with Lord Barclay is a wish that goes unfulfilled for many ladies."

Wilhelmina eyed Lord Restin and pulled no punches. "I gather, then, that it was a lark for you to thrust me before Lord Barclay to dance."

Lord Barclay wanted to laugh. *Ho, Johnny, how does it feel to be censured by this impertinent baggage?*

Lord Restin's mouth dropped open, and he said, "I ask that you accept my apology. You are correct; I did it as a lark, not on you, but on my friend."

"True, my lord, but at my expense, with no thought of my embarrassment."

Lucien raised his brow. *Grandy's little baggage friend shows no respect.*

Johnny swallowed, "Again, I apologize. It was wrong of me to use both you young ladies to irritate my friend." Then he grinned, "But it turned that the two of you know the waltz. You can't imagine how exquisite to see two strangers dance as if they've been practicing for such a night. That is why, Miss Thaylor, everyone soon left the floor to watch the most sought-after Earl waltz and you following his every step. It was the talk of the *ton* for weeks," Lord Restin bowed fully.

"The talk of the *ton*, no doubt, my lord, because you politely omitted saying that the Earl was waltzing with a nobody, and that gave it questionable interest."

Stunned and unable to speak, Lord Restin knew this young lady was no fool.

Wilhelmina made a curtsy.

Lord Barclay steamed as he swallowed a long swallow of whiskey. *Johnny could always talk himself out of unusual predicaments; evidently not this one. But that mahogany-haired witch can really waltz.*

Lady Julia listened while keeping an eye on her grandson. *He is truly upset—this isn't like him. He won't admit he enjoyed waltzing with Willie. This will be very interesting.* "My dear, you are *my* guest. You are enjoying your visit at Seahurst, am I right?"

"Yes, my lady." *Until now*, though she kept those words to herself.

"And I enjoy having you. Please stay for a few more days. It will take that long to arrange proper transportation for your safe return to London." She eyed her grandson. "Will you agree, Lucien?"

"Fine… fine. Do as you wish. You would anyway," he grumbled.

Wilhelmina caught Lady Julia's soft wink. "Thank you, my lady. If you will excuse me, I think it best I forego dining with you this eve."

Lord Restin, corners of his mouth turned up, suggested, "Join us for a glass of wine, Miss Thaylor." Not waiting, he offered, "To forgiveness? Memories?" smiling he raised his drink.

Always a gentleman, the Earl nodded and did the same.

A satisfied pulse settled within the dowager.

Lord Restin decided to keep the conversation flowing in order to keep this striking auburn-haired visitor from leaving. For some reason, she irritated his friend, and he'd like to discover the reason. *That waltz—it's not like Lu not to realize he and his partner were the only ones dancing in the ballroom… why?* Lord Restin then listened to the two ladies trying to catch up on what they were saying.

The Earl of Grenmoor didn't join in; he stared out the window with rain beating against the panes. *So, this brazen ne'er-do-well is going along with Grandy's marriage scheme… I won't have it. Tell any story you like, but I'm not buying it… eloping?* He wanted to laugh at her idiotic story. He was beside himself with anger that he controlled as he thought the mahogany-haired wench a husband hunter and, in a conspiracy, to capture his attention. Adding to his internal disharmony, he took in her attire—*her exposed arms are brown like a farmer's wife and that face—rosy and beautifully weathered, why she doesn't wear bonnets.* Realizing what he was actually thinking, he became annoyed with himself as never had he denounced any person for what they wore or how they looked. This eclipsed anger blinded him to the lady's natural gentle bearing.

"Want to freshen your drink, Lu?"

"No thanks, Johnny." Lucien slipped into a chair, not saying much but began to take in his grandmother's charlatan. It was then he noticed the dainty pin Miss Thaylor was wearing on her shoulder; a curl seemed to have caught on that pin. He kept studying the pin, forcing to control his surprise that he remembered it. It was once a favorite of Grandy's, and she gave it to her godchild, Edith Marlowe's daughter, Lady Karen. *Now how in the devil is it in this ne'er-do-well's possession? Could Grandy's impertinent guest openly thieve?* Lucien rubbed his forehead. "That's an interesting brooch you're wearing, Miss Thaylor. Is it an heirloom?" Lucien's bitterness spilled over in his voice.

I can do this. This bad-tempered aristocrat. Wilhelmina automatically touched her pin and sweetly smiled, "I can't say it is a family heirloom, but it will become one now, my lord, as it is a gift from my father, and he considered it a treasure."

Lucien eyed his grandmother. *She knows something—those two are planning and plotting.* He got himself another drink, looking over at Johnny in question. His friend held up his glass—it held enough liquor—and Lucien set the crystal decanter down.

Lady Julia raised her handkerchief to cover her smile. *Karen must have given it to her much-loved vicar. Karen was very possessive of my gift. It pleases me that Willie has it now.* She knew Lucien to be fuming and masking his vitriol temper. *I can't break my word and tell him about Karen.* She looked at Wilhelmina. *She takes after her father, as I see few traces of Karen.*

Lost in thought, she heard Wilhelmina saying, "I bid you goodnight, my lady."

The dowager eyed her conspirator. "Goodnight, Miss Thaylor. Sleep well, and do carry on as you have. You are most welcome at Seahurst. Rest well, my dear."

Wilhelmina brushed a kiss on the old woman's cheek, slightly curtsied to both lords, and without haste, walked gracefully from the room.

The silence in the room ended shortly after the door closed. Lucien leaned forward and chastised his grandmother, "Having this unexpected guest raises my suspicions once again over what we discussed when we last spoke." His eyebrow lifted. "Grandy, do not under any circumstances continue with matchmaking. I'm serious, for if you and I are to continue having our comfortable relationship, it will stay if you *stop!*"

"Listen to me, grandson," she looked over at Lord Restin, "and you too, Jonathan. I did not plan or have any idea that Miss Thaylor was going to come to Seahurst. The first night she arrived, I naturally made her comfortable, and the next day, she was polite but said nothing to indicate exactly why she was here, except saying that she was Lady Edith's ward. She did give me a letter from my friend, Edith, and that is why I extended my invitation for her to remain. It was a day or so later that she talked about Lady Agatha's elopement and their needing the few days to make their sail date. That is all there is to it. Miss Thaylor has been good company, and I am enjoying her visit. That is all."

Lord Restin spoke first, his eyes gleaming to match his grin. "You mean, my Lady, Lady Agatha really did elope?"

"Yes, that was the purpose of the letter. Lady Edith knew and sanctioned her granddaughter's elopement with the barrister's son, James. Miss Thaylor's part was only to help them."

Seething, Lucien wanted to shake his grandmother for encouraging this fraudulent, impertinent baggage to remain. *Maybe Grandy didn't plot Miss Thaylor's visit, but is she doing it now? I must not let that cheeky, green-eyed vixen get under my skin, because she has, ever since she said no to a dance and then had the audacity to exquisitely know how to waltz... perfectly.* Every time he thought of that waltz, he wished to find another excellent waltzing partner so he could forget her and that evening as if it never happened.

"And so, I admired her loyalty to her best friend, as she explained it to me as soon as she could. There is no conspiracy, Lucien. Why, I don't think she even likes you." Then looking at Lord Restin, she said, "And I'm sure she doesn't think well of you. Not that I blame her."

"Right you are, my lady." Lord Restin held his drink and tipped it to the dowager. "Miss Thaylor is an innocent, and," he smiled, "quite lovely, even though I must say, she has a barbed tongue. My apologies if I offended you, my lady."

"You have not, Jonathan, but do take care."

"Since the two of you have chosen to revere Grandy's houseguest, I will say nothing." He offered a warm smile to his grandmother. "I'm very pleased with your restoring Seahurst. The changes remind me of days gone. A very pleasant welcome upon returning; you've done wonders."

"As much as I would like to accept your appreciation for these changes, I cannot. None of it has been my doing, but I did give my direction for it to come about."

"Grandy, I don't understand." Lord Barclay's eyes narrowed, "Then to whom do I pass my kudos?"

As though it wasn't unusual, she clearly said, "Willie."

"Willie! And when am I going to have the satisfaction of meeting this Willie who has not only rearranged my home but also takes it upon himself to ride Zephr?" Obviously aggravated, he went on, "He leaves orders regarding the care and feeding of *my* horse. This lad is incredible." Pacing, he continued, "Jaggers informed me that this Willie dines with you. Am I to have the privilege of joining the two of you?"

Lord Restin saw his friend in turmoil over a mere lad and horse. *Something has set my friend into this unbelievable state. I best not say a word.*

Lady Julia appeared to think nothing was amiss. "Willie and I do dine and discuss important matters that interest us both." Watching her grandson, she knew she must be overly wary on how she carried on. "You did tell me to engage someone to help me, did you not?"

"I did," his voice softening, "I'm not complaining, Grandy; it just seems that when I have inquired about anything… why, even staid old Jaggers boasts, 'Willie did this' or 'Willie did that.' It has become disconcerting." He leaned against the mantel. "I apologize. It appears that in some regard, I've become a curmudgeon."

Lady Julia smiling, her silver eyes aglow, said, "I believe it's time to dine."

Lord Barclay took his grandmother's arm, asking, "And is your Willie going to join us?"

"Possibly, though many times, I dine alone. We'll have to wait and see, as I've never required Willie's presence unless there is something that needs attention. Dining together is not obligatory."

When seated, the three enjoyed their meal. Willie did not appear. Lady Julia didn't mind, and Lord Barclay thought to have a good talk with the lad in the morning.

Chapter Eleven

Dawn, Barely Daylight

Dressed in her breeches, boots, an extra warm sweater with her hair stuffed under her cap, Wilhelmina hurried to the stable. *I know Zephr is Lord Barclay's horse, and after today, I won't be able to ride Zephr, but I'll have Zephr back before the Earl rises.* She didn't sleep well and was anxious to have the pleasure of one more gallop on the extraordinary black beauty.

She didn't see Robbie, so the young stable hand and Willie brought Zephr from his stall to be saddled. This did not seem odd as everyone knew Willie rode the black stallion almost every day. So together, they readied the impatient horse.

The unpredictable horse was obviously in a hurry to be on his way, trotting forward, unwilling to be delayed. Another groom came to help. No one liked handling this particular horse being constantly amazed at Willie's gentle nature with the black beast and her ability to ride him.

Patting Zephr, she spoke softly to steady him, and in a few minutes, was smiling and thanking the lads for their help. Riding astride, she and Zephr were off heading for the cliffs, knowing they'd feel salty air blanket their faces. The morn's misty dampness invigorated her. Soon, the sun might well break through, and she rejoiced, loosening her hold on the reins and allowing Zephr to gallop, knowing this beautiful animal felt as free as herself.

The Earl of Grenmoor entered the stable twenty minutes after Willie had left. Unknowingly, Robbie offered his toothless greeting. "Good morn, mi'lord. Ready for your ride?"

Lucien was in an exceptionally good mood. The damp air felt good, and taking Zephr out to a full gallop on this misty morn set yesterday's disquiet at rest. He eagerly looked forward to riding his prized powerful horse over his wet isolated land. "Good morn, Logan. Make haste and ready Zephr."

"In a dicker, mi'lord." Logan left to fetch Zephr. He returned with no horse; his face bore a worried frown.

"What is wrong with you, Logan? Where the devil is my horse?"

"Well, you see, mi'lord… it's like this," he scratched his forehead and unconsciously turned his cap to one side of his head, "You see, Sir, Zephr ain't here at the moment. I mean he ain't stolen, it's just…"

Incensed as never before, Lucien interrupted with a steel edge in his voice. There could be no misunderstanding for Robbie Logan. "What in blazes are you babbling about? Bring Zephr out here, now!"

Robbie was shaken. "The lads… they didn't know… you see, they didn't know you were back, or they would have never saddled Zephr up this morn."

Gritting his teeth, Lucien asked with deceptive calm yet with his dark eyes flashing, "Saddled Zephr? When? Why?"

Robbie shuddered. *There's going to be the devil to pay for this.* "Like always, most every morn, as day breaks… usual like… so you see," his voice resigned that His Lordship was not happy. "We can't say where Zephr is this minute, mi'lord. But I know for certain your horse is all right." Nodding his head and wanting to assure His Lordship, he explained, "You see, Willie came and…"

"Willie?" The Earl's demeanor exploded to violence that Robbie never heard before. "You are telling me that this Willie has Zephr? *My horse?*"

Logan's tone, cautious, nervously tried to justify Zephr's missing. "You see, mi'lord, evidently, Willie just didn't know you ride Zephr in the morn. I'm sure that's it, mi'lord. You see," he beseeched His Lordship to understand, "Willie's been riding Zephr just about every day, rain or shine, and the lads know that, so they didn't know not to saddle him today. Willie came, and I was out back in Meadow Ten." Anxious to have His Lordship understand, he continued, "Willie's an early riser," *like you,* but he didn't dare say it, "and they didn't know…" His voice trailed off; he was shaken—repeating again in a lowered voice, "The lads didn't know."

Lucien's temper was beyond the stablemaster's ability to comprehend. *When I get my hands on this Willie, I will throttle the lad once and for all.* He ordered, "Saddle Zairian and be quick about it." Sarcastically, he questioned, "Zairian has not gone off with Willie, too, has he?"

Robbie didn't answer and rushed about to bring Zairian forward.

When Lucien was mounted on the radiant chestnut and about to ride off, he looked down, scowling and contemptuously asked, "Does not Willie like to ride this piece of horseflesh?"

Robbie bit his tongue, he did not know whether he should say it or not, his *nibs* being in a waspish mood.

"Well?" Lucien growled as he turned Zairian and eyed the troubled stablemaster.

Robbie knew he had to answer. His Lordship was waiting. "Willie rode Zairian a few times, mi'lord, but after riding Zephr just one time, said Zairian's heart didn't match Zephr's—said he's a good ride, but not like—" he rubbed his chin and knew he had to hide grinning, "the Earl's black beauty."

Angered beyond words, the Earl kneed Zairian into a gallop, heading out to where, Robbie didn't know. Robbie took off his cap and scratched his almost bald head. *Seahurst's a big place. Oh, Willie, for your sake, I hope you don't meet up with His Lordship.*

As Wilhelmina cantered back into the stable yard, her cap stuffed in her waistband with her auburn hair curling from the dampness and falling freely from being windblown and with rosy cheeks, sparkling green eyes and happiness filled laughter, she waved to Robbie.

"Ooh, Willie, there is going to be the devil to pay as sure as I know those clouds hold rain."

Laughing, she asked, "What's wrong, Robbie? Did you forget to close the gate and the Earl's horses have run free?"

"I only wish that was my problem. No, no, Willie," he blurted with not the least of lighthearted banter, "The Earl came down this morn to ride Zephr, and you had already taken him, and the Earl was hotter than coals in a fire. I think 'e went to look for you. 'e had to ride Zairian and didn't like it at all."

So as not to raise any more anxiety in her friend, she said easily, "I'm sorry, Robbie. I didn't realize the Earl was an early riser. I'll explain to His Lordship, and I promise it will be all right." Handing the reins over to Robbie, she said, "I better get up to the manor and change clothes. When His Lordship returns, if he should ask, please tell him I've gone to see Lady Barclay."

"I'll do that, Willie. I'm sorry, but you can't ride Zephr as long as the Earl is here. The lads know about it, too."

Wilhelmina patted Robbie's bony shoulder. "I know Zephr is the Earl's horse, and I wouldn't have taken him this morn if I knew he liked to ride early. Not to worry."

Comforted, Robbie boasted, "You're a real prize, Willie… you sure are. None of the other ladies ever treated me so good."

She accepted his complement, smiled, and walked off toward the manor waving, not letting him see her worried expression.

When Wilhelmina explained what occurred at the stable, Lady Julia released a chuckle, easing some of the Wilhelmina's worry. "Lady Julia, this is serious. I mean no disrespect to Lord Barclay. I owe him an apology. I didn't think riding Zephr this early would be a problem. It was mindless on my part and another thing is poor Robbie; the Earl gave him a rough set-down. I have to make this right. As furious as the Earl is, I hope to reason with him."

"Stop admonishing yourself, Willie. I know you would not have taken Zephr if you knew that my grandson rode first thing in the morn. I guess I forgot to mention it. There is no need for you to apologize."

At once dubious, Wilhelmina lightly reproved, "Lady Julia, I trust you are not involving me in some ploy to disturb Lord Barclay. It's obvious that he finds me below his standards, and though I have great respect for you, I will not be a party to intentionally bring anguish upon anyone. I made that mistake once, and it will not happen again. No plots, plans or misconnections… no way… no more."

She's a spunky one. "Willie, I assure you that I feel as you do. You must know that I would not deliberately bring hurt upon anyone, especially my grandson." *This is better than if I planned it. Grandson, you said you could not abide self-centered, simple-minded, sniveling young women. You've met your match, Lucien, and I'm going to make sure you know it.*

Puzzled by the sudden silence, Wilhelmina said, "I do not understand. Surely, I should know why you are asking me not to apologize to the Earl."

The elderly woman reached for Willie's hand. "Please do me this favor and withhold any apology. I will explain things to you in due time. Just be Miss Thaylor to him and Lord Restin," she said with a gleam in her silver eyes, "but around me, you are Willie. Agree?"

Uncertainty caused her to bite her bottom lip. "I'll trust this is the right thing to do for now." Narrowing her eyes and eying her host, Wilhelmina said, "I'm ignorant as to your motive, Lady Julia, and I don't like it. So, tell me what is going to happen when the Earl insists on meeting the *lad*, Willie? Prolonging my identity will not be helpful.”

“Sit down, if you will, and listen. My grandson is very dear to me, and what I am doing is for his own good. You must believe that. You will be doing me a great favor by going along with this semi-complicity. All I am asking is that you be Miss Thaylor—nothing else. I assure you that in the end, I will resolve everything that matters, and if my grandson should be angered, it will be completely on my shoulders. Now, dear Willie, you ride any other horse in the stable, but of course, not Zephr. I will take care of this morn’s little misstep. Regardless of what my grandson espouses, I do have a say here in Seahurst Manor, but that is not to be interpreted as any disrespect toward the Earl of Grenmoor.”

Wilhelmina stood with her back straight and her arms crossed. She wasn’t buying everything Lady Edith’s friend was aggressively voicing, but as her guest, she’d temporarily agree. “Yes, Ma’am, but know that I find your reasoning questionable; however, I’ll go along for a while. That’s all I will promise.”

“Thank you, Willie. We shall let matters remain as they are until I say otherwise.” She kept her catlike smile hidden, pleased with this outcome. “Now, I would not be surprised if, at this moment, Lord Restin is searching the manor for Miss Thaylor. Keep in mind that he is a tease.”

Feeling her suspicions had merit, *Lady Julia is up to something—she has been quick to forgive my playing impostor.* “Lord Restin’s smiles and flirting mean nothing, I’m sure.”

Smiling while shaking her head, Lady Julia ordered, “Go and enjoy the rest of the day. Do try to forget about the Earl and Robbie. Everything will be fine.”

Wilhelmina nodded. She would do as Lady Julia dictated, though she was bothered. *I can only hope that the Earl of Grenmoor will be as forgiving as his grandmother… though I doubt it.*

Unknowingly, she left Lady Julia highly satisfied and beaming while awaiting a visit from her grandson.

Chapter Twelve

The library's sliding doors were partially open with Lord Restin standing in the room, watching Wilhelmina descend the stairs. Grinning broadly, he gallantly vocalized, "Miss Thaylor, I've been looking everywhere for you—hither and yon."

Recognizing the teasing from the handsome man's tone, Wilhelmina continued down the stairs. *Regardless of his antics, he is a charmer.* "Why? Pray tell, my lord."

Exuding profound warmth, his tone amusing, he continued, "I have been left to my own wiles as my host has forsaken my company for that of a horse. Can you believe such an absurdity? A horse rather than my charming company? Will you allow me to be your servant and turn my day glorious?" He made an overstated cavalier bow.

Laughing, she joined Lord Restin and impishly returned, "The Earl of Grenmoor chose a horse firstly? My, oh my." *I would prefer riding Zephr, too. The Earl must know the joy that his beautiful stallion gives his rider.* "Upstaged by a horse, dear me, my lord." She curtsied.

They were both laughing and did not hear or see Lord Barclay standing nearby. Jonathan stood with his back to him while Wilhelmina was standing sideways. As she was looking at the blond lord, her eye caught the Earl's reflection in the windows' pane, his frown magnified by his muscle clenched jaw. Realizing he was eavesdropping, she exaggerated, carrying on with Lord Restin. "However, do not lament, my lord. You must trade being cast off as a means to rise above rejection, move onward and conquer, the unknown."

"Hold, dear maiden; if you will permit us to adventure together, I will protect you from the fearsome dragon waiting to spew his fury," he exaggeratedly begged.

Wilhelmina's giggles lit up her face and her green eyes shined. Jonathan was completely taken with her vivacious bearing. "As humbled as I may be, my lord, I must decline your generous offer, so you must journey on alone."

Lord Lucien Barclay had heard enough nonsense. His violent mood filled the room. *This husband hunter is in for a shock. I'm on to her—the scheming vamp. Johnny's acting a fool. What's come over him!*

Jonathan saw his friend's undisguised ire. Grinning, he inquired, "What happened, Lu? Did the big black beast throw you?"

"Very funny, Johnny." He stared at Wilhelmina. When he watched his friend and the mahogany-haired lovely enjoy their tête-à-tête, it doubled his irritation. The friendly intimacy between them gnawed. Not in a generous mood, the Earl boorishly stated, directing his words to Wilhelmina, "I know that you are my grandmother's guest, Miss Thaylor, and it behooves me to ask, however, if you will find this Willie person for me *at once*. I would appreciate it. Evidently, Jaggers is attending to some other major eventuality and cannot do so." He hesitated a second, raised his eyebrow and grumbled, "Then you and Lord Restin may continue to carry on."

Lord Barclay's condescending tone angered Wilhelmina. His sardonic manner was a thorn she couldn't remove. *He may be the titled Earl of Grenmoor but to insinuate that I am carrying on with Lord Restin is overmuch.* Acknowledging Lord Barclay, she barely made a minuscule curtsy and graciously said, "Good morn, my Lord." Her green eyes darkened as her tone, unyielding yet pacifying, said, "It is true, my lord, that I am Lady Julia's guest, and I may fulfill a favor someone asks of me." This time, she made an obvious deep curtsy, rose, peered at him without moving an eyelash, and said, "I trust that will be satisfactory with you, my lord?" She did not weaken. "But," her ire coming to the forefront, she did not realize she put her hands on her hips while taking two steps forward and, looking up into the Earl's staring eyes, said, "For your information, *Sir*, Lord Restin and I were not carrying on. Lord Restin explained that you preferred a horse's company rather than his," she smirked, "I might add that Lord Restin got the better deal; the horse surely did not!" She turned, nodding to Lord Restin and walked smartly from their company. The two men didn't know that when Miss Thaylor's back stiffened, it strengthened her resolve not to be talked down to.

Lord Lucien Barclay was speechless. No one had ever dared address him in that manner, especially someone of the female persuasion and in his own home.

Jonathan's laughter pealed loud and clear. "I say, Lu, I do not know what has come over you. Whatever it is, that fiery guest of Lady Julia's is not intimidated by your title or your unpleasant mindset." He was goading his long-time friend. "What have you always called the female gender? Oh yes, I believe it's that they are simple-minded snivelers and always ready to drape themselves all over you. It seems that today, the great Earl of Grenmoor has met his match." He poked Lucien with his elbow. "Miss Thaylor is not simple-minded, and she certainly isn't a sniveler, and we both know sure-fire that she is not draping herself all about you. You know what, Lu? I like her. I really do. She's like a fresh breeze I haven't experienced in a long time."

Lucien raised that eyebrow. "Certainly not a gentle breeze, Johnny; more like a gale."

"What is it about Miss Thaylor that seems to rile you? Her dancing, maybe?"

"The devil, Johnny, though I agree the spitfire is different from other women. To top it off, she doesn't seem to notice—or if she does, she cares not one whit about her dress, arms exposed, and unruly hair… no doubt she has a motive for being here in Cornwall, and I'm curious as to how she plans to obtain her goal. The only thing I'll admit to… the lady knows how to waltz."

"You're talking in riddles." Defending the lovely woman, Jonathan added, "You certainly are cynical, Lu. I would bet she is not after anything and has no ulterior motive. You're just in an unforgiving mood."

"Listen," his tone hardened, "no female is without a motive of one kind or another. Think! Why would a young beauty be out here in the middle of nowhere and not off where she can dress properly and attend afternoon teas and evening balls?"

"Perhaps, she has no interest, or it may be that she has no sponsor. Maybe, she doesn't have the background; after all, she is addressed as *Miss*. Why not ask your grandmother?"

Lucien dropped into a favorite leather chair, propped up his feet, and rested his hands behind his head. "Good heavens, Johnny, don't tell me you're that naïve. I would wager that dear Grandy's guest is a hunter, and I don't mean for the four-legged species."

"Ah, Lu, you think everyone has only marriage on their mind. There have always been women doting on you with hope. They're like bees hovering to be drawn to your hive. How you get away with it is beyond me. You insult them by paying for bedding them and they still wish to be your paramour. But now," the mood changed serious with a tinge of wonder, "there is Miss Thaylor who doesn't measure up… rather, she's just the opposite of your interpretation of women, and you more than sharpen your tongue and scowl when she is around and come across as a self-important noble. This is not like you. Why?"

Lucien turned his head to look at his long-time close friend who hadn't sat down, but stood near the cold fireplace, though it was ready to be fired. "That's quite a narration of my life, Johnny." There was a trace of bitterness in his tone. "The one word you omitted is *trust*, and until I find a woman, which I doubt exists, that I can trust, then I'll continue on and pay for bedding as its consensual. I don't offer diamonds or pearls for them to flaunt. Call it cold-hearted and arrogant, but I'll never be accused of heartbreak. It is pleasurable at the time and nothing more." Lucien stood. "You know me well, my friend. I am who I am. There are only two people I trust… Grandy and *you*. And if Grandy keeps interfering in my life, I might have to exclude her and trust only you."

Jonathan shook his head. "I can't imagine how I've earned your loyalty, Lu. Just so you know, I've always respected and treasured our friendship."

"I know." Lucien acknowledged their mutual understanding and then said, "How about I suggest Grandy that she work at making a match for you, the Earl of Ventry? You require an heir, I believe."

"Don't remind me… I'm waiting for you, and then I'll consider being shackled, too." Jonathan plopped down in a chair and spoke with conviction, "Although I might not mind being chained to sassy, lovely Miss Thaylor. I think I'll ask Lady Julia about her. I find her more than interesting."

"Johnny, you are being taken." Lucien was upset. He didn't care for Miss Thaylor, and suddenly, he didn't want his friend to be interested it her. "Surely, you're jesting. You're falling into her trap."

"Trap? What are you talking about? Are you serious?"

"I believe Miss Thaylor is a husband hunter and Grandy and she are conspiring for me to accept her as the next Countess of Grenmoor."

Jonathan laughed, "You've got to be kidding. Marry her… you? Lu, I'll bet you a hundred pounds you are wrong about that beauty conniving to marry you." Laughing more, he added, "Why, even with all your title and wealth, she doesn't even like you."

"Save your money, Johnny. If I'm wrong, I'll apologize."

"You are in a bad temper. Did Zephr not perform to your expectations?"

"I did not ride Zephr this morning as I planned. It seems this Willie rises before dawn and was gone before I set foot in the stable."

Flabbergasted, Jonathan's mouth fell open. "You mean he took Zephr? With you here?"

"Yes, and to top it off, everyone in the stable is ready to defend the lad. Dealing with that was enough to take out my anger on just about everyone." What Lucien didn't say was that returning and finding his grandmother's guest acting innocent and flirting with his friend added to his morning's upheaval. He was unable to understand why that firebrand provoked him. *She certainly wasn't sniveling or self-centered. She doesn't even realize how striking she is with those fired-up green eyes and thick, dark, auburn hair, and her tanned face and bare arms that add to her charm.*

"Tell me, Lu," Jonathan was watching his friend, "what erased that scowl, turning it into a smile? What or whom were you thinking about? Evelyne Carstairs, right? She has it all and would make a beautiful countess."

"You think she'd made a beautiful countess, do you?" Not waiting for an answer, "Then you marry her."

"Lady Carstairs... *my* countess? I'm not wealthy enough as I only have three estates. She's waiting for you."

Lucien laughed and shook his head—his mood lightened. "Speaking of Willie, I guess I won't hang him yet. I admit, there's admiration for him the way he handles Zephr with ease and with no abuse, and believe me, that horse is a handful. Logan said Willie never uses a whip or takes one when riding. I've decided to let this Willie continue to ride Zephr, but only when I'm not here. Zephr has never looked better."

"So again, the horse comes first, and ladies second, or even last. Lu, you'll never change."

"You just don't understand my perspectives regarding horses, Johnny. You care nothing for the animal except that it will move you from one place to another. I'm telling you, when it comes to animals, you get what you give. Take Zephr... he asks for nothing more than a little care and food and gives his contented thanks with a gentle nudge and an inspiring ride. As for those supposedly gentle females you vociferously justify, admit that they expect to be coddled, petted, given constant attention—and don't forget, they expect to receive expensive gifts. They first think of themselves, and then, in marrying you, they have done you one gigantic favor." Lucien's mood turned. "Be honest, do you not find it all rather tiresome and boring? To be married to one, as I've described, would make life a living torment. Marriage means 'chained for life', so I will prolong it as long as I possibly can. I am in no rush for a life of ennui."

"After marriage, you'll stay the course, and there will be no mistress? No extra bedding?"

"As I've said, once married, there will be no other women. No mistress in my life and there sure as hell," his voice hardened ruthlessly, "won't be any other man in my wife's life."

"Maybe you'll be lucky and find that special someone, and when you do, you better hope she doesn't tell you to take yourself, your title, your riches and your horses and be gone. You're not easy to please, and you're heading toward a lonely life."

Lucien couldn't help but chuckle. "The trouble with you is that you love all women and then break their hearts. That's where you and I part company." Lucien then said matter-of-factly, "Don't fool with Lady Julia's guest in that fashion, Johnny. Grandy won't like it," he hesitated and then added, "and neither will I."

Stunned, Jonathan gaped. "Will you be troubled if I decided to become better acquainted with Miss Thaylor? I mean in a serious manner."

"You don't know who she is or where she's from; what kind of background she has, and who her parents are; and why she became the ward of Lady Marlowe. And she's a *Miss.* Perhaps a lady, but certainly not titled."

"You've always judged a person by their character rather than their background. You're surprising me. I like her, Lu, and it matters not to me about her ancestry."

Lucien smothered the memory Miss Thaylor seemed to arouse in him. *That waltz.* "Suit yourself, Johnny. I could care less."

"If I didn't know better, I'd say you have an interest in Miss Thaylor, too."

Answering almost too quickly, he snapped, "That little conniving hoyden, I think not. Just bear in mind that Grandy has plans for her. I just know it! And don't think for one second that her guest is all that innocent. Best watch yourself, or you'll be betrothed."

"You really believe they are conspiring together?"

"Definitely. I know Grandy is much like your aunt, Lady Edith Marlowe. They thought they could maneuver me into marriage with Lady Agatha, but I proved them wrong. If I know my Grandy, she hasn't given up."

"Me thinks thou protest too much. Besides, Miss Thaylor is not like the others. Have you not noticed her complexion is not milk-white? Her hair is not coiffure, and her fingernails are cut close and unpainted, and her gowns are unadorned." Jonathan winked, "But of course, whatever she wears, she's beautiful. There is nothing artificial about her."

Do you think I'm blind? Of course, I've noticed—not only that—but there is a grace about her that shines. "Are you through espousing her attributes?"

Grinning, Jonathan assailed, "You *do* like her. Attributes, you say."

"I won't dignify that with an answer."

"Well then, Lu, I shall visit with Lady Julia and seek her permission to pursue the lovely redhead."

Suppressing his dismay, yet not comprehending why, Lucien cautioned, "Suit yourself, Johnny, but this isn't like you… have care."

Chapter Thirteen

Sitting in a straight-backed chair, Lady Julia Barclay handed a cup of tea to Lord Restin. "This unexpected request for a visit is a surprise, Jonathan."

The Earl of Ventry smiled generously at the woman he'd known all his growing years. "I asked for this private audience, Lady Julia, because it is a personal matter." He set the untouched tea upon the small table beside him.

Lady Julia raised her eyebrow at Jonathan, who, being familiar with the Barclay trait, withheld the smile wanting to break through. "I'm intrigued as to what an old woman can do to help a young scamp as yourself." Her voice softened, "If it's funds you require, I'm certain—"

Interrupting quickly, he said, "Oh, no, my lady, surely not."

"Firstly, Jonathan, in the privacy of this room, you may call me Grandy," she reminded him, "you used to address me that way a time ago. You may be older, but I still see you and Lucien as young rapscallions always trying to outfox me."

Grinning, he said, "I never knew we were so obvious."

Her silver eyes twinkled. "It was all part of both your growing years."

Lord Restin's strong affection for this grand lady never wavered. "Thank you, Grandy. You may not believe this, but when you would scold Lu about learning his bad behavior from me, I cherished that, as I thought it gave me some importance coming from you." Laughing, his charm exuded the entire room. "I'm not all that bad, you know?"

Lady Julia tsk-tsked and then asked, "Suppose you tell me what it is I can do for you."

"It is about Miss Thaylor. I am very seriously thinking about courting her."

Lady Julia leaned forward while setting her teacup and saucer down. *Jonathan is not supposed to be smitten with Willie. My stubborn grandson should be.*

"You see, Grandy," he continued, "if I may have your permission, I would like to get to know Miss Thaylor beyond a mere acquaintance."

Keeping her tone light, she said, "Miss Thaylor is an extraordinary young lady."

"Exactly my sentiments." Jonathan rose and paced a few steps, not knowing in this same room, Lucien ordered his Grandy to cease her matchmaking.

"You do realize that Miss Thaylor has a mind of her own," Lady Julia chuckled, "She's sassy when she's irked. Too, she is not part of the *ton*. You are, Jonathan. Won't that be a dilemma for you?" She had to try to discourage him from pursuing the one person that was right for her grandson.

"That's what is so attractive about her. Miss Thaylor's humor, and yet, she appears to be a no-nonsense person. And if she is my countess, the *ton* will accept her." Now, he chuckled. "You probably know she has *backbone*."

"Backbone?" She was surprised yet disturbed that his perception was spot-on correct.

Unable to withhold a broad smile and anxious to tell, Lord Restin continued, "Absolutely! This morn, she set Lu back on his heels. She plied him with a few choice words of her own making, including his horse, and then literally left both of us standing in the library with our mouths gaping." Jonathan went on describing this morn's happenstance with Miss Thaylor. "After, Lu and I were discussing Miss Thaylor, and I accused him of being jealous when he overheard Miss Thaylor and me teasing each other."

Inwardly pleased, yet not wanting Jonathan to know of her surreptitious interest, casually using her napkin and taking her time, she blotted her mouth and then said, "And just how did Lucien handle it?"

Jonathan returned to sit down, not missing the veiled unspoken interest from Lady Julia's disguised tone. *There is a flicker of interest in her voice… maybe Lu is right; she is hiding something.* Not smiling, he mulled over his reply while watching the white-haired sly woman whom he just learned was never outfoxed by the two of them. *Oh, Grandy, I'm on to you… you want Lu to be smitten with that gorgeous redhead, not me. I'm not giving up.*

"Well, Jonathan," she pressed, "Was Lucien upset?"

No doubt about it, Lu, she is matchmaking, but I don't think Miss Thaylor is aware of it. Eying the grand old woman with a new perspective, he coyly replied, "Lu was annoyed about my insinuating his being jealous. He said he has no interest in Miss Thaylor or any woman in particular." Wanting to prickle this meddling of this woman he revered, he added, "But then, Lu is seeing Lady Evelyn Carstairs more often than any other woman." He mused, "Though he vehemently denies any interest in her, I disagree." Grinning, he purposely added, "We both know we must provide an heir, and I think Lu is taking his obligation serious." Then throwing more kindling on an already hot fire, feeling the tickle run through him, Lord Restin continued, "It makes me know I have an obligation to my family, and that's why, I think Miss Thaylor is as good a person to be my countess as I will find."

Not missing the white knuckles as Lady Julia gripped the arms of her chair, she was not pleased with all that he'd said. "How may I help you, Jonathan?"

Nonchalantly and being offhandedly naive, he offered, "Miss Thaylor is your house guest. I would ask that you permit me to accompany her around Seahurst and take in Cornwall with her… enjoy her company, and too, she'll get to know me."

"Are you planning on riding?"

"Oh, no. I ride when I must, and I really doubt whether Miss Thaylor rides well enough to control one of your beasts. I will take one of the carriages… with your permission, of course."

Lady Julia stared at the handsome blond man. *Miss Thaylor not ride and unable to handle a horse—this is an answer to my prayer—she will make up her own mind, but grandson, can you be so blind?* "If Miss Thaylor agrees, Lord Restin, I expect you to be a gentleman at all times. I should have Miss Thaylor's maid go along; however, I will place my trust in you as long as this riding stays within the boundaries of Grenmoor, so as not to cause negative gossip toward my guest."

"I give you my word, Lady Julia. I will conduct myself as a gentleman, especially with Miss Thaylor."

"Very well, but keep in mind that Miss Thaylor is my guest, and the blessing you aspire to must come from your aunt Edith, Miss Thaylor's guardian."

"Aunt Edith? Why? Who is Miss Thaylor that Aunt Edith has become her guardian?"

"Those answers must come from Lady Edith. I am not privileged to say; in fact, I haven't the answers to your questions."

Disconcerted, Jonathan, weighing the revelation of his aunt's guardianship of Miss Thaylor, rationalized—a touch of anxiety in his tone, "Perhaps, I shall not pursue Miss Thaylor until I have Aunt Edith's permission; that way, when I propose to Miss Thaylor, all will be right. I will travel to London in the morn as I'm anxious to talk with Aunt Edith and have an understanding. Then, I am going to do all I can to get that beautiful, uninhibited redhead to take me seriously. Grandy," his voice lowered but fierce, "I am captivated and will be honored to have Miss Thaylor become my Countess of Ventry."

Unsatisfied with this outcome and knowing she had to keep Wilhelmina's stay at Seahurst longer, she tendered her answer, "I wish you the best. I'm sure Miss Thaylor's choosing to become betrothed will be made wisely."

He said nothing but thought of what Lady Julia said; did it have a double meaning? Was it in his favor? He wasn't sure, but time would be the indicator. He could wait a while longer before starting his conquest of Miss Thaylor. He would talk with Aunt Edith about this important undertaking of wedding the confident, lovely lady. Guarding his thoughts—disbelieving in one sense that within these last forty-eight hours he is seriously thinking of marriage, looking at Lady Julia and not completely trusting her regarding Miss Thaylor, and having to leave with Lucien still at Seahurst, he still had to do what had to be done. "You're quite right, Grandy. Miss Thaylor will choose wisely. And after I talk with Aunt Edith," he brazenly winked, "I'll pursue Miss Thaylor until she says *yes*."

Lady Julia lightly admonished, "You've always been an upstart, Jonathan," yet smiling, added, "always dear to me."

Lord Jonathan Restin, Earl of Ventry, leaned over and kissed the dowager's wrinkled cheek. "And you will always remain endearing to me, Grandy. If you will excuse me, I will find Lu and let him know I'll be leaving." He bowed, and the Earl of Ventry departed, leaving Lady Julia with much to think and plan.

* * *

That evening, Seascape Drawing Room

Lucien was in a better mood. Completing their meal rather than remain to have a brandy, the two earls chose to have coffee with Grandy and Miss Thaylor in the drawing room.

"I will miss this," Jonathan said, "the company of two exceptional ladies along with Cornwall's adverse weather, but I have duties to attend."

"You really mean to leave in the morn, Johnny?"

"I must. I intend to visit with Aunt Edith and then attend to matters that I've neglected. Perhaps I'll see you all in London."

Lucien looked at his grandmother. "What say you, Grandy, are you willing to spend time in London town and see about the household at Barclay Square?"

I've got to keep both Lucien and Willie here in Seahurst. "I said I planned to spend time in town, but not until I have every matter here at Seahurst looked after. When we've settled that, we can adjourn to Barclay Square." Her tone purposely insinuated she would make all decisions.

"Grandy," Lucien uttered, "I'm warning you… don't go there."

"What's up, Lu?"

"Never mind, Johnny. You do your thing in London, and we'll be along." He eyed Wilhelmina, surprising everyone. "Miss Thaylor, will you stay two weeks more and accompany my grandmother in our coach? It will be safe and a more comfortable ride."

"Or," Lord Restin burst out, "you can come with me tomorrow morn. We'll be company for each other."

Dumbfounded by Lord Barclay's gentle request and then hearing Lord Restin's ridiculous offer, with her humor itching to tease, Wilhelmina angled her body toward Lord Restin and seriously persuaded, "My Lord! Just the two of us traveling alone? It will not do. Why, to save *your* reputation, I'd be forced to propose marriage—and seeing that I don't wish to marry," she shook her head regretfully, "so I think not. I'll travel with Lady Julia." Laughing, she added, "Wouldn't you be in a pickle if I accepted?" Her laughter showing her white teeth against rosy, tan skin and, as usual, that one loose curl falling over one eye that she momentarily pushed behind her ear while the lighted candelabra's candles reflected her green eyes into emeralds, the three stared at the picture she made as well as her outright humorous absurdity. Her smile faded when she turned toward Lord Barclay. "Thank you, my lord, for inviting me. I'd be delighted to journey with Lady Julia."

Lady Julia could barely hide her joy. "Then it's settled. Jonathan, you will visit us at Barclay Square, and if I feel up to it, I might just see that we give a ball."

Lucien couldn't fault with his grandmother for thinking of having a ball, as at one time, Barclay's famous ball was an exclusive affair. One hoped for an invitation, and when it came, it was cherished. Lucien glanced at Miss Thaylor. *To waltz with you. I haven't forgotten.*

"Splendid, Lady Julia." Lord Resin went on. "Miss Thaylor, right this minute, I insist that you save the first waltz for me."

Miss Thaylor smothered her want to smile and turned to the Earl. "Do you think, my lord, I'll remember how to waltz?"

The Earl of Grenmoor knew when he was being mocked, and he didn't mind it one iota. In fact, a pleasant jolt dashed through to his head—memories. "It is too bad, Miss Thaylor, that we do not have an orchestra to see if you remember the waltz. If I remember correctly, you dance it well." Then a thought traversed, and he spoke without a smile, but his tone deep and smooth as velvet, "If there is a ball, then it is my duty to have the first waltz to test your ability and also the last waltz to ensure that you won't forget."

Jonathan, silent but not believing what his friend implied. *Not Lu... he never makes overtures to anyone. What is he up to with **my lady**?*

Lady Julia was beyond pleased and overjoyed.

Wilhelmina, quite taken by the Earl's direct compliment, gathered her wits and brazenly suggested, "To test my dancing skill, my lord, perhaps we could hum the music now and see if *you* remember?"

Lucien couldn't help but smile... it was a warm smile as it reached his eyes.

Jonathan warred, "I think not, Miss Thaylor, as Lord Barclay will purposely step on your toes and blame the music."

"You found me out, Johnny. We'll have to wait for Grandy's ball."

Lady Julia spoke, "I haven't decided if there will be a Barclay Ball, though I believe it is a grand idea, and of course, Miss Thaylor will receive an invitation with Lady Edith."

"I can't really say, my lady. If my ship sails before your ball," she spoke with finality, "I'll be at sea, though I'll be imagining all the dancing and enjoyment."

Lady Julia didn't hesitate to reply, "That's true. Let's hope you sail *after* our ball."

They were enjoying their coffee when Lord Barclay spoke to Miss Thaylor, "Did you locate Willie for me and tell him I'd like to meet with him?"

"Yes, my lord, Willie is willing to meet with you in the morn after the usual morn ride and definitely will not ride Zephr."

"This Willie is an impertinent lad, Grandy. Where did you find him?"

"Willie appeared and said horses were a favorite and liked them. Robbie said Willie has the *touch*, so I allowed Willie a free hand. Willie's company has been invigorating to all of Seahurst, as you can see."

"After I see him in the morn, I'll tell you what I think of the lad."

"I'm afraid not, dear. I sent Willie to Devon for supplies." Seemingly not concerned, she explained, "I didn't know you asked Miss Thaylor to get Willie for you."

"When did this come about?" He eyed his grandmother with suspicion.

"Shortly before tea this afternoon. When Cook said we were running low, I saw no reason to wait a few days for delivery."

Wilhelmina couldn't sit by, hearing Lady Julia craft more untruths. "If I may be excused, I'll say good night. Lord Restin, I wish you a safe journey, and please, if you will, relay to Lady Edith that I will see her soon." She stood, curtseyed to Lady Julia and then to Lord Barclay, and left.

Lady Julia, knowing what she said and was doing was wrong and that Wilhelmina would no longer agree to be a party to her mischief, lifted her cup of tea and found it cooled. Still determined, she thought, *I need these two weeks to make Lucien see what a treasure Willie is, and then I'll admit why I instigated these falsehoods.*

Meanwhile, Wilhelmina began to plan her return to London and ready her sail to America to Aggie and James. She liked Cornwall and its multiplicity of weather, especially the freedom of donning breeches, and riding Zephr and now, Zairian. She'd rise early as usual and gallop across Grenmoor and later meet and try to explain to Lord Barclay how Willie came about. *If the Earl will release a bit of the charm he had this eve, maybe, she will be forgiven this charade.*

Mostly, she thought how she would miss Lady Julia but certainly not her arrogant grandson, the famously handsome Earl of Grenmoor. *Aggie, our charade was the right thing to do, after all. You would not be happy with the Earl, especially that you don't like riding and he seems to thrive from it. He exudes power like Zephr, and I must admit, it magnifies his mystique. So, Aggie, my friend, we did the right thing—you are with the man you love, and hopefully, I will find someone, too.*

Climbing into bed, Wilhelmina had to grant one undeniable point, that without a doubt, the Earl was not an old man as Aggie derided. *I won't ride in the morn; I'll wait for Lord Barclay to return from his morn ride and tell him the truth.* Her mind settled, Wilhelmina closed her eyes and slept.

Chapter Fourteen

Next Morn

Lord Barclay joined Lady Julia and Wilhelmina as they were breaking their fast. He was still in his riding clothes. Having a good ride on Zephr, he was in a placating mood and decided it was time to undo his previous rude conduct, surprising both ladies when he asked, "Do you ride, Miss Thaylor? I could show you about Grenmoor if the weather holds."

The dowager barely managed to conceal choking on her toast.

Wilhelmina blinked, and thinking to tease this very good-looking, virile, obstinate man as she brazenly waltzed, diffidently answered, "Yes, I do ride, only…"

Being courteous and thinking she did not want to admit that she could not sit a horse well, Lord Barclay interposed, "Perhaps it would be better if we were to use the curricle."

She casually said, "Thank you, my lord; I have discovered the Cornwall weather is definitely unreliable, but that's what makes it interesting."

"Then, we must hope the weather will hold as the curricle will be without a top. It is more enjoyable to use it that way, but be aware, you will be windblown."

Unknowing that her smile initiated sunshine into the room, she said, "I look forward to the ride, and without a top will make it more a challenge. I worry not about being windblown."

The Earl of Grenmoor could not help staring at the beautiful woman. Her openness, along with her golden complexion, became strangely appealing to him. Feeling pleased with his decision, he said, "Shall we say in the morn tomorrow at the half-past the ten hour, if that is not too early for you?"

In all innocence, she replied, "That will be fine, Lord Barclay, but will you not be pressed for time if you ride your big black horse?"

Not expecting her regard but pleased, he answered, "I see you have heard of Zephr." Proudly with his dark eyes warm, he continued, "Zephr is my wondrous black stallion, though not one that settles easily. I usually ride at daybreak, so there will be plenty of time for our drive."

Lady Julia listened to the easy discourse between the two people she was fond of. She could only hope her plotting would prevail. Being ever so careful, she knew it was necessary to criticize her grandson's plan. "Really, Lucien, I do not think it is a good idea to take Miss Thaylor out in the buggy, especially with Cornwall's unpredictable weather."

"Grandy," he gently rebuked, "I thought you would be pleased. Did you not remind me about our Barclay custom?"

"That is so, but I cannot have my guest catch a chill. And what about a chaperone?" The old woman sounded adamant.

Wilhelmina didn't want to miss riding with the Earl, even in a carriage. She wished to see Seahurst from his viewpoint, so she quickly injected, "Please, Lady Julia? I will dress warm, and I'd like to see more of Seahurst in any kind of weather."

"There you are, Grandy," Lord Barclay said, his tone lighthearted, "after all—Miss Thaylor has not had an opportunity to see much of anything while visiting. We have no choice but to honor your guest's wishes."

Feigning reluctance, Lady Julia finally relented. "I believe I must yield to the both of you; take Tess with you."

"Impossible, the curricle seats only two, as you well know. Do you propose Tess run alongside?"

"Don't be facetious, Lucien."

"There is no need for concern. Miss Thaylor and I will be fine. We will ride only on Grenmoor land."

Overly excited and not understanding this sudden elation building within her, she offered assuredly, "We will manage, my lady."

Lord Barclay found himself gratified at putting these matters right with this saucy firebrand. *Yet once again, she is boldly reassuring Grandy.* Even so, he discovered he was actually looking forward to the next morn's outing. Here was a female not concerned about the weather or worried about her hair blowing wil-nil. It should prove an interesting outing.

Lady Julia Barclay sat in her patted chair, working diligently to bury the deep smile that warmed her whole being. *They both are such innocents.*

* * *

The sun was peeping through the cumulus clouds as the Earl of Grenmoor helped Miss Thaylor into the two-seated open curricle.

Wilhelmina's dark velvet green pelisse hugged her body. Her matching velvet bonnet with its wide ribbons tied snugly under her chin left her long auburn tresses hanging freely below her bonnet.

Lord Lucien Barclay could not help but observe her green eyes fused splendidly with her outfit. His voice deep with undisguised admiration, he said, "May I say you look very fetching, Miss Thaylor?"

While her stomach turned somersaults, she courteously replied, "Thank you, my lord." She was thrilled by his compliment, but more so by just being in his company. He was so different from their first introduction and previous encounters. She wanted to remember everything that befell this day so she could tell all to Aggie. Indeed, the Earl was indescribably kind; this must be what Lady Julia signified. Still, in her mind, she knew Aggie and the Earl would never have suited, as their personalities would never have meshed. Aggie didn't care a fig for riding all that much, only using horses to show off her new riding habits. "And may I say that you also look well, my lord?" Then she blushed, having spoken so freely. She didn't add that his tanned complexion from riding made him seem all the more magnificent.

Taken aback by her forward appraisal, he nodded, "Thank you, Miss Thaylor."

The familiar groom stared at Wilhelmina. *She sure looks different in a dress; not the Willie I know.* He remained silent as he nodded to her and then said, "Hello, Miss."

Smiling, she acknowledged in her usual melodious voice, "Good morn."

Lord Barclay glanced at the groom and at Miss Thaylor, slightly shrugged his shoulders, as never did a stable hand ever speak unless first spoken to. And never had any of his acquaintances recognized a servant, other than to give an order. *Oh well, this spitfire is not the usual piece of fluff.* Jolted, he wondered why he'd even think to compare this headstrong woman as an acquaintance. Thinking back to that first morn in the library with Johnny and having been

85

given a vociferously dressing-down, he smothered a grin. *Oh, yes, she is surely different.* And for some strange reason, he was gratified about it. He felt he was going to enjoy this outing today and happy it came about.

Sitting straight and somewhat comfortable in the tightly spaced curricle next to the masculine Earl, she could feel her heart fluttering. What was the matter with her? Her insides were jittery. She could sense the body warmth emanating from him as he filled the seat with his overpowering size. Too, the fact that the Earl's attitude was no longer insolent gave her unexpected joy.

It was unacceptable that a single lady would be alone in the company of a man, but Wilhelmina cared not one iota. She was in her glory and knew it was the presence of this tall, handsome man beside her. *I best be careful; this will not do. I am out of my element and best I remember the Earl is only being agreeable to me because of Lady Julia reminding him I'm her guest. I don't belong in his elite society, but I will enjoy this day and be myself, though I better watch my busy mouth and not spew too many opinions. It could spoil the day.*

The Earl gently fluttered the ribbons, signaling the golden matched pair to move forward. They started with a smooth trot.

"So, Miss Thaylor, is there anywhere special you would like to go? Possibly overhearing some place that raised your curiosity? Cornwall is beautiful if you understand its history."

Knowing she couldn't reveal that she had ridden over much of Grenmoor land and that it was imperative to stay away from the Earl's tenants, she thought of the wild stretch of moors. "I have heard of the moors, Lord Barclay. Do you think we might travel there?"

The moors are not nature's most appealing vista, but of course Miss Thaylor would not know. He told her of their craggy, rocky lands, all brown in color and useless, the only exception being that the turf was taken from it and used for fuel.

Without thought, she contradicted him, "If the moors provide fuel, then it cannot be useless. I should like to see it."

He raised his right eyebrow at her correct presumption and firmly said, "Very well, we shall visit the moors."

The moors were quite a ride from the manor. Neither of the curricle's occupants spoke as the sound of the horses' hooves sounded melodious in their clop-clop across solid ground. It was a restful sound that inspired no conversation. Both persons were quiet in their own thoughts. The sun peeked through the clouds now and then, offering a bit of brightness enhancing the day.

Suddenly, breaking the silence, Wilhelmina cried out, "Oh look, my lord, the land is covered with yellow flowers! Even with the clouds shutting out the sun, they glow and reach for the sky." She eyed the seemingly unreadable man and couldn't withhold a tease. "I can see what you mean when you say the land is brown."

"Tell me, Miss Thaylor; are you always so cognizant of everything voiced?"

"But of course, my lord, how can I not be?"

The Earl of Grenmoor liked her spirit and couldn't help laughing. "Getting back to those beautiful yellow flowers you admire, never try to pick them."

"Why ever not? Do you know what they are called?"

He noted that she did not accept his warning but countered it with more interest. Like her query to know more, he was pleased to answer. "Those yellow flowers you are so taken with are called *furze,* or better known as *gorse.*" He chuckled. "They are very spiny and, consequently, are left alone to spread their beauty over a lot of wastelands. Not only are they prevalent here in Cornwall, but they also spread themselves in places across the continent."

She could not contain her exuberance. "Is not nature absolutely amazing, my lord? It allows some things to say, 'Do not touch me. I belong to this land,' while other beautiful flowers are plucked and taken as one's own." Her eyes shone even on the cloudy day, and she spoke from her heart. "Wisely using spiny thorns for their protection, the furze is still a beautiful flower, do you not agree?"

As the wheels were swallowed in minor holes, Lucien gripped the ribbons as he peered down, taking in her mahogany curls hanging below her bonnet while she earnestly took in her surroundings. A bit awed, he agreed, "Yes, Miss Thaylor, there is a lot of beauty here even if coated with thorns."

Aware that the Earl of Grenmoor was being polite even with her busy tongue, she was delighted by his rejoinder. She sensed more ease with him then she'd ever expected.

"You know, my lord, they say beauty is in the eyes of the beholder, and to me, these moors possess their own unique perfections. I see the brown patches as we approach them, and they seem solid and strong against the elements from the sea." Her voice, unfeigned, she continued, "One could come to a place like this totally unencumbered to think and even relax." Then quickly adding with a wide smile, displaying her lovely rosy mouth, "That is, if the weather would cooperate and let one enjoy this wondrous world of isolation." She put her hand up to shade her eyes, staring out. "It must be staggering to be out here without protection, with the rain pounding the moor and the wind blowing; frightening, really, even if one is bundled to stay dry."

"Ah, Miss Thaylor, your guileless intrigues me. How ever did my grandmother find you?" He spoke without suspicion and didn't seem to particularly expect an answer; it was just an unexpected pleasing comment.

Wilhelmina choked inwardly. Deceiving Lord Lucien Barclay, she sensed this supposedly temperamental man was not going to appreciate the game Lady Julia initiated and she consented to go along. She was quiet, letting his statement pass, and then changed the subject. "Do you think, my lord, we can travel over the moors toward the sea?"

Not noticing anything strange in her request, especially coming from this inquisitive, surprisingly likable person, he responded, "As sure footed as these horses are, Miss Thaylor, and that they travel most always by instinct, I think not. We had better keep their safety in mind and stay on the path. It would be difficult to pull the carriage across the moors and around the bogs, rocks, tora, and brooks."

"It does appear a bit inhospitable." She lowered her voice, "Yet, it is so quiet with only the wind for company. I like that."

He didn't mention that he too found this a place for solitude. A breathing space with its unkempt landscape. Looking at her tanned cheeks and bright eyes, he halted the horses and the carriage rocked to a stop. "You are a strange one. You have a ready smile and an exceptionally vital, telling outlook that you portray often," they stared at each other in the ringing silence, "and you appear to like the company of people. Still, you vie for this solitude and placid life. Where do you really belong?"

Unabashed, she spoke openly, "What you have said about me is quite true, my lord." Her voice changed to reverence. "My father was a vicar, and naturally, people would seek him out regularly, regardless of the time of day. He did not mind, and I accepted it as our way of life. However, one rainy afternoon, we had no interruptions… I remember it well." Lord Barclay heard melancholy break in her voice. "The two of us sitting quietly in our cottage, the only sounds were the clock ticking and the rain pattering against the windowpanes. I sat with an open book, not reading. We were both absorbing the quiet… tranquilized with our own thoughts. My father smiled at me and said that I should never forget that solitude is a precious gift. I should respect it, treasure it, and offer it to others when possible." She looked over at the Earl and said simply, "There was sadness within him that afternoon… I only wish I knew why. He said I was the best gift he could have ever received." Unconsciously, she touched the Earl's arm. "I was abandoned at his church, and he said that I belonged to him that very minute." Tears formed but didn't fall. "I was so very lucky." She looked away, hiding her embarrassment of telling too much, then half-smiled and said, "I apologize, my lord. I've spoiled your quiet with my prattling."

Momentarily speechless and fascinated at her remarkable intellect, he only nodded.

"Just one more thing, my lord. I do enjoy company, yet I treasure the solace of isolation. As my father said, *it is a treasure*, and I couldn't agree more. It is not something you buy; it is a free commodity for each of us to take, respect, and enjoy. If used wisely, it can be enriching without the need for material things, including an abundance of funds."

Never before had Lord Lucien Barclay met a woman that wholeheartedly understood the need for solitude. He was in awe of this forthright, outspoken termagant with her understanding of life. "It's obvious your father's love connected so well with you, Miss Thaylor. Your grasping the importance of enjoying quiet opportunities available is unusual, especially to liking seclusion without having to make an absurd excuse for it."

"My father's words stay with me; I'll value them always." Feeling cramped from their long ride, she tried to move her legs. "Please, my lord, may we not stretch our legs for just a few minutes?" So taken by their perceptive aloneness on the moors and the gentleness of the man, she did not think it was a request he would not accede to. Besides, she wanted to prolong their outing, knowing it would soon be over, and she would never again be alone in his company.

"I do not think it would be wise, Miss Thaylor. We will most likely get wet, as it is. Those clouds hovering have darkened. We must return to the manor."

Wilhelmina didn't heed his warning. Without thinking, she hopped from the carriage unassisted and ran a few steps and turned, ran to spin. Enjoying the wind whipping her pelisse and gown away from her, it then took her bonnet, blowing it off her head, though it remained tied, hanging loosely on her back. She was laughing, excited and merry. Her long auburn tresses blew every which way, covering her face one minute, and then blowing away and up high, tangling in the air. She did not care; she was enraptured with the moment. She did not give any consideration to Lord Barclay's call, but continued to spin around again and again, distancing herself from the carriage and the waiting Earl. Suddenly, she slipped and stumbled over her own feet, losing her balance and falling on the wet ground. Her foot caught on a flat slippery rock; she could not move. The pain shot through her leg; still, she did not cry out; only her features unmasked her pain.

The Earl of Grenmoor was beside her instantly, concerned yet smothering his anger over her ignoring his caution and doing as she pleased. Kneeling at her ankle, feeling it through her dampened slippers, he testily exclaimed, "I consider your actions to be witless tomfoolery. Why did you not listen to me?" He continued to hold her ankle. "I believe it is only twisted, not broken." Sarcasm pervaded, "I trust you are quite satisfied, Miss Thaylor!" He stood over her with one knee soaked and soiled from tending her. His boots were muddied.

Hearing the adversity in his tone, she responded likewise, "Thank you, my lord. I appreciate your concern. If you will be so kind and aid me so I may remove myself off the ground, I will gladly return to the carriage, and we can be on our way."

At that moment, the wind calmed. It was eerie, as a massive black cloud moved overhead, ready to blanket the moors with its downpour, adding to the already ominous feeling surrounding them. Only the sound of the sea connected, adding to the horses' wary movements and the windless silence turned their situation threatening.

Once again, she is issuing me orders. This will not do. Offering his hand, Lord Barclay continued his barrage, "You cannot walk on that ankle, Miss Thaylor. I shall have to carry you."

With her jaws set tight, joining the frown covering her face, she obstinately shot back, "No thank you, *Sir*, I can do this myself."

The temper of the Earl was about to explode. Any other female he knew would be anxious to be rescued and held in his arms, but this sassy vixen was trying his patience. She was the most contrary woman he had ever met. Ready to catch her but also ready to show this smart little know-it-all she was wrong, he removed his one hand from her waist and let go of her arm.

As Wilhelmina put her weight on her foot, she almost cried out at the pain and was about to fall but was caught by the powerful man. Quickly, he lifted her into his strong arms, not waiting for her to vent her pigheadedness. It was at the moment the black cloud burst; its icy downpour and sharp needles were unrelenting. The wind started to batter the two people with fury. She held tightly to the Earl, pressed against his broad chest, her cheek cutting into his silver buttons as he plodded over the slippery, wet earth.

Settling her not too gently on the seat, he moved around to the anxious horses, speaking quietly to them. He hand-turned them as he sloshed alongside to aim in the right direction. The horses were difficult to steady, but his strength holding their halter calmed their unease. Climbing in beside her, he loosened his grip on the reins to allow the very wet golden horses have their way to take them back to the stables. They would use their instinct to return safely to their dry stalls and food.

Lord Barclay shouted over the blowing wind and cold rain, "You little idiot, this could have been avoided if you had heeded my warning!"

It was impossible to see where they were going. They both had their heads bent to buck the wind. Wilhelmina's bonnet hung limply down her back, dripping with water, as the deluge plastered her tangled hair to her head. The Earl's hair was also plastered to his forehead, with water soaking his still, tightly bound queue. The afternoon light disappeared as they moved, little by little, forward through a wall of rain. The horses were a blessing taking them back to Seahurst Manor.

Unable to talk or hear, Wilhelmina discerned the Earl's last words calling her an idiot. She was seething as rain hammered her head and body, all the time thinking of the pompous lord having the audacity to call her an idiot and seemingly blaming their saturated predicament on her. If her ankle did not hurt so, she would shout her message to him loud enough to be heard all the way to London and insist on walking back to the manor. Any kind feeling she previously embraced for this noble man vanished. She pulled at her soaked plissé—she was cold.

Holding onto the reins, the Earl of Grenmoor decided it was impractical to try to comfort this young, mindless minx. Sitting silently beside him, he had to admire her plucky stamina. There was no question that her ankle was throbbing and hurting, yet she said not a word as whipping bitter winds kept torturing them with sheets of icy rain. The carriage was too small to remove and offer her his water-soaked coat. He could only hope they would not come down with the ague. His anger was returning in full. When he returned her safely to Seahurst Manor, he would never offer to be in her company again. The devil with Grandy's admonishing him about his manners; someone should have taught this sassy minx the meaning of obeying and heeding guidance. *Once I deliver her to London, I'll be glad to be rid of her.* His cold soaked clothes penetrated to his skin as he looked over at the water-soaked redhead huddled next to him with her head bent and arms crossed—her gloves, wet clothing covered with filth—her hair saturated as though glued to her head, along with her pained ankle, yet she said not a word while icy cold rain hammered them totally. Unexpectedly, that very special soft place in his heart seemed to open as he had an overwhelming feeling of wanting to hold her close and offer her comfort. *Watch it; you are definitely looking for trouble. Stay away from her.*

The storm hadn't abated as they arrived at the manor. They were greeted by his grandmother and what seemed to be the entire Seahurst staff.

The Earl carried Miss Thaylor directly to her rooms and deposited her on the lounge near the fire. His grandmother, Jaggers, Tess, and three others had followed him. *You'd think I carried in a princess.* In a cool, impersonal tone, he ordered that Mrs. Bainsboro be called to attend Miss Thaylor's ankle. He gave her one last glaring look; his dirty saturated clothing with water dripping from his hair and down his face, he stormed from the room.

Lady Julia knew better than to follow her grandson or question him at this moment.

Everyone was busy following the Earl's orders.

Lady Julia stood quietly, worried. "Child, are you alright?"

Wilhelmina nodded. Tears filled her eyes. "I just had a silly accident. I twisted my ankle. I'm sorry for causing this fuss. Lord Barclay is terribly angry."

"Do not concern yourself about my grandson. We all have our moments. Jaggers is locating Mrs. Bainsboro; she will care for you properly. She has a magic touch, and you will be up soon. I'll leave you to have a warm bath—take a long rest."

"Thank you, my lady."

Then, turning her back to Wilhelmina, as her wet clothes were being removed, Lady Julia wanted to soothe her fear. "I want you to take as much hot broth as you can and stay under the covers. I will come to see you in the morn."

Wilhelmina tried not to grimace from the pain as they moved her foot. "Thank you, my lady." Holding back her tears, she apologized. "I should have known better. In truth, the Earl had warned me, but I wouldn't listen." Choking to smother her tears, she said with awe, "The moors… so different, yet there is something remarkable in its isolation. Regardless of the Earl's anger over my ignoring his caution, I'm pleased to have seen that part of Seahurst."

Lady Julia eyed her candid guest with affection, "I haven't visited the moor in years, but I do remember its isolation. Not to worry, my dear, no apology is necessary. I'm sure whatever happened was only by accident. Rest well."

Dabbing her eyes with the corner of the linen towel, Wilhelmina smiled. "Thank you, my lady."

The dowager motioned to Tess. "If Willie needs me or anything special, you have Jaggers tell me immediately. Is that clear?"

"Yes, my lady," Tess curtsied.

Lady Julia left.

Chapter Fifteen

Lady Julia rose earlier than usual and waited. When Jaggers informed her that her grandson was breaking his fast, she hurried to join him.

Lucien was sitting at the table, staring out at the heavy mist. The long glass windowpanes seemed to bring the silent vacuous weather indoors preying on the preoccupied man.

"Good morn, grandson."

He turned, surprised, and raised his eyebrow in the famous Barclay tradition. "Good morn, Grandy. This is unusual, is it not?"

Ignoring his question, she asked, "Did you have a good ride on Zephr this morn? I had hoped you would have remained in to be sure you did not catch a chill. Then you are well?"

"You mean your faithful Jaggers did not report that I fared well?"

"Don't be impertinent."

Eying his dearest grandmother, he politely answered, "I did ride, and it was most invigorating."

The superbly coiffure, white-haired lady said in an agreeable censured tone, "As you well know, your own man, Crooks, is as faithful to you as Jaggers is to me." She smiled endearingly and moved to join him at the table.

He immediately stood and seated her on his right. Sitting down again, he casually said, "I dismissed everyone from serving this morn. May I serve you, Grandy?"

Knowing he was disturbed, she said, "Just tea, please."

The tall man moved with grace for so powerful his stance. At the sideboard, he poured her tea, adding one lump of sugar, and returned to join her. Sitting once again, his tone mild, he said, "I am well, Grandy. Thank you for inquiring."

The dowager, dressed in her usual black, long-sleeved gown, with her cameo pinned on her left shoulder, reached for his arm and patted it. "Lucien,

I could not understand your anger last eve. Surely, it cannot be because you were saturated from your outing."

He eyed her over his cup of coffee, silent.

She continued, wanting to find out all she could. "It certainly is not the first time you have gotten soaked." Her voice amiable, she continued, "Why, I bet, during your ride this morn, you got another damping."

Silence. He didn't respond.

Lady Julia wasn't giving up. "Miss Thaylor certainly didn't complain about being wet, and knowing her as I do, she has built-in endurance." Thinking she might be pressing Willie's qualities a bit much, she took another tack, vigorously stating, "I tried to discourage your outing, did I not?"

Lord Barclay peered at his grandmother. He just didn't trust her on this. *She's here—rising early. She's up to something. I can feel it.* Still, he couldn't get a hold of the reins, so to speak. "Grandy, what exactly do you want me to say? That I was careless with your house guest? That I let that defiant but determined cheeky female get hurt and possible catch the ague that can harm her for the rest of her life? Do you want me to admit it was my misstep for not taking proper rain clothing on our so-called outing? And that I should not have taken the curricle?" He stood, not having eaten any food, and walked to stare out of one of the long windows, his back to his grandmother. He shook his head, trying to understand why that windblown, saturated firebrand would not heed his words and why it bothered him so. *She is obstinate in every sense of the word, yet I feel admiration for her even though she's difficult to deal with.*

So, thought Lady Julia, he blames himself for Willie's being injured and wet. He holds himself responsible. "Lucien, surely you cannot possibly believe Miss Thaylor or I would ever think that such nonsensical suppositions have one iota of merit. We know Cornwall weather changes in a blink. As for twisting her ankle, no one can predict something like that will occur. Miss Thaylor told me it was a frivolous accident she brought on by her own recklessness."

Lucien turned and said pointedly, "I should have been more on guard and not allowed her to get out of the curricle." He frowned, disgruntled, adding, "She does not listen and does what she feels doing. She has an independent streak in her; the likes which I have never encountered in a female before." He shook his head, "She just doesn't listen."

Suppressing her smile and realizing that her house guest was a thorn in her grandson's orderly life, she offered, "I agree that Miss Thaylor is quite self-determined. It seems her father raised her alone and allowed her more freedom that is not permitted in our elite female persuasions. She said her father encouraged her to use her mind and make decisions, enabling her to rely on herself. She said he wanted her to enjoy living."

Grumpily, Lucien retorted, "That's unheard of."

Lady Julia sipped her now tepid tea. "It is, but her charm proves her father instilled her with profundity that she's taken to heart. She is well and no serious harm; a twisted ankle will mend quickly, and we will depart for London as planned. We will only be delayed a few days… not serious at all."

Eased somewhat by his grandmother's enlightenment, he nodded and concluded that he may have been overly suspicious, admitting that Grandy's guest doesn't have any interest in him at all. He was sure now that she was not acting. *She owns an outlandish personality and is not the least inhibited by anyone, especially me.* He choked back a laugh. *She's spewed her indignation many times without thought of who I am. Indeed, she is a rare female.*

Lady Julia recognized a collected calm embrace her grandson. "I visited with Miss Thaylor this morn, and she is in her normal good spirits. She apologized again for causing a fuss."

He remembered her wet mahogany hair plastered on her head with rain dripping off her long dark lashes and soaked with cold rain; she bucked the downpour, saying nothing about the pain she was enduring. He admired her tenacity and found himself charmed by her sassy attitude. *She is unique.* He was grinning.

Lady Julia didn't miss the change come over Lucien. *All will be well.*

For just that moment, lost in his own thoughts, he forgot his grandmother was with him. She was quiet.

"I think, Grandy, the next time you visit Miss Thaylor, I should wish to go with you."

Not surprised but pleased, she protested strongly, "Grandson, you cannot visit Miss Thaylor in her private rooms."

Not to be deterred, he uttered, "Hang it all, Grandy. You will be with me." He returned to the table and began to devour cold food. Looking at his only relative, he added, "And even if you were not, I would go."

"Lucien!" she reproached.

"As you have often said, *we Barclays have a mind of our own*. I only want to see how she is faring. I owe her an apology for my boorish behavior."

Lady Julia was pleased and knew not to show it. She tilted her head to one side. "Oh."

"Worry not, as I am not going to compromise the little firebrand." His smile broadened. "Besides, she will no doubt have that maid of hers hovering over her. Where did you find that obedient servant? Did she come with Miss Thaylor?"

"You must mean Tess? I asked Jaggers to select someone to assist Miss Thaylor while she is my guest. Tess was working in the kitchen and Jaggers decided Tess would do."

"Of course, Jaggers is always right."

Lady Julia smiled as she set her napkin on the table, having arrived at a mental decision. "To assure you that Miss Thaylor is well, you may call at four and have afternoon tea with Miss Thaylor."

"I wasn't planning on waiting that long."

"I suggest that you do." Her firm tone brooked no opposition.

The Earl of Grenmoor winked, "I obey your command, my lady." He stood to aid his grandmother from her chair.

Lady Julia returned his mocked surrender with a shake of her head as Lord Barclay kissed her cheek, unknowing that his Grandy was in one of her conniving moods.

Lady Julia immediately proceeded with her manipulations while Lucien was checking on Zephr, positive this would bring her two favorite persons together.

The clever dowager ordered a blazing fire to be burning in the library and ordered tea and coffee to be served. Jaggers complied with His Ladyship's wishes. Everything would be ready, and he would see that they were not disturbed.

She could easily leave her two favorite people alone in the library but not so in Willie's private rooms. There wasn't any doubt in Lady Julia's mind that Lucien and Willie would come to value each other's company if they could converse with no preconceived assignation. They might discover how well they suited.

Pleased with her decisions, Lady Julia relaxed and departed to her private quarters to await her grandson.

* * *

Lord Barclay began to guide his grandmother toward the other wing in the manor. He felt good and would have whistled, except he knew this display of exuberance would definitely have Grandy take notice. *It would not do for my cagey grandmother to suspect something other than I'm just happy Miss Thaylor is in good health.* He was only proving to himself that Miss Thaylor had not come down with a cough. Eying his grandmother, he said, "You look lovely as always, Grandy."

"Thank you, grandson. You look well put together—dashing." He had the Barclay straight nose with a solid jawline. His raven eyes exacted his grandfather's along with stubbornness. Lady Julia loved her grandson with all her being and forgave him his few negligible faults. "We must go to the library, Lucien."

"Are you getting a book for Miss Thaylor? What title? I'll get it."

Lady Julia walked on and did not answer. Jaggers was standing at the library door. Looking at Lady Julia and receiving a slight nod from Lady Julia, Jaggers moved slide open the library doors.

Wilhelmina was sitting before the blazing fire, gowned in a plain day dress. Sitting on the sofa with the lighted fireplace behind her, she looked up as the doors slid open. A worried frown darkened her green eyes, and she blinked as her pulse seemed to double beat looking up toward the door and seeing the handsome Earl and not Lady Julia. *What is he doing here? He seems as surprised as I am to be here.*

Lord Barclay's step faltered at the unexpected picture she presented. It was obvious she didn't expect him as he seemed to freeze in place. The shine in her beautiful hair accentuated by firelight actually caused him to stare. *She is enchanting.* The natural picture she portrayed forced his heart to skip a beat.

Lady Julia stepped aside, glancing at Jaggers and barely nodding her approval, and moved into the library. "I'm pleased you're here, Miss Thaylor."

"Lady Julia!" she tried to hurriedly explain, "When Jaggers arrived with your footman to see me immediately downstairs, I was not prepared. Forgive me, my lady, for I was told you wanted to see me at once, without delay." She tugged at her sleeves and then quite naturally pushed a lone curl behind her ear, and went on to say, "I'm afraid I'm not at all presentable." She hastily added with concern, "I thought something drastically happened that you needed me."

Lady Julia, not the least concerned about this set up she had concocted with Jaggers, said, "I believed a change of scenery would be nice for you. Both the Earl and I wanted to be certain you are on the mend and in good spirits."

Lord Barclay was enthralled. Her rosy complexion, along with her innocence, was prevalent; he wanted to go to her and assuage her embarrassment. Instead, he just stood and gaped like an inexperienced lad as rapture built within him because of her.

Taking the Earl's silence for disgust and disapproval, Wilhelmina looked away and stared at the burning logs.

Lady Julia hurried to Wilhelmina to assure her guest. "I did not want to cause you any inconvenience during your convalescence. As my guest, you have no need to apologize." Then, she patted the young girl's hand. "Perhaps, I should apologize for my grandson. Usually, the Earl of Grenmoor is more cordial… especially as this is teatime."

Coming out of his obvious stupor, a rarely seen broad smile crossed his handsome face. "I was surprised to see you here, Miss Thaylor, and looking marvelously well." *I would like to add beautiful.*

Lady Barclay, cherishing the moment, unobtrusively sat down—away from them.

Wilhelmina couldn't help but blush, secretly pleased with the Earl's compliment. "Thank you, my lord. I'm afraid I am unable to stand." She shifted her position to extend her bandaged ankle and slipper.

The Earl's mouth twisted into a threat. "Please, Miss Thaylor, stay as you are." He moved to kneel on one knee to check on her wrapped ankle and frowned, yet gently asked, "Does it pain you overmuch?"

His voice reached her warm yet with a touch of force. "Oh, no, my lord, hardly at all; only when I try putting my weight on it." She hastened to explain, "Of course, it was a foolish thing that I did. I refused to listen, and now, I must accept my comeuppance." The tone in her voice became shaky as she said with sincere feeling, "I'm truly sorry, my lord, for causing you this inexcusable disruption. I really must stop following sudden inclinations that just suddenly erupt." She turned from a serious tone to unexpected laughter. "Though when returning, it's a wonder we didn't frighten everyone being soaked and our hair hanging every which way. We were a mess."

The same joy seemed to connect with Lucien that time they had waltzed together. With her head tilted and laughter ringing in his ears as her rosy mouth opened, showing off her rosy tongue, Lucien Barclay, Earl of Grenmoor, was captivated. One minute, she was repentant and apologetic, and the next, she was boldly telling him he was a mess. He would have liked to thoroughly kiss that rosy mouth spewing nonsense, and then, he wondered if anyone ever had the opportunity. A surge of jealousy jilted him. He could not believe this was happening—his unexpected warm concern over Grandy's lively houseguest. *Get hold of yourself, old man. Miss Thaylor is not your concern.*

Wanting to disguise the impact she had on him, he replied not too pleasantly, "That is not the point, Miss Thaylor. How we looked is unimportant. What you seem not to understand," he admonished, "is that you could have become seriously ill."

"But it did not happen, did it? So, we shall not concern ourselves further, my lord."

Lucien was outraged at her sound of dismissal, considering the matter closed. He was about to speak, but she went on.

"As for my sore ankle, I accept full responsibility as I have previously stated. I assure you that it is not necessary to apologize for something that was not your doing. Mrs. Bainsboro thinks I will be about in less than half a fortnight." Looking at him, she was adamant. "Not to worry, my lord, I don't believe there will be a repeat performance," she was actually grinning, "as we are not likely to traverse the moors together again."

The Earl of Grenmoor was flabbergasted. *This impertinent little baggage is systematically ordering me to put this matter to rest.* Irked, he responded, "Why you—"

Lady Julia could not let this go further as much as she was enjoying their little set-to. She did not want it to get out of hand. Knowing that other ladies must always coo over her grandson, she could tell that he was not only astonished by Willie's saucy attitude, but to be told to forget the entire incident—she withheld the urge to chuckle and spoke instead, boldly interrupting her grandson, "I think it is time to ring for tea."

Having forgotten his grandmother's presence, he only nodded and moved to pull the cord.

Wilhelmina turned slightly to look at Lady Julia and said in a wearisome tone, "I am trying to explain to Lord Barclay that…"

"Never mind, dear." The dowager's tone was warm. "Let us stop offering apologies and enjoy our tea, though you prefer coffee?"

Wilhelmina nodded.

Lord Barclay moved to assist his grandmother near the small table as Jaggers and a serving maid set the tray. They left at once, and Lady Julia began to pour.

"Nothing for me, Grandy." He was still irritated. "I do believe I need something stronger than tea." He reached for the whiskey decanter.

Oddly, Wilhelmina felt free, tired of the great Earl of Grenmoor treating her as an infant without sense. *The devil with him, I had to set matters straight.*

Not much was discussed. The last fifteen minutes of the hour seemed to drag. Lady Julia didn't worry as she continued to plan. "You must be tired," she said, looking at Willie. "I'll ring for Jaggers to have you helped to your room."

"Thank you, Lady Julia. I think I may be able to manage if I may lean on Tess."

Still agitated, Lord Barclay said, "Do not call anyone, Grandy. I will assist Miss Thaylor to her rooms." Looking at Wilhelmina, he said, "You are to stay off that foot until it is completely well. Is that understood?"

Surprised, Wilhelmina sat open-mouthed with nary a word forthcoming.

Lady Julia, playing her game, eyed her grandson. "Do you think that is wise, Lucien?"

Exasperated at Grandy's caution of his entering the little minx rooms, he uttered, "Really, Grandmother, you do agonize over much. I suggest you cease with all this caution. I assure you, Miss Thaylor will be very safe." He wanted to add that he was not about to take any liberties, not that a stolen kiss would seem the thing. He could feel his pulse jump.

Entirely pleased, Lady Julia looked at the fire burning low. She did not want to chance her grandson seeing the twinkle in her eyes. "I am only thinking of my guest," she lightly reprimanded.

Wilhelmina was still gaping at His Lordship.

The Earl of Grenmoor peered at his nemesis. Miss Thaylor's rosy mouth was slightly open, holding that tart tongue. He could not believe she was not rattling off orders that seemed to be her wont. Sarcastically, he inquired, "Do

I have your permission, Miss Thaylor, to help you?" He raised that Barclay eyebrow, daring her to refuse. "I do believe I can manage to lift you safely without direction."

Reluctantly, she had to admit that the great broad-shouldered man thrilled her senses, but outwardly, she would not give him that satisfaction of knowing. "If after our harrowing sojourn of yesterday, my lord, you feel you have the strength, I should be delighted to accept your generous offer."

Lady Julie knew Lucien was fuming; her adoring grandson had never met the likes of Wilhelmina Thaylor… *my Willie. Yes*, she thought, *they will suit just fine*. It took all her willpower not to burst laughing. Moving toward the door, she stopped, seeming a bit agitated. "Very well."

Lucien gently picked up Wilhelmina—she felt good in his arms as she smelled of soap, not a cloying perfume. It rattled his senses. "As you wish, Grandy. It seems today is my day to obey everyone's command."

"Why, Lucien, whatever do you mean?"

His dark eyes glittering, he answered, "I think you know exactly what I mean." But his mind was abruptly diverted when Miss Thaylor's fingers touched his skin when moving his hair at his nape, causing a shockwave to course through his body as she maneuvered her fingers to hold on, while using her other hand to lightly grip his coat for balance. Her lustrous hair fell forward, accidently brushing his cheek as his body temperature rose, his breathing vanished and he hid his gasp for air, while this lightweight vixen unknowingly turned his strength to mush.

Lady Julia warned, "I trust you know the way," her monotone brooking no discourse. "I must leave, so do not tarry over your charitable undertaking."

Infuriated, he bellowed, "Really, Madam!"

Fortunately for Lord Barclay, Miss Thaylor's gown hung low and covered his groin area. He shifted her to be sure she would not feel his predicament. Tess was waiting and hurriedly opened the door wide. Lord Barclay quickly set Miss Thaylor on the lounge, turned, and fled. Looking over his shoulder, he saw her surprised stare. At the moment, he had to get out of there before the obvious bulge was noticed. "I will see you at supper, Miss Thaylor." Before she could reply and thank him, he was out the door.

Wilhelmina bit her lip. What did she expect? Certainly not any special attention. After all, he was the Earl of Grenmoor; he was nobility while she was a vicar's daughter. He could never find her interesting. *He has too many moods to contend with, anyway.*

She let Tess help her prepare to rest. Soon, she would be in London, and the indomitable Lord Barclay would be back among his beautiful *ton* lady friends. What did she care! She had sailing plans to make and start a new life.

Chapter Sixteen

Seahurst Manor, Five Days Later

The Earl of Grenmoor gathered the playing cards, having won another hand at cribbage. He had easily marked off the holes, skunking his opponent. The evening was pleasant and his mood teasing. "Remember, when you decide to challenge anyone to any game, Miss Thaylor, it's best to know your opponent."

Lady Julia was all smiles. "Did you let my grandson win, Miss Thaylor?"

Wilhelmina could not hold back her chuckle. "But of course, Lady Julia. Although, I also think His Lordship has luck of drawing the best cards."

"Oh no, you don't, admit it… you ladies aren't able to take on an expert as myself." He enjoyed the evening. This guest of his grandmother's was most aggravating, but also with a generous sense of humor. He had enjoyed passing some time with her these last five days. Her ankle would soon be ready for traveling, and he looked forward to going to London. Before he could comment with a bit more teasing, Jaggers entered the Seascape drawing room.

"Beg pardon, my lord, but Rudyard from the East Twenty is at the door. He needs to speak with you. There seems to be great trouble at the cliffs."

Lucien was up and walking with great stride. "I'm on my way."

Wilhelmina jumped up to hurry along.

The Earl turned. There was no gentle tone, and he was in a hurry. "Where do you think you're going?"

She did not hesitate or give thought to her reply. "I'm going with you. I may be of some help."

He was in a rush and had no time for such nonsense. He ordered her to remain with his grandmother, adding, "I'm sure there is nothing you can do. We have people on Grenmoor that will do all they can."

Being her true self and knowing that every helping hand was always necessary, she said, "Really, Lucien, do not be a dunderhead. We must not waste any more time."

Just then, the Earl of Grenmoor wanted to shake some sense into the headstrong, brazen redhead, but he had no time. He did not miss her calling him by his first name, as if it were acceptable. Why did she get under his skin and always disobey his orders? Once more, before stepping from the room, he said in a harsh tone, "You have recovered nicely from your injury; stay put with Lady Julia. Is that clear?" He did not wait for a reply, expecting the spitfire to obey him. He turned and was gone. Jaggers closed the door quietly.

Wilhelmina was beside herself. She was angry. Just when she thought they were getting along well, and traveling to London would be pleasant, this overbearing, presumptuous man was ordering her again, hawking his noble authority over her.

Standing before Lady Julia, Wilhelmina fumed. "Lady Julia, would you mind all that much if I did not stay? I am sure I might be of assistance at the cliffs."

The dowager's voice was not without worry. "I dislike going against my grandson's orders, but I also know that your father taught you to do what you are able in helping others. It is your nature, so do be careful, my dear."

Hurrying, Wilhelmina had to don her breeches and put on warm clothing. The night was wet, cold and brutally blowing. She knew she could get a ride to the cliffs dressed as Willie, for she would not take a horse at this time of night. She would take a dray as, without a doubt, it would surely be needed.

"Tess, please get all the blankets and coverings you can for me to take, and ask Jaggers to have them loaded in a dray. I'll need a driver. I'll meet them at the side door."

"May I come with you, Willie?"

In a hurry, she called over her shoulder, "If you wish, Tess, but do dress warm; it won't do for you to become ill."

Impatient to be on her way, her movements were surprisingly effortless with her tender ankle. She was certain the Earl had left, so she could be on her way.

Wilhelmina and Tess were riding in the dray with Sean, a young groom left at the stable. Wilhelmina was wearing her breeches, her bulky warm sweater, jacket and knit cap with her long hair stuffed into it. She was tense, wanting to be on the beach to help. "Hurry, Sean. Why is it taking so long?"

"Easy, Willie," his young voice said with assurance, "I'm going down this narrow lane that will take us to the shore. It's longer, but we will be able to reach anyone there with these horses." The wind did not hold back its mighty force as rain pelted them without mercy. "I must be careful as the horses need to set their own pace in the dark." He shivered, adding, "It would be better if there was a moon."

"I'm sorry, Sean. I know you're doing your best." The wind whipped them again and again and again as they sat huddled on the bouncing wagon. "I don't ever remember going this way."

"When you were riding Zephr, you usually took the high road. This lane is hardly used, that's why we have to make our own tracks now."

Always attentive, Wilhelmina reached for Tess's arm. "Are you alright? You haven't said a word in the last half hour."

Tess was shaking, as much from the cold and the fear of the unknown as well as being bounced about. "I'm all right, Willie," she shouted over the wind.

Tess could not see Willie's smile, but she didn't miss the softness in her voice as Willie leaned toward her ear. "Don't worry, we'll be all right."

"Here we are," an excited Sean yelled. He pulled up amidst three others.

A large fire was burning as they worked to keep it going. The rain couldn't triumph over these Cornish people, as now, the wind helped fan the flames. There were Grenmoor people milling about everywhere.

She looked around trying to spy the Earl, but she did not succeed. Perhaps, the darkness was a kind of blessing. She would just do the best she could and hope their path didn't cross with all the upheaval taking place.

Without asking, she set right to work. She gave orders to the men standing about. They knew her from the manor and didn't question her authority.

A ship had gotten off course and crashed against the rocks. Few survivors were being brought ashore. Everyone was completely saturated, but the traumas for those from the battered sinking ship were in dire straits. She saw they were wrapped in blankets and put onto the drays. "Take them up to one of your homes and get them in the warm. Your homes are closer than the manor and you know these survivors cannot stay out in this weather any longer exposed to the cold."

She worked with them many times—they respected her as well as liked her. They moved with haste to obey her command. Two men jumped up and one dray started to leave.

"Wait," Willie yelled, "we have a woman here." A man struggling to carry her was joined by another to help. She was weighed down with her torn clothing, her shoes were gone, and her long hair was hanging and dripping with sea water. Willie ran to her and literally tore off her sopping gown and immediately wrapped her in a blanket. The trembling woman was in a state of shock. "Please make sure that your wife gives her something hot to drink, and then she'll have to remove the rest of this lady's clothes." She yelled above the wind, "And be sure you do the same for the men you are taking with you. They must not be left in wet clothing."

Rudyard couldn't help but smile, though no one could see it. "We know what to do, Willie. We'll take care to do it right."

She ran to the dray, yelling, "I'm sorry, Rudyard, of course you do."

The aged drayman reached down and touched Willie's woolen cap, "Remember, the tide is going to be rolling in, so watch yourself and don't get caught and taken out. There will be no shore here in a little while."

Wilhelmina, ever thoughtful and kind, shouted, "I hear you. And you be careful, too. Get yourself warm. Go!"

She turned and looked to see if there were more survivors. There were none around her, but there was a lot of commotion a short way up the beach. One man was holding a torch and Wilhelmina recognized Crooks, the Earl's valet. She saw him bending over someone in the sand. "Oh, please," she murmured, "let that not be the Earl." She hurried to the group of men standing with Crooks, forgetting about her disguise. She moved closer and saw it was a man with a white shirt ripped and hanging from his body. His pants were plastered in place with his legs and feet bare. He was moaning, but his language was one the people did not know. "Petite enfant," he kept uttering.

Before Crooks could comment as he was well-versed with French, one man anxiously asked, "What's he saying, Willie?"

Hearing the name Willie and seeing Miss Thaylor, Crooks nearly dropped the torch he was holding up. He was no dummy, quickly surmising the connection with His Lordship's grandmother.

At the same moment, the Earl came staggering from the sea, and someone yelled that they heard a cry from a floating box. Without thought, the Earl called for a torch and returned wading into the water. Everyone could make out the floating crate being bashed by strong wind and waves and then disappear. The Earl persisted against the mighty sea, holding the torch high. Wading into the water already covering his chest, he spied the crate, but a wave washed over him, and the torch was no longer alive. It was dark, and

Wilhelmina prayed that he would be safe, but she knew he would continue to try to reach the crate—she hoped that he would find the crate and return without mishap, knowing the water was icy cold and the wind bashing the water hindered any rescue of getting help to the Earl.

The Earl of Grenmoor dove into the wave, hoping his sense of judgment was on target. The water was so unbearably cold, it numbed his tired body, but he was determined to continue or lose his life trying. Taking another deep breath, turning to his left, he touched the crate and heard a mewing sound. Miraculous, surely, God was helping him. Unable to do more, he held tight as another wave crashed against him. The mewing stopped and he knew that it was covered with cold, salty seawater. He was so tired, yet with sapped energy, he hauled it toward shore with the next wave, choking on sea water that he could not escape.

He thought he heard someone yell for help—it was probably his faithful Crooks. Someone was trying to take the crate from him; his hands were so cold he could not release his grip. He was numb and freezing.

The men were pulling the Earl and crate to shore. Everyone was water-soaked, but that didn't matter as at the moment, all they could think was to take care of the Earl. He had done what none of them would have had the courage to do.

"Willie," someone shouted, "we all best get out of here, the tide is rising and will swamp us." There was no doubt about it; the sea had already risen to their knees.

The Earl heard someone call Willie, and then he lost consciousness. Inside the crate was a small child, soaking in cold seawater. Willie grabbed the first blanket and wrapped the child in it. She squeezed the child's chest gently, forcing it to cough. It was then she barely heard a small sound—like a cry. Hoping she was right, she called out, "Hurry, take this child with the man calling for his petite enfant, his small baby. I must check on His Lordship." Willie was saturated with the sea as well as the rain, but her thoughts were for the Earl of Grenmoor.

She saw Crooks struggling to carry his employer. "Mr. Crooks, I have an empty dray with dry blankets over there. What can I do to help?" Her anguished voice was not missed by the valet as he sloshed through the rising tidal waters.

Men were following and hauling things that were washing on shore, but the shore was disappearing, and they worried they would be caught in the crashing waves.

Without thinking what Crooks would judge as her right, she ordered, "Each of you take hold of the Earl and help us get him in the dray. Please hurry." Crooks said nothing but accepted their help. The Earl being a big man, his dead weight nearly did the older valet in.

A wave came in and knocked Wilhelmina off her feet and began to pull her into the sea. Being wise enough to know not to fight the current, she let her body go limp for a second and then dug in her heels as the icy water began to recede, giving her just enough strength to pull herself up. A big, callused hand grabbed her by her sweater and brought her up above the water line.

Chattering from the cold, she offered her thanks.

"Aw Willie, you don't need to thank me. Come on, everyone is up and about to be gone from here. Can you make it?"

"I can. Thanks to you."

They sloshed through the incoming tide and just reached a higher space when the waves seemed to unleash all its fury and break from the sea in torrents.

They were all wet and shivering. Willie hurried to the dray where the Earl was lying covered and unconscious.

"I'm taking him to the manor," Crooks stated matter-of-factly. "We have to get him warm."

Deathly cold, everyone waited for someone to decide they could all return home themselves; all was done that could be done.

"That's a good half hour ride from here, Mr. Crooks." Willie turned and called to Mr. Sidden, "Your home is the nearest, Jack; do you think you have room for the Earl? It's too far for him to ride in his condition."

"We'd be honored, Willie. Come on, best we go. You best get out of those wet clothes before you come down with lung trouble."

Not thinking of herself for a minute, she turned and shouted for Robbie. "Robbie, where are you?"

"Over here, Willie."

"I know you're soaking wet, too, but do you think you can ride to the manor and let Lady Barclay know that we are safe? Take Tess with you. Then later, bring clothes for the Earl and also for Mr. Crooks. I know he will want to stay with His Lordship."

Crooks smiled in spite of his freezing condition. *This Willie, or should I say, Miss Thaylor, is a wise one. Wait until the Earl finds out.* Just those thoughts warmed the valet. Crooks spoke out, "Robbie, have Jaggers give you a case of brandy. It is well-earned."

Grinning with blue lips, Robbie saluted the lordship's valet. "I'm off, Willie. I'll take the horse Crooks rode."

She suddenly called above the wind, "I forgot, what about Zephr? We can't leave him."

"Oh no," Robbie groaned, "I can't ride Zephr. No way. You know that."

She made her decision on the spot, not hesitating. "Everyone, get on your way. Mr. Sidden, you take Mr. Crooks and the Earl with you this minute. I'll take Zephr back to Seahurst and see that you get more dry blankets and dry clothes."

Crooks was more indecisive. He knew what Zephr meant to His Lordship, but he also knew that Zephr was hard to handle. With that long ride to the manor to take care of the horse, she could catch lung fever. As the dray began to move, he called, "I don't think you should try to ride Zephr." He pleaded, "Come and warm yourself with the rest of us. It is too long a ride on that uncontrollable stallion."

Willie was adamant. "Get along with you, all of you. We are dallying over long. You must get yourselves warmed and in the dry." Shouting over to Crooks, she said, "I'll be fine. I know you will take care of the Earl, but you take care of yourself, too." She left and headed for the nervous, unpredictable Zephr.

Robbie heard some of the words Willie crooned to Zephr over the roar of the sea. "You'll be home soon, you big beauty, and we'll see you get some extra sweets." He still couldn't figure how Willie managed to get in the Earl's stirrup, but there she was with her legs dangling, keeping the black stallion on track.

"We're ready, Robbie."

Both of them were shivering as they were the last to take off toward Seahurst, knowing they would find warmth and dry clothes.

Chapter Seventeen

Four Days Later, Seahurst Manor

Distressed, Lady Julia sat beside her grandson. He was feverish and thrashing in his bed. Her aging body did not have the strength to help keep him quiet.

Wilhelmina, in the Earl's room, said, "Let me help, Mr. Crooks. We must not let him use what energy his body still has."

"I agree." The personal valet and friend to the Earl of Grenmoor being very worried, said, "I fear the Earl is overly warm. This is not good."

Lady Julia, using her handkerchief and blotting her eyes, said nothing.

"Lady Julia?" Willie used her arm and swiped at her eyes to hide her tears. "If you will permit me to use a method my father believed in but one that his doctor scoffed at, I think it will help bring down the Earl's fever."

"What is it, Willie?" This angst had aged her these last days since the shipwreck. "You know Lucien is my only concern. I'll trust you to do what you can in my grandson's best interest in getting him well." She hesitated, hoping she was not wrong in giving this young woman her consent. "If you are certain, it will do him no harm."

She knelt beside the dowager. "I am not certain, but I truly believe it will help. It has worked before at my father's insistence. It will not cause him further distress. If you will permit Mr. Crooks and me to try, we will do our best."

At that moment, the Earl began to thrash again. Wilhelmina moved to help the Earl's valet as she continued to talk with Lady Julia. "Please, we must attempt to lower his temperature."

Troubled, Lord Barclay's grandmother replied, "Yes. Do what you can, please."

Not wanting to waste time, Wilhelmina spoke to Crooks, "I need cold water and towels. Father believed that to bring down a fever you had to help cool the body." Speaking with caring to Lady Julia, she said, "I am thankful that you did not permit His Lordship to be bled. Father once told me he was sure that doing so weakens the patient, making it more difficult to fight the illness."

Lady Julia was so distraught, she placed her confidence in this caring Willie, whom she had come to respect. "Let us try your father's method, then. My grandson needs all the help we can give him; staying in the sea for so long a time has depleted his energy to fight these chills."

Crooks was already returning with towels, and the Seahurst staff carried pails of cold water.

Wilhelmina quickly took a towel and soaked and squeezed the chilly water from it, then transferred it to the Earl's forehead. "Mr. Crooks, if you will please keep the towels coming, for we must continue to do this to help cool his body's temperature." She carefully moved the covering to the upper part of the Earl's waist, not exposing his personal body parts. So intent on her work pressing cold compresses on his naked, dark-haired chest, she had no time to think of embarrassment while doing what she knew was necessary. She didn't give one thought that this was the handsome man she admired who usually became frustrated and angry at her.

Lady Julia said nothing as she reached for her grandson's listless warm hand. She could feel his rapid pulse beat.

Between Crooks and Wilhelmina, they continued their administrations without stopping. The Earl tried to throw off the cold cloths that covered him, but to no avail. If Crooks didn't reach over and stop him, Wilhelmina did. "Oh, no, you don't," she would scold.

Keeping busy with cooling the muscled torso, she kept thinking of his snappish, arrogant manner. She'd give anything for him to voice his sarcasm at her again instead of lying ill and incapacitated.

Changing the towel on the Earl's chest, Wilhelmina asked, "Mr. Crooks, would you mind seeing that some broth is brought for the Earl? We must get some warm liquid into him—also, something for Lady Julia and yourself." She smiled. "None of you have eaten for a long while. We can't have the Earl's favorite people getting sick on him now, can we?"

Crooks admired this woman, known to everyone as Willie but the Earl. He smiled to himself, thinking how His Lordship ranted he was going to strangle the lad, Willie. Crooks couldn't get over this bit of a woman riding that beast that only the Earl was able to handle. *Oh yes, the Earl is in for a big surprise.*

Looking at the busy and constantly active, non-complaining but tired young lady, Crooks responded, "Thank you, Miss. How about yourself? You haven't left the Earl's bedside since Lady Barclay had him brought home."

Lady Julia came out of her lethargy, and her gentle voice ordered, "Jaggers," knowing he was nearby for her as always.

"I'm here, my lady."

"We must have broth for my grandson, and also, please see to a repast for all of us." She eyed her young guest standing over her grandson with regard plainly visible. *If anyone knew that this young lady was tending Lucien in his private quarters, unclothed, she would be unable to survive the scandal put upon her; yet, I need her confidence to pull my grandson back to health.*

Wilhelmina looked over at Lady Julia and then back at soothing the Earl, and said in with gentle softness, "Try not to worry, my Lady."

Jaggers acknowledged, "I'll return shortly."

Lady Julia spoke, "I can't do without this grandson of mine. He is loving and loyal and always ready to do my bidding," then chuckled and it eased the tension, "of course, if it suits him."

Wilhelmina's hair was pulled back and tied high on her head, yet strands fell, but she didn't seem to notice or care. She continued toweling the Earl with cold compresses. "Lady Julia, how could he not be all those things to you? You are most deserving."

Lucien suddenly thrashed, and the covers very nearly exposed his vital parts. This time, Wilhelmina could not help but blush. The black nest of hair at the top of his lower body was there for them to see. Crooks quickly covered His Lordship.

Wilhelmina turned to change the cloth covering the Earl's chest. She broke out into a smile. "It's working!" she almost shouted, "I believe His Lordship is not as warm."

The worried dowager rose and felt her grandson's forehead. "I think you're right; he is cooler. You've done well, child." The dowager's worry eased. "Now, you must let Crooks continue with the toweling while you take a respite."

"I'm fine, Lady Julia, truly, I am. Especially now. I was so worried for His Lordship. I want him to be well for you as well for himself."

Eying the tired, auburn-haired woman, she said softly, "But not for yourself?"

Wilhelmina couldn't hold back a blush even if she wanted to. Not giving a reason to answer, she turned to Crooks. "If you will continue bathing His Lordship—though now it is important not only to keep him cool, but we must be sure he maintains a comforting warm body. The damp bedding will have to be changed."

"Worry not, Miss. I'll have a footman aid me. Thank you for looking after His Lordship. I've known him all his life and his well-being is my main concern."

She nodded. "I think, then, that I will take a few moments to freshen up." Standing, ready to depart, she added, "You might try cooling his upper thighs, also."

"Of course, Miss. I will do so immediately."

Nodding to the both of them, she hurried from the Earl's room.

Lady Julia smiled, positive that Lucien nipped at Willie's heart. All this caring and worry about Lucien meant more than her friend was willing to admit.

It was then that the Earl spoke clearly and without pause, "Red… sassy… listen…" His words turned mumbling and incoherent and faded.

Lady Julia looked at Lucien's loyal valet, her eyes gleaming. "Did you hear what His Lordship said, Crooks? Is there any reason for my thinking that he could have a tad of feelings for our Willie?"

"I really cannot say, Ma'am."

"Oh, posh, you wouldn't tell me if you knew. Your loyalty belongs to the Earl, and you know, Crooks, I would have it no other way. But I suspect you know more than you are willing to say. Am I not right?"

Crooks kept changing the cooling cloths, "Ma'am, I'm afraid I don't understand."

"Humph," she uttered, though pleased.

Jaggers entered with a tray of food and tea arrangements.

Lady Julia's demeanor brightened. "Jaggers, the Earl is going to be well. Our Willie did the right thing."

"She's a wonder, she is, my lady."

"We can agree to *that*, can't we, Crooks?"

"My lady, if you will allow, I'll have the Earl's bedding replaced."

"Of course." Lady Julia took her tea and scone and moved across the room to give Crooks and the footman privacy to care for her grandson.

The Earl was resting on dry bedding, with Crooks applying cold cloths to the restless body. He hadn't replied to Lady Julia's question.

Wilhelmina returned, freshened, her auburn hair brushed back and tied with a fresh velvet ribbon. Her dark blue day dress without frills suited her. Her green eyes were shining. She walked directly to the Earl's bedside, felt his forehead, and laid the back of her fingers on his neck below his ear. It was a slight caress. She glowingly voiced, "His Lordship is much cooler, my lady. Though I do think we must continue cooling him but keep him covered and warm. We don't want to overdo."

"I have every faith in your father's remedy and also faith in both you and Crooks. Do what you believe is right."

Wilhelmina eyed the tired dowager. "Lady Julia, why don't you take a respite now that His Lordship is on the mend? You haven't rested at all."

The petite older woman looked over at her grandson, and seeing him resting comfortably and no longer thrashing about, agreed. "I will leave Lucien in your care for a short while, Willie. Would you mind too much?"

Crooks gazed at the older, guileful dowager. His eyes told her he was aware of her scheming. He remained silent.

Totally unaware of their silent messages, she said, "Do rest well, Lady Julia, and have no care. I will look after our patient." Softly, she said, "Mr. Crooks, if you will help me hold up the Earl, we can try to get some broth into him. He will need nourishment to regain his strength and helping to fight off this fever."

As they worked together getting the large man in an upward position, Lady Julia sat back and nibbled on a scone and sipped tea—elated with Willie minding her grandson, regardless that it was in the intimate privacy of his rooms, with Lucien bare under his covers and Willie a maiden. She cared not, for she wanted her grandson healthy and back to his grand bearings. Crooks would see to Lucien's needs. There was not a shadow of doubt that Lucien had the best care.

"I will leave the two of you to look after Lucien. I know I am leaving him in good hands. Please call me if there is a serious change."

"Please do not worry, my lady." Crooks assured, "The Earl is a strong man and too stubborn to let any illness get the best of him."

It was then that Lucien tried to turn his head and refuse being spoon-fed the broth. He was in a semi-conscious state. Without giving thought of her circumstances, intent on feeding the Earl, she admonished, "No, you listen to me, Lucien William Barclay. You will hold your head still and take a few spoons of this broth. Do not think for one moment that I will tolerate any disobedience from you." So resolute was she in her course of action that she literally forgot about those around her. Then, it was as if Lucien was suddenly conscious as he stopped moving as she held his chin in her hand and carefully fed him the broth. He swallowed and took two more spoonful before he began to fight the situation again.

"I think we did fairly well, Mr. Crooks. Don't you agree?" She set the unfinished broth on a tray and gently wiped the Earl's mouth with a linen napkin. "We will try to feed him a few spoons more every half hour and keep the cooling cloths on his forehead, but they shouldn't be icy cold anymore. In fact, it would be good if you put some sleepwear on His Lordship now that his sweating has ended."

Crooks was most impressed with her knowledge, and then, there was the fact that she called him *Mister*, surely aware it was not necessary, but then, she respected everyone. Crooks had never met a lady like her in all his travels with the Earl. *She is giving, and there isn't a selfish thought to her own self or seeking some kind of benefit.* He wanted to laugh, wondering what this lovely redhead would think if he told her His Lordship always slept only in his bare skin, regardless of where he was and that he owned no nightwear.

"Here, let me help you with His Lordship." Crooks held him as Willie straightened his pillow. The valet voiced his concern to Lady Julia, "Why don't you rest a bit?"

"A splendid suggestion, Crooks." Lady Julia walked to her grandson's bedside, felt his forehead and laid her veined hand on his unshaven cheek. "If you can hear me, Lucien, you must let everyone help you so you can once again be up and around. Lord Restin is coming to visit in a couple of days; you will want to talk with him, won't you? Rest, my dearest." She patted his face and walked from the room. She did not look back for fear her tears would be visible.

"She loves him so, Mr. Crooks. We must do all we can to keep His Lordship cool, yet warm." Without realizing what she was doing, Willie gently laid her hand on one side of the Earl's face.

"If I may say, Miss, the Earl of Grenmoor is most caring about many things. A fair man he is and can be counted on, always."

"The Earl of Grenmoor is definitely sure of himself and his opinions. I doubt he listens to others." She winked at the valet, teasing. "But now, we are in charge, and there is nothing he can do about it."

"I doubt His Lordship would approve or agree with your outlook, Miss."

"Why, Mr. Crooks?"

"I really can't say, Miss. And my name is Crooks—it is not necessary to apply *Mister* to my name."

He knows why the Earl doesn't like me. I'll not push for that answer. Wilhelmina busily removed the tray and picked up some of the towels. "I'll take care of these; it will give you time to get the Earl into his sleepwear."

"I'll do that. Also, Miss, it would be wise to just keep the Earl covered as we have. I believe he will be more comfortable seeing as he moves about so, and sleepwear linens will only entangle him." Crooks hesitated in explaining the Earl had no sleeping clothes at all.

She tried not to blush and nodded. Together, they fixed the Earl's pillows, covered his torso up over his chest, and continued with the cool compresses on his brow.

Wilhelmina looked at Crooks; he was so tired. He'd never left His Lordship since the shipwreck, taking only snatches of rest. Gently, she suggested, "When I return, why don't you get some rest? I'll stay with His Lordship, and if he awakens or needs your help, I will call you at once."

Crooks studied the woman that had bamboozled His Lordship. Hiding his smile, he thought of Lady Julia plotting to entice both of these persons into a romance; one that, he had to admit, was just what His Lordship needed. *This Willie is no piece of fluff as His Lordship refers to the ladies trying for his affection.* And, Crooks, knowing the Earl, was astonished, finding that this redhead never hesitated to voice her viewpoint and didn't seem to be enthralled over his title or him. Smothering a yawn, he said, "If you are sure, Miss. I'll be in the next room and can be here in a second or two. You're right; I could use a bit of a nap if I'm going to be of any value to His Lordship when he awakens."

She walked over to Crooks and took the cool cloth from him. "Go," she mildly ordered, "You are an angel in disguise, and angels need their rest, too. I promise I will call you should the need arise or if the Earl calls for you."

Reluctantly, Crooks moved to leave. Looking back at the determined woman, he said, "Thank you, Miss, for caring for His Lordship. I know he can be difficult, but he really is the finest man I know."

"You need not thank me, Mr. Crooks. One must always help and do whatever is necessary without exception. I do realize being in the Earl's rooms is not done and most unsuitable, yet how can it be wrong—especially when it is helping Lady Julia? I have to be here."

"I do not differ with your thinking." He offered a slight bow and closed the door, leaving Wilhelmina alone with the Earl for the first time in four days. He leaned against the door, listening, and as tired as he was, he waited with a broad smile when hearing Willie begin to talk to His Lordship. He heard her authoritative tone with a bit of wry temperament. "Now, Your Majesty, you listen to me… *you* will get well, and *you* will no longer worry those who love you. Is that understood? Your dearest grandmother and valet are beside themselves. Don't think for one moment that I am unaware of their worry, so you are going to get well, and you are going to let me help you." Her tone brooked no opposition. "You, my dear Earl, are going to follow *my* orders, and you will do as *I* say."

Hearing her admonishment, Crooks moved from the door to rest his tired body. *Yes, my lord, you are in good hands. And I cannot wait to tell you this bit of news.*

Wilhelmina set the broth closer to the Earl's bedside, then sat on the bed and carefully, but with difficulty, lifted his head and tried to spoon-feed him again. "Come on, Lucien," she blatantly cajoled, "just a couple spoonful. Come on, don't give me any grief. You will take at least three mouthfuls, and you will swallow them! I shall not permit you to dribble them away."

Before she accomplished her task, she was wearing some of the broth, along with it on the linen she placed under Lucien's chin. In his semi-conscious state, the Earl was not cooperating, but Wilhelmina's determination would not give in inch, and without his knowing it, she gave him four mouthfuls, even though some of it spilled on both of them. Cleaning up their mess, she looked down at his sleeping form—he lay still with his eyes closed, and his handsome face wasn't scowling at her. She reached and let her fingers trace his brow and then her thumbs lightly pressed around the corner of his eyes and down the side of his cheeks. She couldn't help herself as she leaned over and let her lips rest for just a few seconds on his—surprising her, as they weren't soft and mushy, but firm. She let the tip of her tongue touch his lips, she didn't know why—it was a simple reaction. It seemed as if they burned her, but it was a delightful singe, and then, she could feel her pulse beat a bit quicker. Not concerned, she couldn't seem to stop. Gently, she covered the sides of his face with both her hands and let her fingers trail down to his neck and on to his chest. She bent over and kissed him near his ear. The feeling within her was magnified by a strange, warm awareness, assaulting the quiet within her. He moaned, and she used her thumb, pressing the corner of his mouth. "Shush, you're going to be fine." She leaned in once again, brushing her lips on his. She caught her breath and knew why—she was in love with the Earl of Grenmoor. It shook her as she tried to control the sudden confession and turmoil spinning inside of her head. Quickly, she moved back and stared at the man she knew didn't like her, and when he'd learn she was Willie, he'd probably throw her out of Seahurst. Twisting her fingers, gathering her wits, she knew she had to keep her feelings to herself. Taking a deep breath, she went on to cool his brow and ensure he was resting comfortably.

She leaned over the Earl, her breast just above his face. She was busy trying to adjust this pillow when he grabbed her waist and pulled her upon him. His strength was incalculable. Struggling to break his grip, she felt heat breathing on her breast. It was so deliciously warm and astonishing her that she almost forgot to move, but when he began to nibble at her breast through her clothing, she was so startled that her strength became surprisingly powerful. It worked; it broke the hold on the ailing Earl's grasp. Shaken, she stood back, straightening her dress and smoothing her hair that had fallen from its velvet ribbon. Staring at the Earl's closed eyes, his breathing a bit faster, he spoke clearly, "Deedee darling, don't stop." Then he was silent.

Tears formed, and she could not hold them back. What was the matter with her? The Earl did not belong to her. What was she thinking, taking over as if he was hers to look after? His unknown uttering shot through Wilhelmina that he had desires for this certain woman in his elite society. *Thank the good Lord, no one knows what a fool I am.* Upset yet grateful for awakening her from her reckless dreams and realizing how she had taken over in openly caring for the Earl, her idiotic heartfelt thoughts toward this man of aristocracy, and she a vicar's daughter, cut straight into her being. *Foolish and definitely, outrageously stupid of me.* She forced her feelings to turn into the nurse form she was supposed to be while keeping her deep-seated love secreted inside of her. She attended to the Earl as a patient, and without any other regard than getting him well for Lady Julia. She would go to London and across the sea to Aggie as planned. Swiping at tears, she thought, *I want to be truly loved and have children, and I must concentrate on finding a regular man; perhaps, Aggie and James will know someone.* Her heart heavy, aching for the man she could not have.

The sun had set, and wind began whipping around the windows. Even with the heavy velvet window coverings, it blew, telling Seahurst's occupants they were in for another good blow.

Lady Julia was back in Lucien's room, and Crooks had awakened after a long-needed sleep. He felt renewed and ready to take on the night's vigil.

Wilhelmina met them both with a warm smile. "The Earl will recover and soon be snapping orders."

Lady Julia noticed Wilhelmina didn't use Lucien's given name as before. She said nothing but hoped there would be familiarity between the two of them. Both she and Crooks went to Lucien, and he was sleeping soundly, his brow cool.

"Oh, Willie," the dowager's voice filled with elation, "I cannot thank you enough. I truly believe you saved Lucien's life. I am so pleased you insisted that he not be bled, for surely you were right—it would have weakened him. Don't you agree, Crooks?"

"I certainly do, my lady." Looking at Willie, he asked, "Do you want me to continue with the cool cloths?"

She looked over at the sleeping Earl. Her heart was ready to burst, but no one could know. Her tone conciliatory, yet cool, she said, "I think not, Mr. Crooks. His Lordship is doing well. I would bet that by morning, he will be his self again and wanting a huge meal."

Both Lady Julia and Crooks were surprised at Wilhelmina's cool demeanor. What transpired during the hours between the two of them that had her seemingly indifferent now? Surely, Lucien hadn't wakened to scold her, or did he say something that she should not have heard? "Oh, dear," she exclaimed.

Wilhelmina didn't understand what Lady Julia was referring to, but she assured her, "Please don't worry, my lady, you will have your healthy grandson back with you in no time at all."

Lady Julia reached for Wilhelmina's hands and gently pressured them, looking at the tired young woman. "Thank you, again, dear Willie. You astound me with your caring. I believe Lucien couldn't have made it without you."

Wilhelmina could not trust herself to say anything; she pressed her lips together, looking over at the sleeping man.

"Is something wrong, Willie?"

Needing to ease this kind woman's concern, she immediately said, "Oh, no, my lady, nothing. I do think I need some exercise, if you don't mind. I shall take a turn walking about and also let the staff know that His Lordship is well. But first, I must change my gown," she laughed, "The Earl and I had a bit of a tussle when he refused to take my serving him broth."

"Do what pleases you, my dear. You must be exhausted; you have done more than anyone when we needed you most. Crooks and I will look after Lucien."

Giving the Earl one more glance, she nodded and quietly disappeared.

Lady Julia looked at Crooks. "Something happened. Do you know what occurred?"

"I have no idea, my lady."

"I mean to find out what went on while we were away. Are you certain you can tell me nothing? Believe me, Crooks, this is only what is best for my grandson."

Indignant, Crooks raised himself up and looked down at the petite older woman. "I know nothing that would have changed the young woman's manner. When I left, I overheard her admonishing the sleeping Earl and telling him he would do as she says and get well. I was relieved to leave him in her good hands."

"Then we will have to just wait and see and work at this problem." Her tone was adamant. "As there is one, I am sure."

Chapter Eighteen

Wilhelmina, having slept soundly, was awakened in her darkened room with only the glow from slow-burning logs offering light with the heavily covered windows keeping in the warmth. She stretched like a contented kitten and then came to grips with the time—it had to be late. She was concerned, as no one woke her. Could the Earl have taken a bad turn and Mr. Crooks failed to get her? That didn't seem right. Hurriedly, she dressed in a simple, dark-colored gown, trimmed at the collar and cuffs with wide black velvet ribbons. Not bothering with her hair, she pushed loose curls behind her ear. She had no inkling of the time, and thinking that it was late, she did not want to ring for Tess. Unable to button up the back of her dress, she threw a shawl over her shoulder and headed to check on the Earl.

Just about to round the corner that would take her to the Earl's quarters, she heard Lady Julia bid her grandson a good eve—Jaggers was at the dowager's side. As they made their way in the opposite direction, they did not see Wilhelmina's approach.

Quietly, not wanting to disturb the Earl but wanting to see that he was truly well, she thought to peek in on him and then return to her rooms for the balance of the eve. Pleased that Lady Julia was in high spirits, she'd relax and have supper in her room.

In her haste, Wilhelmina did not carry a candle to light her way, though it did not matter as she was quite familiar with the hall. She walked softly and saw the Earl's door was left slightly ajar. It was not like her to eavesdrop, but when she heard her name, she halted as the Earl's words knifed into her being.

"Miss Thaylor! Can you believe it! Johnny, that impostor passing herself off as a lady and all the time she's that fraudulent person known as Willie?" He laughed and Jonathan joined him.

Jonathan couldn't stop laughing as he admitted, "I will say, Lu, she had me fooled. How did you discover all of this about her?"

"Crooks. Thank god for Crooks. When I was iced to the bone down on the shore, he said the people were doing all that Willie asked of them. They were actually following her command even though they knew what must be done." Lucien sounded astonished. "I have a hard time believing it. But Crooks, I trust, said that when he spied, it was none other than our little fraud, Miss Thaylor, otherwise known as Wilhelmina, or better yet, *Willie*. He said she moved about dressed in breeches and looking like a young lad."

Together, both men broke out with laughter.

Disgraced, Wilhelmina fled back to her private rooms. Tears burst and ran freely, literally falling onto her gown. She entered her room and was startled as Tess was there with a tray.

"Oh Miss, you scared me. I thought you were in the dressing room."

Wilhelmina tried to dry her tears, she turned her head and used her shawl to dab her cheeks.

Tess noticed and worried for her. "What is it, Miss?" Thinking her mistress was worried about the Earl, Tess, added, "His Lordship is all right, Miss. He's right as rain, he is. Why, below stairs, they say he is ordering himself trays of food. They say he told Crooks he was starving." She praised Wilhelmina, "You did a real good job caring for His Lordship, Miss. Please don't fret none."

Getting herself together, she answered, "Thank you, Tess. I admit I worried."

"I was surprised you weren't asleep when I tapped on your door. I know you must be hungry. I have a pot of coffee, just the way you like it."

Wilhelmina smiled as she fabricated a story to cover her tears. She could not let anyone know that she overheard the Earl and his friend laughing at her. She was too humiliated and embarrassed. "You're very thoughtful, Tess." She gave the young maid a reason for her being distraught. "I was on my way down to the kitchen as I thought it was much later and everyone would be asleep, but I couldn't button my gown, so I threw on this shawl." She half-smiled. "Then I realized it wasn't as late as I thought and hurried back to dress properly."

Tess wasn't that feeble; something else had upset her fine mistress, but she would not say a word. "Let me help you, Miss. I'll button your gown."

"No, I think I'll forget about it. You have the tray for me, and the Earl is doing well. There is no need for me to tend him this eve. Mr. Crooks will as usual. I think I shall relax in a warm bath and spend a quiet eve."

"Good for you, Miss. Why, I have never seen anyone so worried and looking after His Lordship like you did. If anyone deserves a good rest, it is you."

"Tess, what would I do without you? Thank you."

"Oh, Miss, you are special to me and to all of us."

"Even when I take over and become bossy?" She couldn't help but grin.

"Why, Miss, no one here minds you giving them orders. You order by asking. Why, it has been so much fun with you about being Willie..." she blushed, "I mean..."

Wilhelmina touched Tess's arm, "Worry not. I know what you mean, and it is all right. We are friends regardless of how I'm dressed, are we not?"

Elated, the young plump maid happily answered, "Oh yes, Miss, and proud I am that you do consider me your friend. There is nothing I would not do for you. Just ask."

Wilhelmina's voice was just above a whisper, "Perhaps, Tess, I might just do that." She stepped out of her gown and Tess quickly assisted her with a robe.

Mentally, Wilhelmina was crushed and needed to be by herself to sort things out. *I must be very careful not to reveal my feelings for the Earl. I'm a fool to even consider the great Earl of Grenmoor might share an interest in plain me. Aristocracy bands together.* "I won't need you this eve, Tess—take the rest of this day for yourself. Just leave the tray until morn. I may read a while before going to sleep. There is no need for you to wait for me."

Tess couldn't believe her good luck. "Thank you, Miss. I'll be here first thing in the morn. Do you think you'll ride?"

"Perhaps... yes."

"I'll be here for you."

"No, no. I'll slip down to the kitchen and have a cup of coffee and go directly to the stable. There is no reason for you to rise early. I have all my things right here and donning my breeches is quite simple. I'll be fine."

"But Miss, Lady Barclay will not approve of me not being here for you. Especially after all the time you've looked after His Lordship."

"I have a fair understanding with Lady Julia. Now go, enjoy your eve and take a long morn, too."

With Tess gone, Wilhelmina had time to consider her complicity from the very beginning, and then continuing until it had now become embarrassing.

She wanted to weep. She was definitely out of her league, and she knew she had to do something. But what? How? Mortified at being laughed at and determined not to have to face the two lordships and pretend... *curtsey to them... I will not!* Shamed, she had to think of something.

* * *

Wilhelmina shouldn't have run off as she would not have only been astounded but would have reveled with delight over Lucien's words.

Lord Lucien Barclay and Lord Jonathan Restin never minced words with each other. "I'll tell you, Johnny," Lucien's laughter subsided, "I have never held so much wonderment for a young lady. To think that she, and of course, Grandy, is just as calculable in this, could do such a thorough job of subterfuge." His voice, tinged with awe, continued, "And to think all that mahogany hair hidden under a cap and being so slim in stature rode Zephr as though that black beauty was not a stallion but a gentle gelding is absolutely miraculous. It is beyond my comprehension how she handled Zephr that blustery night and brought him home. Crooks said no one would go near my horse." Lucien gasped. "He would have died, Lu, if not for Willie. It seems everyone knew about Willie and her connection riding Zephr—everyone but Crooks and me." Lucien shook his head. "Zephr has a mind of his own and must be controlled, and that little impostor did it and did it superbly." The Earl's face and tone revealed euphoria over her control of *his* horse. "No wonder she is so sassy and impertinent. Oh, wait until I confront her. I am going to have some wiles to perform on her," his voice was filled with happy mischief.

Jonathan studied his friend, as he had never heard Lu speak so engagingly about the opposite sex. To Lu, women were just flighty wenches full of fluff and avarice that had to be tolerated, because it was their way. "I think, Lu, you are having second thoughts about Miss Thaylor. This is not like you, as you're usually indifferent with the ladies."

Lucien eyed his friend, wondering how this conversation had turned, and Johnny's tone became somewhat disbelieving. It was then that he remembered that Johnny was seriously thinking of pursuing Miss Thaylor. "Worry not, Johnny, all I want to do is meet Willie... in person." He laughed, "Willie's my kind of *guy*," continuing to tease, "riding my beautiful stallion deserves some pay-back as well as praise."

"Hold on, Lu, I'm serious." Jonathan began to pace and then stopped beside his friend propped up in bed, "I think you are confusing the issue."

"Certainly not."

"Are you forgetting that Willie and Miss Thaylor are one and the same? Yet you talk about confronting Willie when all along it's going to be Miss Thaylor."

"And you don't think I know the difference? Johnny," Lucien moving his hand back and forth for emphasis, "my interest is getting back at the brazen redhead that treated me as one of her staff." He chuckled, "You've witnessed her impertinence, and then, she had the temerity to walk off as though it was her right."

Jonathan's grin reached his eyes.

"I have every right to get *even*, though I'll not really mean it, but I don't want her to know. Let's see how she handles it. Agree?"

"I'll go along with you as we remember this is pretend," he laughed, "but still, I think our little lady will be a force to confront."

Lucien did his best to camouflage his unexpected feelings for Miss Thaylor. "No doubt you're right, but I want the opportunity to see her reaction."

"Truthfully, I do too, but know that I'm not in your corner." Jonathan dropped in the chair near Lucien's bed. "I really like her, Lu. She's phenomenal. I mean to carry through with courting her as soon as I talk with Aunt Edith. Lady Julia said I must have my aunt's consent. And when I get it, I am going to do all that I can to win Miss Thaylor's affection and whatever name she chooses is fine with me. She's going to make a great Countess of Ventry; she'll be magnificent."

"Yes, she'll make a lovely countess." For the first time, Lucien became a shade envious of his friend, not letting on but knowing in his heart that Willie was just the kind of woman he had been searching to become his wife… his countess. He wouldn't renege on his word. *Most likely, she would turn me down after my miserable disposition and attitudes I've lobbed at her.* Lucien's smile was sincere. "I apologize, Johnny. I never said, but Grandy has been plotting and planning for me to marry, and I thought all along that Miss Thaylor was part of it. Then there was Zephr… that was the last straw for me."

Jonathan laughed. "Can you believe that winsome, magnetic woman rode that black beast of yours? Remember when we first saw what we thought was a lad racing Zephr across Grenmoor?" His voice was filled with awe. "Why, that was Miss Thaylor. I can't believe how spirited she is."

"She is that." And Lucien meant it.

"So, Lu, you're sure you're all right with my capturing Miss Thaylor for my own?"

"Just remember that her sassy mouth is going to drive you up Ventry castle walls. One thing you will find is that she never listens and does as she pleases."

Jonathan grinned, "Having her as mine, I won't mind at all." He looked over at his bed-ridden friend. "If I thought for one minute you might also be serious about her, Lu, I would say we should let the best man win. I don't want this to cause friction between us—our friendship means a lot."

Lucien's gut knotted. His head told him to admit the truth, but Johnny being his best friend, although Willie turned to be something special, he had no right to think she would ever consider him a suitor. Fustian, he was sure she wouldn't. *Why, she doesn't even like me.* So, he warned half-seriously, "You're digging your own burial, Johnny, and don't look for me to help you climb out of it. If I know you, in a few months, you'll be backing off, and Grandy will hold both of us responsible if that saucy redhead is hurt or embarrassed." Lucien thought he covered his feelings well. "So, be sure. As for me, no, thank you."

Relieved, Jonathan admitted, "For a moment there, I thought you might be leaning toward finding out more about her. I really know nothing. I asked Lady Julia, and she told me to talk with Lady Marlowe. I don't understand how my aunt is involved with Miss Thaylor. Why the mystery? If there is one, I'll find out."

"It is odd, as Grandy invited Lady Agatha Landry, your aunt's granddaughter, to be her guest, and it comes to pass she has Miss Thaylor instead." Lucien shook his head, "Why is Miss Thaylor your aunt's ward? I remember Miss Thaylor saying that her father was the vicar at Marlfordshire, near Marlowe lands, and that he died. Where Lady Edith comes into the picture, Miss Thaylor didn't say."

Jonathan adamantly declared, "None of that matters a fig to me. We've always said intelligence along with quality is what our women friends lacked," he grinned, "and Miss Thaylor is certainly not lacking in any of those." His brow wrinkled and then he brightened, "You're right; the Marlowe and Marlfordshire border each other. Had I not heard of your illness, I would be in London now, getting answers." Jonathan teased, "Well, of course I came because of you, but then I thought I could get another glimpse at Miss Thaylor. Where is she, by the way? I hear she never left your side while you had a fever."

"Speaking of my nurse, I thought for sure she would be about giving orders again. She must be resting. Crooks said she was insistent about staying on with him and helping all the while I was high with fever."

"She sure is something, and what a surprise when you told me about her actually being this fabulous Willie everyone is so taken with."

A smirk crossed Lucien's face.

"What's so funny?"

"Tell me, Johnny, what are you going to do when Miss Thaylor asks you to go riding? She rises at dawn to ride—weather be hanged… rain, mist, wind, or sunshine—she's goes to the stable," really grinning, he added, "*early!*"

"I never thought of that. We'll have to work something out. Why, I'll buy her the best stable this side of London, and she'll have her choice of any fine horses." He lightly reached and knuckled Lucien's arm. "How about selling me Zephr? What a wedding gift!"

Glaring, Lucien gritted his teeth. "The devil, I will. Zephr is a handful. I would worry if Willie owned him. Oh, no… Zephr stays with me."

Jonathan chided, "Would you be worrying about Willie or about your horse?"

Lucien threw a pillow at his friend.

Chapter Nineteen

Just Before Dawn

Wilhelmina pulled on her breeches, wool stockings and boots, planning to hitch a ride with Jenkins, who brought supplies and took outgoing missives to the mail coach coming through Penwyn. Her plan was to get out of Cornwall. She'd go to Lady Marlowe in Marlfordshire and explain only that she was anxious to sail and see Aggie as they planned.

Wilhelmina's heart filled with a pulling ache that wouldn't leave. *Wise up… I know the Earl of Grenmoor thinks I'm a cheat, and he'll never think otherwise. He's a nobleman, and I'm my father's daughter.* Knowing she loved the persnickety aristocrat, she had to keep it bottled inside of her or she'd really be a laughing joke to them all—more so than she was now.

She'd have Jenkins deliver her thank-you letter to Lady Julia on his next delivery. It was the only way to thank Lady Julia without fully explaining.

Gathering a few things and stuffing them in one bag, and then pulling on her shirt, heavy sweater, and raincoat with her hair stuffed in her cap, she was ready. Now, all she needed was to sneak down the back stairs without being seen by Jaggers. She knew he never missed anything, and it was with hope that with the Earl no longer in danger and all worries gone, Jaggers would be less cognizant about the morn's happenings, and her departure would go unnoticed.

Wilhelmina slipped out and made it down the drive; a mist hung in a thick haze, blurring the moon's light. Her face wet from tears, she used her arm to swipe at them as she called out to Jenkins. She waited for him make his deliveries, and now, as he hadn't yet given the horses their way, it wasn't difficult for him to stop.

He looked at her when she climbed onto the seat next to him, explaining she had to take the mail coach at Penwyn without fail. Jenkins knew of her; who didn't… and him being a stoic kind of person, only nodded and took her with him, only thinking that if this one wanted to leave Seahurst before daybreak, who was he to say?

Jenkins dropped her off in Penwyn with a nod when Wilhelmina thanked him. With her hair stuffed inside her cap and wearing her raincoat with the muffler wrapped against the dampness, also to hide her face, she waited for the mail coach arriving within a half hour. She could purchase a seat and be on her way, knowing that part of the way, she'd have to change to another coach to travel on. Certainly not like coming to Seahurst in one well sprung coach and in modest comfort. Though fear augured its way into her, adding to her stress, she knew she had only one option, and that was to leave Seahurst quickly. She could not stay and face humiliation and more embarrassment, especially from the man she loved. *I'll not let him laugh at me again.* Taking a breath, she had to overcome her apprehension of traveling alone, forcing her mind to remember that she made the trip to Cornwall and wasn't totally unfamiliar with the journey. *I can do this.* She stiffened her back and gripped her bag.

So far, she ran into no problems dressed as a boy. The mail coach had two other passengers, both men, and after having eaten at Six Bells, they climbed into the coach. The heavy-set man took most of one seat—she sat with the other. Neither said a word; both men yawned and closed their eyes. As they bounced down the road, Wilhelmina pushed her fist into her mouth to keep from making a sound. *He never liked me, and he never will.* She bowed her head as though sleeping, as she needed to hide her watery eyes. She thought her chest would burst as her breath caught in her throat. She must have been shaking as the heavy-set man nudged her with his foot. "You okay, lad?"

Wilhelmina jumped and almost screamed but caught herself in time and nodded.

"First time away from home, is it?"

Her stomach churning, she just nodded.

"You'll be okay. Wait and see... everything gets better."

She nodded again and mumbled, "Hope so."

He closed his eyes, but she knew he wasn't asleep. The man sitting next to her never said a word or made a sound.

Wilhelmina settled in, put on her gloves, and tried to keep her raw emotions in check. She didn't dare close her eyes for fear that her cap would come off.

When the rickety mail coach stopped and readied its passengers to transfer to another mail coach, Wilhelmina waited off to one side and then noticed a handsome coach with a coat of arms; its crest carried a glow. A uniformed man was trying to calm his horse that was tied at the rear of the coach. Without thinking, Wilhelmina walked over and reached to comfort the huge beast.

"What do you think you're doing? You want to get stomped?"

By now, she was next to the golden stallion and talking softly to it. It seemed to calm but was still sidestepping. She carefully reached and ran her hand over his neck and turned as another man walked toward her. He wore fine, tailored clothes—reminding her of the Earl, and she said, "Sir, if this is your horse, the leather bit in his mouth is pulled too tight. It is cutting him. He doesn't like it. If you loosen it and allow his mouth to heal, you probably won't have any more trouble."

The man's mouth fell open. He couldn't believe a mere lad could tone down his horse and without thought tell *him* what to do. But he looked at Samson, and indeed, his mouth was raw with traces of blood. He yelled for his coachman and ordered that it be attended to immediately. He turned to Wilhelmina who was walking away. "I say there, let me pay you for your sound advice." He couldn't stop looking at the lad's most alluring green eyes. *What wouldn't any young lady give to own a pair like that? They are mesmerizing, and the lad doesn't have a clue.*

Wilhelmina shook her head. "Not necessary," she replied, lowering her voice as best she good, "Glad to help your beautiful horse."

"You like horses, do you?"

"Yes, Sir."

"I'd like to do something for you. Samson is my favorite of all my cattle."

Wilhelmina didn't know what to say. She had to catch the next coach that was getting ready to leave. And then it hit her; she looked back down the side road and saw two other mediocre coaches, certainly not as fancy as this one, but knew they carried his staff and baggage. Looking at the crammed mail coach, she quietly asked, "Do you suppose, Sir, you could transport me further down the road? I'm on my way near to London."

Seemingly pleased to repay the kind lad, he said, "I believe so."

A lady within the dusty lacquered coach stuck her head out the window and voiced, "Gerald, I don't think so. We must be on our way."

"Oh, pardon, Ma'am," Wilhelmina gave her best performance of a simple lad, "I meant if I could ride in one of the other carriages following. I promise not to make a mess."

The woman pulled back her head and said not another word. Gerald, Samson's owner, called out to someone named Nash and had him take Wilhelmina to the first following carriage. She thanked the man with a nice manner, noticing his black hair had silver streaks. *Not like Lord Barclay's.* She was on her way.

They bumped along; she, Nash, two maids, and an elderly woman. She saw that four grooms were in the other carriage following them. No one spoke, but finally, one of the younger maids asked where she was going. Wilhelmina, not wanting to talk to give herself away just shrugged her shoulders. The other older maid smiled and said what a good-looking young 'fellow' she was. The older woman told her to mind her business and then went on say that His Grace wouldn't appreciate any goings-on.

His Grace? I've done it again. Speaking out to aristocracy… a duke! But no one will ever know. Wilhelmina smothered the smile that wanted to break open.

It seemed to take forever. Wilhelmina was offered food and given a blanket against the cold. Evidently, having His Grace put her in their care counted.

When they stopped at Peabody's stream to water the horses, Wilhelmina went to Nash and said she would ride no further; thanking him, she asked that he convey her gratitude to His Grace. She still didn't know the duke's name and wasn't going to inquire, as it wasn't important. Samson benefited from her knowledge, and in turn, she was rewarded with transportation. Her troubles ended when leaving Cornwall. She'd not see the Earl of Grenmoor again, or Samson's owner.

Marlfordshire was just over the rise from the stream. She skirted the village, not wanting to be recognized, and hiked through the meadow until she reached Marlowe lands.

The Duke's coaches left. Wilhelmina kneeled and scooped cold water into her cupped hands and splashed her face, and then, she laughed, her laughter joining Peabody's rushing water splashing over rocks and pebbles. She felt free, with no more pretending. She whipped off her hat and let the wind fly through her tangled hair. She started walking, occasionally picking a flower and twirling it between her fingers with thoughts of Seahurst, Lady Julia, and of course, the Earl of Grenmoor. How was he? He was anxious to get to London, her twisted ankle halting his journey, and then he could have died from lung congestion and high fever helping to save lives. Memory blossomed as the Earl's words crowded her mind when the fevered Earl called for Deedee, thus telling the Earl must already have a favored lady. *He said don't stop... stop what?* Wilhelmina shrugged, not knowing what to think. *I've got to forget that stubborn-arrogant haughty Earl and accept the absurdity, thinking that he could even like me a little bit.* More determined than ever, she tossed the wilted flower, pulled back her shoulders, stiffened her back and moved her steps at a quicker pace. *Aggie... I'm coming.*

Chapter Twenty

Marlowe House, London, Ten Days Later

Wilhelmina stepped down and out of the Marlowe coach, taking the short walk to the gray brick manor with its magnificent mansard roof, glistening windows and huge dark forest green door that opened before she reached it.

Smiling, with her arms open, Lady Edith Marlowe said, "Finally, my girl has come home to me. I had Haley notify me the instant the coach rounded the corner."

Lady Edith grasped Wilhelmina right there and then stood back, taking in Karen's daughter, *her granddaughter.* Her heart tripped seeing their identical smiles, but Wilhelmina's green eyes belonged to her father. She noticed the drawn look but made a point to say nothing after talking with Julia.

"It's so good to see you and thank you for sending your coach with Mrs. Coggins. I promise, Lady Marlowe, I won't be underfoot long; just until I can arrange passage to sail."

Lady Edith, her light gray hair matching the gray damask gown, her blue-gray eyes warm, put her arm around Wilhelmina while guiding her into the dowager's favorite drawing room. "Willie, my dear," *how I wish I could say granddaughter,* "you are not ever to think such nonsense as being underfoot." She squeezed the red-haired beauty's arm. "I'm sorry I wasn't there to greet you. I had no idea when you planned to leave Seahurst." Waiting for an explanation, she guided Wilhelmina to a comfortable chair, pulled a cord and ordered tea and coffee, then smiled. "I remember you prefer coffee."

Wilhelmina took a deep breath. She knew she had to explain and thought she had it all worked out, but now, it seemed wrong. She'd tell from the beginning with Agatha and James and Lady Julia and Seahurst and the Earl, but she would exclude her love for the authoritarian Earl of Grenmoor.

"I had to leave, my lady. I made a cluck of myself. I just couldn't hold my tongue, and then, Lady Julia didn't help matters. What I mean is, she asked me not to reveal that I was Willie to the Earl and his friend, Lord Restin." She removed her small bonnet and tossed it off to one side, stalling while pushing a few loose tendrils behind her ear. Finally, taking a visible breath, she said, "The Earl was angered that Willie rode his prized horse, Zephr. That stallion is beautiful—he has natural grace and speed and gave me his heart." Wilhelmina beamed, but didn't know it as she continued, "To freely gallop is the only way to ride, and Zephr gave me so much joy." She sort of chuckled, "There were some funny moments." She sat back in the chair. "I rode astride with Lady Julia's permission. and though I surprised the staff and everyone at Seahurst, they accepted me. They were so very nice." Her voice filled with amusement. "They called me *Willie,* just as my father did as I wrote to you." She bit her bottom lip. "I still can't imagine why Lady Julia did not want me to tell the Earl that Miss Thaylor and Willie were the same. His Lordship was angered and looking for Willie, but Lady Julia said not to worry. It became an absurd situation. I couldn't go against Lady Julia's wishes. Yet, it was dishonest. I knew the Earl would be outraged." Suddenly, her beautiful leafy green eyes glinted mischievously as the corners of her mouth turned upwards, "And he was. Then, everything exploded, and even though I was reluctant to be an impostor, I was one, and then I didn't have the courage to face what I had been doing." Wilhelmina's voice lowered with intensity, "I couldn't tell Lady Julia was part of my second fraud, so I cowardly slipped away without telling anyone."

"But now the Earl knows that you are Willie?"

"Yes. His valet, Mr. Crooks told him. Oh, that's another story, but to make it short, a boat crashed on Grenmoor's beach and everyone, including the Earl, were there to do what they could. I donned my breeches and hitched a ride to help after the Earl told me not to; as Miss Thaylor, I was to remain with Lady Julia. Well, most everyone knew I rode Zephr and wore breeches, so at the beach, they called me Willie, and Crooks heard, and then, the Earl caught cold from the icy water and almost died, and after seven days, he did make it. Then, I overheard Lord Barclay telling Lord Restin who I was, and they were laughing." Wilhelmina's color paled. "I'm ashamed to say I couldn't take the embarrassment and shame of all that I was part of... I didn't want to mislead anyone further; as I said, I sneaked away."

"Go on, tell me." Lady Edith reached to touch her granddaughter. "Nothing is so shocking that it can't be put right. Julia boasted how you made friends with everyone. That doesn't surprise me." *Julia has written all that transpired, but she said something must have occurred while Wilhelmina was caring for Lord Barclay. She knows not what but is certain the two of them are well-suited. Lord Barclay was furious when he found Wilhelmina had sneaked away and successfully at that.*

"I know Lady Julia wrote to you about our being delay coming to London."

The maid wheeled in the tea cart with coffee's aroma hitting Wilhelmina. Her stomach gurgled, but only she knew. There were meats, rolls, and pastries for her to indulge, and she did.

Lady Edith waited with her tea and a scone. She gathered her granddaughter wasn't being completely candid, but she'd try to figure out the missing parts once Wilhelmina continued.

Setting her coffee cup down and folding her napkin, she laid it next to the empty cup and said, "Thank you, my lady; delicious as I remember."

"Aren't you going to continue calling me Grandmother?"

Wilhelmina's green eyes appeared dewy. "I thought you asked that I do so for Aggies's benefit… I miss her. We were close almost like sisters."

If you only knew, granddaughter. "That is not the reason. Will you allow me to call you my granddaughter? It would please me."

Wilhelmina's warm smile brought Karen into Lady Edith's heart. "I'm honored, *Grandmother*, but know that there seems to be a mystery here as to how I became your ward. I don't recall Father mentioning the Marlowes. I look forward to hearing about it from you."

Mystery? Not really… a secret. A bit of stress eased from Lady Edith's heart. "No mystery, my dear. I heard you were alone when the vicar died." She reached over and touched Willie's arm. "How could I not want to claim you as my own? Now just one more question: how is your ankle? Julia wrote that you twisted it. How? Does it pain you?"

Wilhelmina blushed; she couldn't stop the heat invading her complexion. "It was my fault. Lord Barclay and I were on the moors, and I decided had to leave the curricle when he told me not to, and then I tripped, and he had to carry me, and it started raining and blowing cold winds, and he was so angry with me." Lady Edith saw her tear-filled eyelids as she tried to explain without letting a tear fall… "It seems that every time I'm around the Earl of Grenmoor, I refuse to listen, and I guess you could say I become obstinate." Suddenly, her eyes glistened from her tears, "I somehow resented his haughty attitude. He treated me as if I was brainless, and I apologize, Grandmother, as I couldn't keep my thoughts to myself. It seemed I was always contradicting him. Lord Barclay is handsome, and women must dream to be with him. I am not one of them. And too, what Abby and I did was wrong, but it ended to be right."

Oh, oh. I think my granddaughter has a bit of tender for Lord Barclay. Could Julia be right? "The Earl is in demand, but that is his concern, not ours. For now, you've had a long travel, and your Cornwall holiday has been extraordinary. I'm so glad you shared it with me. I think, between the two of us, we can get Lady Julia to tell us about her motive for secrecy."

"I doubt it, as Lady Julie has a way about her. She's gracious and sweet, and one willingly ends getting whatever she commands." Wilhelmina smiled. "If you don't mind, Grandmother, I best rid the dust from my travel. Later, I must learn about sailings and arrange for passage."

Concealing her upset, Lady Edith said, "You're still planning on going on with the plans you made with Agatha? I had hoped you may have decided not to."

Anxious to clarify, Wilhelmina said, "I must sail. I want to. I need to leave England." Wanting to hide her depression, she added, "A new place and a new life. I'm certain with Aggie and James's help, I'll be able to do that."

Lady Edith wasn't giving up, persistent. "But why? I thought staying with Lady Julia, you were enjoying… as you call it… freedom and were looking forward returning to London. Am I wrong with my presumption?"

Wilhelmina needed to leave, or she'd say something to reveal her true feelings. "No, but circumstances occur that change one's thinking. Lady Edith… Grandmother, will you excuse me for a short while and we'll talk later?"

"Of course, my dear. Do take rest." She felt the need to keep Wilhelmina with her, she missed her so. "But I must tell you that Lord Restin visited and asked permission to court you. I refused. I hope you don't mind… in my heart, I believe you would not suit," not telling that she extracted Jonathan's promise not to reveal her long-held secret when he made a special visit to seek permission to court her ward, Wilhelmina Thaylor.

Accepting Jonathan's word to keep Lady Edith's secret, she explained why Jonathan could not court Wilhelmina. Karen and the vicar were in love, and that Wilhelmina was Karen's daughter, and the vicar *was her father.* That Uncle Henry would not permit Karen to marry outside aristocracy. It was secretly agreed that Karen's baby was to be left with the vicar as abandoned… he would raise his daughter and keep *their* secret. Forced to marry the Duke of Rainstone, and you know the rest, Karen died, and we have Agatha because the Rainstone was only interested in an heir. Lady Edith remembered hearing Jonathan's gasp and then his reassurance that her secret was safe with him.

Wilhelmina's mouth gaped. "What? Lord Restin has an interest in me?"

"Are you surprised?"

She didn't say that it was the wrong Earl to court her while hiding her feelings. "Yes… yes, I am. I know he has a teasing sense of humor, but never did it come across as anything else. I'm certain he is jesting."

"Would you consider Lord Restin in a serious courtship?" Lady Edith had to know if that was why her granddaughter's outlook seemed so cheerless.

He and Lucien relished laughing at my Seahurst deception, "Oh my, no, *not* Lord Restin."

Lady Edith was having second thoughts. *I believe it's the wrong Earl my granddaughter has an interest in. Oh Julia, maybe we should not have tried matchmaking… it seems it is only one-sided as Lord Barclay has the pick of any in our social ton, and my precious doesn't measure up. He's not wise at all. That must be why she wants to sail so quickly.* Coyly, Lady Edith asked, "If not Lord Restin, is there someone else?"

I must be careful and not show any regard for that arrogant noble who will think nothing of making me into a funny story and laughing while telling it. Her blood pounding, wanting to hide her bruised pride, eyeing the lady who believed in her and not wanting to think she was stepping above her place, she bit her tongue and fibbed, "No, my lady, I'm off to be with Aggie and James as we planned. I'm not part of your London elite."

Exasperated, Lady Marlowe didn't hold back. "Why, that is utter nonsense!" Her warm smile eased Wilhelmina's tension, "Now, take rest, and we'll talk later. Just promise me that you won't hurry off. Set sail if you must. I'll not deny you from keeping your word to Agatha, but please, won't you stay with me for a visit? I'd like that so much."

Standing and offering a small curtsey, Wilhelmina's warm smile reached her soft green eyes. "Of course, Grandmother, I like being with you. Thank you."

Chapter Twenty-One

Now in London, Three Weeks Later

Sitting slouched with one leg crossed over his knee and not caring about wrinkling his well-tailored clothes, Lord Jonathan Restin was in a petulant mood. He swirled whiskey in the crystal glass again and again—he would stop and then start again and not drink.

Lucien said nothing—leaning back in his desk chair in his private study on Barclay Square, he waited for his friend to break his silence that lay heavily midst between them. Lucien leaned forward, his voice low but commanding. "So, Johnny, are you going to tell me what's vexing you or not?"

Jonathan thought this was what it felt like, being dragged by a horse— bruised. *I gave my word to Aunt Edith.*

Lucien probed, "You visited Lady Marlowe. Is that why you're in a stew? Did you see our impostor and learn why she sneaked away like a thief?" Lucien's upset was obvious that he continued to think of his grandmother's guest and annoyed that she occupied his thoughts. *It's a good thing Johnny has in mind to court that cheeky baggage, so I can finally vanquish her from my mind.* Looking at his friend, he said, "What's the problem, Johnny?" Lucien pointed to the glass in Jonathan's hand. "Tell why you aren't imbibing my whiskey. You've been staring at it this last hour."

I promised Aunt Edith I wouldn't reveal Karen's secret, but then, it makes Miss Thaylor seem unworthy of my courting by not saying why I can't. Lu would understand, but I gave my word. Crestfallen, Jonathan took a deep breath and said, "I did see my Aunt Edith, Lu, and she is against my having any close interest in her ward, Miss Thaylor."

Truly astonished, Lucien leaned back in his chair, eying his friend, and then leaned forward, pushing his glass of whiskey aside. "You're serious?"

"Yes. Lu, I can only say this to you and no one else… I gave my aunt my word, and the reason is personal between Aunt Edith and me. The discussion ends there."

"I'm sorry, Johnny."

"So am I." Glum-faced, Lord Restin added, "Listen to this… when Aunt Edith mentioned to Miss Thaylor that I was interested in being more than a friend, the minx had the audacity to laugh. Aunt Edith thinks she favors someone but is not certain. That must be why she's anxious to move on." He now took a deep swallow from his glass, sounding melancholy. "I thought she liked me." His mouth twisted into an infectious grin. "And we know for certain that she doesn't like you." Jonathan's mouth broke into a wide smile. "That dressing-down she gave you at Seahurst with her red hair being as fiery as her temper," Jonathan continued his voice in awe, "Willie… I still can't believe Willie is Miss Thaylor, and that she rode your black stallion as though it was a pony. My god, she can ride." He moaned, adding, "There is something special about her, Lu, her no-nonsense character. You know, in the end, her manner wouldn't set well with the *ton*." Taking another swallow, Jonathan's voice was serene. "And I wouldn't have given a damn."

"You really meant to make her your countess, didn't you?"

"I did."

"Isn't there any way you can overcome what you can't tell me?"

"No. Thinking about marriage—it would be impossible to spend the rest of my life with someone that has no warm feelings for me and definitely has no interest in becoming a countess."

"Don't turn depressed on me, Johnny. We both have our duty as male heirs, and we agreed to prolong our living single until the last possible moment." Now, Lucien freely offered a mischievous jab. "What about Melissa Blakely? She's had her eye on you for two seasons, and you know she's waiting for you."

"Don't go matchmaking, Lu… you're becoming Grandy."

Lucien laughed. "Heaven forbid. Seriously, Melissa's not bad—good figure, soft on the eyes and from upper aristocracy, and her voice doesn't grind on your nerves. Your family would be delighted," Lucien teased. "Besides, from what I understand, Lady Melissa doesn't care for riding unless it's in a carriage."

"Well, then… how about you?" Lord Restin set his drink down and smirked, "As long as we're matchmaking, are you serious about Lady Evelyn? *She* is into riding and has her own favorite horse."

"Now, you're way off and you know it. She is stunning; however, her conceited personality grates—I must tell the lady that she looks beautiful, and her gown is becoming to make her happy."

"Her father's a duke."

"What's that got to do with it? Melissa's father is also a duke."

Jonathan picked up his glass. "Touché!" Lucien grinned, and then Jonathan's laugher filled the room. He was grinning at his good friend with his voice full of mischief. "Why don't you try for Willie? Now that, Lu, would be something. Why, I'll bet you won't be able to get her to waltz with you unless with force."

"Your bet is safe. You said she's sailing."

"Not right off. Aunt Edith invited her to spend a few weeks with her at Upper James. She wants her to enjoy a few parties and soirées. She talked about Miss Thaylor enjoying some of London's season. Are you interested?"

"The reason I really want to talk with that sassy minx is to thank her first for attending me. Crooks said she really helped him take over my care while I was out of it. Crooks said she did it without thought, and Grandy told him to let her do it her way. I still can't get over Grandy allowing Miss Thaylor to enter my bedroom and me naked under the sheet." Lucien smirked. "I wonder how it came about, and if anything, untoward occurred. Crooks said I didn't lie still when I was feverish. Too, I wonder if that is why she sneaked away without telling Grandy. That's not what an honest person would do, but she wasn't honest, was she? She played us fools."

"So, that's what's eating on you? Oh Lu, she touted us both, and we had it coming. And you just can't handle her bossiness and sass while I find it charming and also hilarious."

It's more than that, Johnny, only I can't tell you. She's special, and Crooks said she stayed with me… never leaving my side. I think I felt her hands move over my face so gentle… yet, I'm not sure. "I'll admit, I admire her tenacity but not the way she sneaked away."

"I thought it clever and brave. Can you imagine any female we know that would do that? Ride in a dusty mail coach dressed as a boy? And to top it off, she did it on her own. Alone!"

Both men's mood shifted, enjoying Willie's lark.

Jonathan stood and stretched. "By the way, I didn't see our impostor as Aunt Edith made appointments for new gowns, so she must have been shopping. Aunt Edith did mention that she accepted Sheldon's party invitation and will be taking Miss Thaylor with her. Are you going?"

"I wasn't, but now that you say our impostor is going to be there, I will definitely show." Lucien's words faded into unconscious warmth, "Miss Thaylor… I still can't believe she rode Zephr."

"I knew it," Jonathan's voice charged, "it's that horse again. Lu, think… it's the girl that's important. You know, there was a time I thought you might be interested in Miss Thaylor, but it turns out, Zephr always comes first. Do we have a bet? She won't dance with you unless you force her, as she won't make a scene like your last waltz when you captured the entire *ton* with your nonchalance waltz." He grinned, "Those curls of hers match her temper. Best be careful, my friend. She just may tell you what she thinks right there for the entire *ton* to hear. After all, she's sailing, and the great Earl of Grenmoor will have to rally after her set-down." Jonathan badgered his friend, "Have you the courage to ask her to dance while all the other willing ladies would die to be in Miss Thaylor's dancing shoes?"

Lucien wouldn't give Johnny any advantage as to what he would do with Miss Thaylor, and he certainly wouldn't give his grandmother one iota of an inkling in his pursuit of the one person that has no interest in him. "My friend, I'm the master at waltzing. She'll fall into my arms."

Chapter Twenty-Two

Night of Sheldon's Ball

"You look lovely, Wilhelmina. You remind me of another young lady."

"Grandmother," she lightly scolded, "I wish Aggie was here in my stead for you. I don't particularly like parties. I only attended the others with Aggie because it pleased you, and now, I'm doing the same again."

You look so much like your mother. Karen would be so proud. "I appreciate it, *granddaughter.*" Lady Edith's heart blossomed being with Karen's daughter. "You are making me very happy. Too, we'll see Lady Julia, and you did say you wanted to have a few words with her. So, it's going to be a beautiful evening." She patted Wilhelmina's gloved hand. "Your gown is exquisite, matching the green in your shining eyes. You are a beautiful lady, and the way your gown crosses over and then falls unimpaired will make eyes turn. My dearest, do not think for one moment that you do not belong in London society… you are first in any class."

Wilhelmina actually burst laughing, "Grandmother, you say the most outrageous things. I'm ready if you are. Only one thing: if Lords Restin and Barclay are there, perhaps if they request a dance, I'll decline, and please agree so that I don't commit an infraction and embarrass you."

So, it is really Lord Barclay she is trying to avoid. I wonder what really happened between the two of them. I must speak to Julia. "I can't imagine why, my dear, as those are two of the most sought-after earls in London," she sighed, "but if it is your wish, I'll do what I can."

The party was well under way when Dowager Countess Marlowe and Miss Wilhelmina Thaylor were announced at Sheldon's. Not many heads turned, and conversations continued. Welcomed by the host and hostess, Lady Edith with Wilhelmina moved to join Lady Julia and others.

Unbeknownst to Wilhelmina, she drew speculation. Some remembered her with Lady Agatha Marlowe and that *she* waltzed with the Earl of Grenmoor.

Now a different Wilhelmina, her gown being superior and her shining mahogany tresses with diamond clips to keep her curls in place, but in all it was her gleaming leafy green eyes that made her stand out. Her tanned beauty being a distraction, her smooth movements and carriage were enhanced by her smile. She was slowly making her way to Lady Julia when she was stopped by none other than the Duke of Baystone.

"Countess," he reached for Lady Julia's hand. "You remain as lovely as always." He turned, giving his attention to Wilhelmina… now staring at her eyes. *Those eyes, where have I seen them?* And then it hit him. *No, it couldn't be… Samson… no, that was a lad; a twin, perhaps.* "Forgive me, I thought for a minute that we've met."

Wilhelmina remembered the man immediately—*Samson's owner*. Her insides knotted as she curtseyed and Lady Edith spoke, "It is good to see you again, Your Grace. May I introduce my adopted granddaughter, Miss Thaylor? I doubt that you have met…"

The Duke interrupted, "I wonder, Miss Thaylor, if you will honor me with the next waltz?"

Keeping mind to answer respectfully and her knees from knocking, she replied, "Thank you, Your Grace. I look forward to it."

She curtseyed, and he had been holding her gloved hand; he gently squeezed her fingers, nodded to others, and left.

Lady Marlowe was surprised as she lifted her fan and said to Wilhelmina, "You have conquered what many have wished to do season after season. He is the Duke of Baystone, and it's known that he rarely invites anyone to dance."

Not that impressed, Wilhelmina asked, "Then why is he here?"

Lady Edith chuckled at her naivety. "I imagine meeting with friends, playing cards and choosing which lady he'll… never mind. There is my friend, Julia."

Lady Julia's smile warmed Wilhelmina's heart. "Lady Julia, you aren't angry with me for disappearing?"

"No, Willie," she whispered. "I knew you were upset with me for the charade we were playing, and it was an ideal way to end it. As long as you arrived home safely, and you did, it's forgotten."

"I'd like to give you a light embrace, my lady," she curtseyed, "though it would be frowned upon. I'll just say that I think you are wonderful, and thank you for my Seahurst holiday. I experienced a new world visiting Cornwall."

Lady Julia was about to say something when two voices intruded, and Wilhelmina knew to whom they belonged. She turned and looked at two handsome men, but the one with dark gray eyes and black velvet hair made her pulse jump as he stared into her eyes, daring her to look away. Wilhelmina didn't; in fact, she just knew it by the quirk at the corner of his mouth and the glint in his eyes.

Both greeted the dowagers and then turned to Wilhelmina. Wilhelmina could feel eyes upon her, remembering their waltz and feeling its impact. She half-curtseyed, just as before, and looked Lord Barclay straight in the eye, not cowering while remembering him and Lord Restin laughing about her. "I'm pleased that you are feeling well and about, my lord. And how is Zephr?"

"I brought Zephr with me. He's stabled at Barclay Square." His tone was impersonal and did not break into a smile.

"There you go, Lu… horse talk again. Aren't you going to ask the lady to dance?"

Lucien could have kicked his friend for making it obvious, and especially with an audience, but he had no choice, and staring at Wilhelmina, he dared her to refuse. "I believe Lord Restin is right. If you will, I would like to waltz with you again, Miss Thaylor." He believed without a doubt she wouldn't openly refuse him. *If she does, so help me, I will forcefully take her in my arms right here and begin to dance.*

Wilhelmina saw the Duke of Baystone approaching. "I'm sorry, my lord, but this dance is taken." She leaned into him and whispered, "And so is every waltz."

The Duke of Baystone appeared. Wilhelmina curtseyed and gently topped his winged arm with her fingers as he led her to the dance floor. Needless to say, everyone in the *ton* choked back a gasp wondering who the redhead was and why His Grace would dance with *her*. The Duke of Baystone and untitled Wilhelmina made a splash as they smoothly glided across the floor in concert with the music. Their smiles at each other did not go unnoticed, especially by the two earls who didn't respond when lovely ladies paraded in front of them.

Lady Julia was pleased, yet worried, as even though living away in Cornwall she knew about the *ton,* and the Duke of Baystone was as sought-after as her grandson. *Oh Lucien, I hope you're smart enough to capture this jewel that entered our lives.*

While dancing, Wilhelmina, in her natural outspoken manner asked His Grace not to return her to her grandmother, but to leave her anywhere but there. His Grace leaned his head back and laughed as Wilhelmina grinned. "I take it you're trying to avoid the Earls of Grenmoor and Ventry. I'll be delighted. I must say, you fascinate me. I'm sure we've met. Do you have a brother? No? You see, there was a lad that actually told me something that helped my horse."

Wilhelmina didn't care if she shocked this nice man… duke or not. Just as the music was ending, she said, "Has Samson improved now that you've loosened the bit?"

People were leaving the floor, but the Duke stopped, stared at Wilhelmina, and soon, they were the only ones left. She brazenly winked into his gray eyes, and with that, he broke into a cheerful chuckle, put his arm around her waist and led her off to the balcony. "We must talk. Agree?"

Smiling, she said, "Of course."

Jonathan couldn't hold back his glee as he saw Lucien scowl.

Lady Julia touched her grandson's arm. "Lucien, ask someone to dance… please?" Looking over at Lord Restin, she ordered, "You, too."

Both men moved to comply with her direction.

Out on the balcony with others nearby yet unable to hear their conversation, the Duke of Baystone, grinning, said, "Now tell me what you're all about."

"Your Grace, I meant no harm."

"There was none taken, and I'm not offended… mostly curious."

"To make my confession quick—I like horses and love to ride. I was visiting Lady Julia Barclay at Seahurst, and because Grenmoor is large, she allowed me to ride as I chose." Wilhelmina hesitated and then added, "My choice is astride. Zephr caught my eye—not only being beautiful but bold." Her voice tendered, "Zephr gave his heart to me."

Leaning on the balustrade and looking into green eyes shining from the reflection of candle lighted lanterns, the Duke couldn't help being mesmerized. Gently, he said, "Do continue."

"As I said, Your Grace, I ride astride."

He gasped, and then a smile crossed the Duke's face and his gray eyes glowed silver as he touched Wilhelmina's hand and softly, gentlemanly chortled, "Boy's clothing."

"Yes. You see, as riding the Earl's prize stallion… well, of course, one couldn't ride him side-saddle." Her laughter held softness. "I don't think Zephr would tolerate a side-saddle, and it isn't joyful riding that way."

"I get it… you ride astride dressed as a lad." Suddenly, he raised his eyebrow; his voice broke with force. "Are you saying that you… *you* have ridden Zephr?"

Wilhelmina bit her lips to stifle a grin, but it still seeped a little. "Yes, and he's magnificent. Zephr has heart, and riding him is like tempting the wind to slow us. In fact, sometimes it was more like racing."

"How could Lord Barclay sanction a willowy person as you are to even get near that beast? I know Zephr, and he may have heart, but he is stubborn."

Now, her laugher sounded like soft chimes tinkling. "Lord Barclay was not at Seahurst then. If he were, he'd never give me permission. As it were, Lady Julia allowed me to ride any of the horses in their stable, and when I saw Zephr, I knew that the two of us would be friends. He is stubborn—probably got that from the Earl—but he has heart, and he shared it with me every time we flew across Grenmoor." Wilhelmina's voice mellowed. "Zephr only wants to have his way to gallop, and we got along without restraint." Her tone changed. "Lord Barclay was furious. I was no longer allowed to ride Zephr. I miss the pleasure that great beast gives its rider."

"Tell me, did Lord Barclay know you ride astride and approve?"

"Oh, no. In fact, all the time, he thought a lad was riding his prize stallion, and when he discovered it was me… let's just say it was time for me to leave Cornwall and return to Lady Marlowe."

"Ah, now I see," his mouth turned up in its corners. "That's why you didn't want me to return you to the dowagers."

"Yes, now you see my dilemma." It was without thought that Wilhelmina in her natural joyous manner didn't realize that she didn't address the Duke as *Your Grace*. Her warm nature wasn't lost on the Duke.

The Duke of Baystone took Wilhelmina's elbow. "Will you do me the honor of allowing me to introduce you to my sister, Lady Henrietta?"

"I'd be delighted." Then she stopped. "You're not going to tell on me, are you? I don't want to embarrass Lady Julia or Lady Edith. Please?"

"No, my dear. I will not say a word."

"Thank you, Your Grace."

When they entered the ballroom, conversation ebbed and started again in a flurry as the Duke gave Wilhelmina's arm a gentle squeeze and whispered in her ear, "Both of your earls are watching us." As the Duke led her to his sister, Wilhelmina knew she was blushing, but she held her head high. To heck with the Earl of Grenmoor.

Having made the introductions, the Duke of Baystone remained with his sister and Wilhelmina, their conversation mostly about horses, especially when the Duke told of Miss Thaylor's love of gallop. It was a short while later that Lady Henrietta suggested they leave, and Wilhelmina leaped at the chance to be away from Sheldon's party. She asked if the Duke and his sister would mind dropping her off at Marlowe residence. *This young lady seems to again be slipping away, and I'm being party to it again.* They agreed, and the Duke went over to Lady Edith relating that his sister and he would take Miss Thaylor home as she developed a slight headache. Of course, no one would tell a Duke no. And it was done.

Lord Lucien Barclay watched as the Duke of Baystone escorted two ladies up the stairway to the exit; one blond and the other a fiery redhead that purposely ignored and avoided him. Lucien turned to Jonathan. "After your next dance, I'm leaving. If you wish to come with me, I'll wait." Lucien moved to take a glass of whiskey from a tray and swallowed all of it.

Chapter Twenty-Three

Two Weeks Later

Wilhelmina entered Lady Edith's morning room, where she usually enjoyed her fast. Today, she purposely sat with the paper folded next to her plate opened to society's tidbits. In one column, it commented on the trio: Duke of Baystone, Lady Henrietta Roach, sister of His Grace and Miss Wilhelmina Thaylor appearing in Hyde Park often in the Duke's carriage or riding the trails on the Duke's exquisite horses. They would be involved in conversation no one dared a stop to visit. Wilhelmina knew she was only mentioned having been in company with the Duke and Lady Henrietta.

One other column stated that Lords Barclay and Restin had been twice seen escorting Ladies Carstairs and Blakley. Could announcements be forthcoming? That shook Wilhelmina, but then she knew her dreams were just that… dreams.

Lady Julia's knowledge of why Jonathan had to forego any interest in Wilhelmina, but she was stunned when Wilhelmina purposely avoided Lucien at Sheldon's party, and then refused to see him the one time he called at Lady Marlowe's home. Knowing her grandson was too proud to call again, her hope for matchmaking lessened.

Wilhelmina's last two weeks were filled with riding and spending time with Lady Henrietta. Because of their mutual interests, they became friends. The Duke usually enjoyed their company and Wilhelmina, in her natural openness, seemed like sunshine to the brother and sister.

Wilhelmina learned that Henrietta's husband died while sailing. His body was found days later. She said she would never remarry and lived with her brother. Henrietta also confided in Wilhelmina that the Duke would not marry, ever. She gave no reason but wanted her new friend to know there would be no matchmaking.

Being truthful, Wilhelmina assured that *that* was not on her agenda as she would be sailing soon and went on to explain to Henrietta in strictest confidence the charade she played for Lady Agatha to elope, about being Willie and then her voice softened when talking about the vicar adopting her when she was abandoned, and adding *I know I don't belong in your society*, and it was then that Henrietta paid Wilhelmina the highest compliment. "You're better than all of us. Don't change."

* * *

Dowager Countess Edith Marlowe, Lady Henrietta Roach and Miss Wilhelmina Thaylor escorted by the Duke of Baystone attended his friend's soirée invitation. Wilhelmina didn't connect Lady Melissa Blakely as the Duke of Morton's daughter, for if she had, she would not have agreed to attend knowing the Earls Grenmoor and Vestry would be present.

Having been received and finding chairs to enjoy the musical, Wilhelmina was smiling and visiting with Henrietta when Lady Julia chose to sit with them.

Taking Wilhelmina's gloved hand, Lady Julia gave it a gentle squeeze and said, "I miss you. How are you?"

"I'm fine, my lady. Keeping…" she stopped talking and stared at the tall dark handsome Earl that was taking the arm of a beautiful blond lady with his head bent to hear what she was saying. Wilhelmina paled as her knotted fingers twisted in her gloves. She couldn't take her eyes off the man that filled her dreams and memories. It seemed that a magic line switched on, and the Earl looked up directly at Wilhelmina and barely offered a slight nod and then moved with his lady to take different chairs across the room.

Lady Julia felt the tension and noticed the knotted gloved fingers as she casually asked, "So what is keeping you occupied? Riding in the park," Lady Julia chuckled, "you've discovered the difference from trotting and galloping?"

With her pulse pounding and trying to get herself together, she lifted her head and didn't realize she had bent after the Earl's cool acknowledgement. "I… I… rather, we, Lady Henrietta and His Grace have invited me to join them, especially when there are horses involved. His Grace has beautiful cattle that I've been privileged to ride. Lady Henrietta is famous with riding. I've learned a lot." She laughed, "But not the same as with Zephr at Seahurst."

Henrietta had been visiting with another lady and then turned to Lady Julia. "I have enjoyed riding these last few days as never before. Miss Thaylor is

150

marvelous and sits a horse as if born on one." It was then that Lady Marlowe spoke, "Vicar Thaylor allowed his little girl the freedom to ride as she wished proving a girl is as capable as or better than some younger men. I'm so proud of her." With those last words, the entertainment was to begin. Wilhelmina tried nonchalantly to locate Lucien, but wherever he'd chosen to sit, she couldn't find him. Little did she know that he was sitting two rows behind her, staring at the head of mahogany hair with eyes narrowed and a frown that would cause someone to wonder what had upset the Earl.

After the musical, the ladies moved about, and Wilhelmina took the opportunity to hurry to the garden. She had to get herself together. Lucien looked so handsome in his crisp white cravat and wine jacket that fit his beautiful shoulders and his gray trousers that Crooks would make sure would not crease. *I love him so,* she thought as she meandered down a stone walk. *If I stay out here long enough, surely he'll be gone, and then I won't have to suffer remembering his laughter at me being Willie.* She sat down on a bench to watch the birds sharing a fountain dripping water. So engrossed in her thoughts she didn't hear Lucien's footsteps.

"I came to find you, *Miss Thaylor,*" he intoned with cold mockery. "You have quite a habit of vanishing." Lucien could see her pulse beat in her neck… a very enticing neck revealed with the gown's low square cut, not permitting her ample breasts to appear, yet knowingly outlining their roundness. He remembered her head and neck resting on his shoulder, and those luscious breasts pressed against his chest when he carried her up the stairs with her twisted ankle. *What is wrong with me? She's a cheat and a liar.* "But that isn't important; I came to thank you for your care. Grandy and Crooks told me how you helped them, and it was your suggestion to cool my fever." He bowed, "Thank you." He turned to leave, otherwise he'd find himself reaching for her and wanting to feel the rosy lips he wanted to devour. *I must be deranged…* He took two steps.

Quickly, Wilhelmina stood. "My lord, don't be under any misconception. I would have done that for anyone." Her heart was breaking, but she couldn't let him think she considered him special. He'd laughed at her already, and she couldn't bear it again.

Lord Lucien Barclay, a man known to be arrogant and cold and about to prove people right, raising his right brow, said, "You, *Willie,* put on a first-class act." His voice threaded with contempt. "You had me fooled, but fortunately, your true colors flourished exhibiting a cheat, liar and a temper that belongs on a street corner." *She doesn't deserve that set-down; why must I behave as a villain with her?*

Water hung on her lashes. *I don't rank in his elite society.* She fought for air as her throat clogged, but her demeanor never wavered. "And I thought you were hiding goodness along with integrity behind that egotistical façade you wear so well, but I was wrong, Lord Barclay, for there was nothing there for you to hide in that empty shell you put on display." She turned, hurrying away in the opposite direction, for she knew her tears already falling would give him more ammunition to laugh at her.

Stunned, hearing her voice as though choking and seeing her tears as she rushed off, Lord Lucien Barclay still couldn't overcome the grip that the fiery redhead had on his heart. *This is the second time her impudence knows no bounds.* He silenced the chuckle that wanted to escape. *Willie, my dear, it seems we make the worst come out when we're near each other. I'm foolish to have ever thought you could care one iota for me or just an Earl.* He stayed a moment longer, unhappy with the outcome of their meeting, keeping his head bent, not wishing to acknowledge anyone, pretending to be deep in thought. He returned to the Morton gathering.

Chapter Twenty-Four

Next Day, Mid-morning, Richmond Race

Lady Edith and Lady Julia were sitting comfortably in the Earl's carriage, enjoying the fresh air as well as the excitement at this small private race day.

"Where is Miss Thaylor?" Lady Julia asked her friend. "I was certain she wouldn't miss this racing event." And then softly, clearly disappointed yet resigned, asked, "Edith, is Willie really going to sail in a couple of days?"

Her voice filled with dismay, Lady Edith answered, "I'm afraid so. His Grace is providing her with passage on one of his ships and will see to her safety." Lady Edith looked about for her granddaughter. "She's with Lady Henrietta. They've become close friends, and I had hoped that would keep Wilhelmina with me longer."

"You haven't mentioned Karen, I gather."

"No. As much as I want to claim Wilhelmina as my granddaughter, I can't do that to my Karen's memory. Fortunately, Agatha has written that in the colonies, they give no special sway to titles or care where you're from."

Lady Julia, looking out across the green meadow, sighed. "It just wasn't meant to be, Edith. My grandson and your granddaughter." She shook her head regretfully, "We aren't good at matchmaking, my friend."

Disappointment being fully apparent, she said, "We tried, Julia, we tried."

* * *

While back in a Richmond stable, Henrietta reminded Wilhelmina, "As soon as you hit the finish line, keep riding back here to Jimmy, and he'll hop on Samson and ride to cool him and return to the winner's circle." Henrietta's liveliness captivated her delight at the daring the two of them were about to do. "That'll give you time to change clothes with Sophie's help and get you there to watch my brother accept the trophy." Grinning, she said, "Oh Willie, we'll do this and," animation left her face, "we won't be able to brag about it." Her mood changed back to amusement. "Though Gerald warned me that it must remain our secret. But it'll be worth it, just knowing we can accomplish what men think only they can do, and we women are helpless."

Smiling, Wilhelmina, dressed in black riding breeches and Baystone's green shirt and vest, with her hair stuffed under the Duke's green crested cap, said, "You and His Grace are certain I'll win, but it'll be Samson that proves you both right. I'm ready." Willie kept her head bowed, her hands gloved, shiny boots trying to resemble Jimmy and bursting with exhilaration as she was going to race against two other horses and Lord Barclay's Zairian. She only agreed to ride Samson if Lord Barclay wasn't going to race Zephr. "Zephr is special to me," she had explained, "and besides, I don't think anyone could beat him."

Sitting astride, no tension, and her green eyes filled with magnetism, she reminded Miss Henrietta to look after Lady Marlowe. *I wish I could look for Lucien.*

Both ladies' hearts swelled with pride, enjoying this thrilling moment to hoodwink everyone with their ruse. "As promised," Lady Henrietta said, "I told Lady Marlowe you would meet her at the race. So, Willie," she teased, "as soon as you cross the finish line, head here; hop off Samson, and Jimmy will take your place. There'll be so much going on that it'll give you time to change and saunter over and join us."

Laughing, Wilhelmina was glowing. "We've gone over and over this. I do believe you're nervous, Lady Henrietta. Worry not—it's going to work. I'm so excited to ride Samson. The Duke is truly remarkable to go along with us." Then she winked, "I've got to be sure my cap doesn't blow off, otherwise it'll be a calamity," and they both chuckled.

"I've got your clothes for after the race, so not to worry. I hope you won't be too flushed to cause anyone to think something is wrong."

"No one cares about me, Lady Henrietta. Will you be with Lady Marlowe and sort of keep her occupied and not worried about my not showing when the race starts?"

"You can count on it."

His Grace, the Duke of Baystone, walked in. His easy steps matched his undiluted strength as he shook his head but was smiling.

He's so good-looking with his gray hair for a man of low age. I wonder why he is against marriage—but I'd never ask... no, never. Wilhelmina, her natural self, swung down off Samson and curtseyed. "Your Grace and Lady Henrietta, as the three of us are here, I want to thank you for your kindness and generosity. I've so enjoyed your company. And thank you, Your Grace, for arranging my sailing on your ship. As I said, your munificence is more than I deserve."

The Duke of Baystone took Wilhelmina's gloved hand. "You are the sincerest and most candid person Henrietta and I have met in a long, long time. We're honored to know you and consider you our friend." Then he winked, "And if I were even to consider a tiny, tiny bit to marry, I'd set my heart on you until you say yes."

Wilhelmina, taken by the sweetness of his words, offered her warm smile and told the Duke he was an outrageous tease.

"And remember," Duke Baystone ordered, "Your last ball before you sail will be the Barclay Ball. You must save a waltz for me. Promise?"

"I... I don't think I'll be attending, Your Grace. You see, I have much packing and getting ready for my trip. I'll have to forego the ball."

"Nonsense! Do you know that an invitation to a Barclay Ball is the most coveted invitation in the *ton?*"

Wilhelmina shrugged. "Not to me, and I don't mean to sound pompous, it's just that I don't think I can dance when I know the Earl will be there and..." she couldn't hide her uneasiness, "as I explained, the Earl and I don't get along. I've only been invited because of Lady Marlowe, and too, the fact that I sail two days after the ball, well, there won't be any reason to question my not accepting the invite."

"What about Lady Marlowe? Won't you be hurting her feelings?"

"I know that my refusing will hurt her, but I'm sure she'll understand. She's been so kind. She's asked me to call her *Grandmother*, but I don't deserve that honor."

Henrietta looked at her brother. They now knew what they suspected over time. Karen and the vicar—old stories that were buried and no one dared say.

The racing horn's sound carried across the meadow. Jimmy ran over to help Wilhelmina mount up again. But before she moved, the Duke leaned over and kissed her cheek. "Good luck, my dear. I hope this isn't a mistake." He eyed his sister and left.

"No mistake," Wilhelmina cheerfully called in her musical voice.

Henrietta patted Willie's leg as she hooked her boot in the stirrup. "Samson," she ordered the horse, "be good to Willie."

The horn blared again, and with her head down, Willie, astride, joined three other horses at the starting line that was just a line scraped in the dirt. This fun race was decided by titled gents to tease who had the fastest horse—for no other reason than their egos. A gun was fired and four horses and their experienced jockeys were off.

* * *

Laughing and unable to stand still, both Henrietta and Wilhelmina were giggling, their fingers entwined with each other while watching the Duke of Baystone accept the trophy—a Richmond Rock with dates and the horses' name painted on it. Cheers were noisy and the Duke's grin lighted standing next to Samson.

Wilhelmina looked for Lucien, and when she spied him, their eyes met as he was watching her and not the Duke. Happy and aglow, she winked at him, though she didn't think he could see it, then she giggled and turned back to Miss Henrietta.

"Are you going over to be with His Grace?"

Henrietta laughingly said, "I can't. I'm afraid I'll tell what we pulled off. I'm so proud of you. You ride as if you're glued to the saddle and literally fly. Samson knows when his rider knows how to handle his reins and then gives his all. You're fantastic."

Ladies Edith and Julia walked over to greet the two friends. Lady Julia spoke first. "You two have had your heads together having enjoyed the race, no doubt about it." She looked at Wilhelmina, and her tone etched with smug delight, "Lucien's Zairian came in second. I don't think he's very pleased, do you?"

Her face showing no emotion but her green eyes gleaming, she answered, "I suppose not, my lady. But Zephr would surely have been first."

Lady Marlowe looked first at Wilhelmina and then at Miss Henrietta. "Am I missing something?"

It was then that the Duke was moving toward them and Henrietta quickly said, "I must go; my brother is waiting. It's been nice visiting…" and before anyone could answer, she was gone.

Wilhelmina, flushed and tired, suggested having luncheon at home, if Lady Marlowe wouldn't mind.

Lady Julia declined to join them, saying she looked forward to seeing them at the ball tomorrow night. "I'm sorry to see you leave us," she softly added, "Willie."

Wilhelmina took both of Lady Julia's hands, so realistic for her to touch a person she liked when she's talking with them. "I'll never be able to thank you, my lady, for your forgiveness and those wonderful days I spent at Seahurst, and the friends I made, and allowing me to ride the true way one can enjoy riding. You've changed my life, my lady. You've taught me to use my strengths and accept goodness in living." She gently squeezed Lady Julia's small fingers, curtseyed, and turned to go.

Lord Barclay appeared, only slightly nodded to Wilhelmina, greeted Lady Marlowe and asked, "Ready to go, Grandy?"

"Yes, Lucien, I am. Where is Lord Restin?"

A half-smile crossed his face. "He's waiting with *Ladies* Blakely and Carstairs for us in the carriage." He reached for her elbow to move on.

Wilhelmina sucked in a breath and wouldn't look at Lord Barclay as she fought her secret feelings for the arrogant, handsome Earl. Crushed, she wanted to run to be away before her temper blasted him for his haughty dominance, but she didn't. Instead, she stood tall, letting the wind do as it would to her hair, blowing it in every direction, not caring as the wind also whipped at her morning dress, and she had no choice but to grasp it and hold it in place while waiting for Lady Edith and Lady Julia to make their goodbyes.

Lord Barclay wasn't all that indifferent to the proud, spirited impertinent lovely. He noted the wind tangling her tresses, and as usual, she didn't give a care. *Just like her,* and that was one of the things that drew her to him—she wasn't fluff and ribbons. *I best get Grandy away before I snap at that unabashed baggage that rode Samson and beat my Zairian.* He gave one last glimpse at Miss Thaylor, wanting to tell her that he saw her red curl slip out from under her cap as she whizzed past on Samson. *You ride with strength and grace… I am so proud for you. Oh, my dear, why must you cheat and lie? I wonder what your retort to me would be if I told your secret.* It was difficult to withhold his smile, but he did.

"Goodbye, Edith. And don't forget, *Willie*," Lady Julia purposely teased, "We will see you tomorrow night."

"Lord Barclay," Wilhelmina lifted her chin, meeting his icy eyes. *I won't lose my nerve* "If I remember how to waltz, and it being my last ball, will you…?" She couldn't continue and faltered, her throat closing up, though she never took her eyes from his. "Never mind." *Even with his display of disdain for me, I wanted one last waltz with him.*

The two dowagers stopped, eyed each other and waited with hope.

"Will I what?" he prodded heartlessly, while choking back a surge of pleasure at the impudent spitfire. Keeping his feelings concealed while noticing her long lashes shadowing her dewy green eyes, he moved a step toward Wilhelmina. *She's foolhardy and sassy and so brave.*

She detected reproach in his tone as his right brow raised, daring her. That's all it took. Irked by his overconfident manner, she lightly shrugged her right shoulder and answered, "I'll be leaving in a couple of days, and I'd like to dance one last waltz with you."

"No!" And he turned, taking his grandmother's elbow, and literally pulled her along with him.

"Grandson, how could you?"

"It is not up for discussion." He wasn't about to explain that she asked for one *last* waltz. Now, it was his turn to introduce her to his bit of scheming and see how she handled it.

Embarrassed, Wilhelmina decided at that instant to go to the Barclay Ball and dance the night away and show his high and mighty lordship she didn't care. *But I do.*

Chapter Twenty-Five

Evening at Barclay Ball

Dowager Countess Edith Marlowe and Miss Wilhelmina Thaylor were announced. They stepped forward to be greeted by Dowager Countess Julia Barclay and His Lordship the Earl of Grenmoor, Lucien William Barclay.

Lady Edith and Lady Julia traded a few words. Then, Lady Julia took hold of Wilhelmina's hand, applied soft pressure and whispered, "I am happy that you're here." She turned to Lucien, "Doesn't Miss Thaylor look lovely, Grandson?"

Wilhelmina froze, looking into his dark, cold eyes. His tall, imposing height wearing impeccable black clothes and white shirt with his perfectly folded cravat took her breath away. He leaned toward her with a polite smile, but his words shocked her, and she gasped when softly he said, "Move on, goose, you're holding up the line."

Wilhelmina's face turned red with humiliation, quickly clashing with her red hair and golden gown. Suddenly, the silk that enraptured her when dressing as it slid down over her shoulders and made her feel special did so no longer as moving with haste, she stumbled. Lord Barclay quickly reached for her arm to steady her; their heat connected, and she pulled away, ashamed. He turned and greeted more guests, but his thought was on the red-haired blushing princess.

After her stumble, there were a few smiles, and younger ladies of the *ton* snickered. Wilhelmina made her way to the ladies waiting room to gain her equilibrium. Lady Henrietta soon joined her. "I noticed, and you can't stay in here for the evening."

"I know." Annoyed at her transparency of awe for the Earl and then stumbling, "I am so inept and," she gritted, "I wanted to be genteel and gracious like the rest of the ladies." Taking a long breath, she said, "I may as well go and make the best of it."

Lady Henrietta lightly shook her head in awe of her wonderful friend. "What we, especially *you* did yesterday; you are magnificent. And your gown is positively striking. Don't forget His Grace will dance with you and *that* will give everyone something to gossip about."

"Thank you, Lady Henrietta, but tell me, do you think that even though this gown covers all of me and with all this chiffon over-covering it, that I look like a wrapped holiday package?"

"Heavens, no!" she laughed, "If you want to know the truth, every man out there would like nothing better than to unwrap the golden package. Wilhelmina, you are covered from head to toe with no jewels and you don't need any… you are a jewel by itself."

"You are outrageous and good for my ego, and you give me confidence to enjoy this ball."

"They will soon open the ball with a dance with the Earl and the Dowager Countess. Gerald told me he will be there for your first waltz and the last, if necessary."

"Really?"

"Why are you surprised? My brother thinks highly of you, and he wants everyone to know it."

"His Grace goes beyond kindness, and so do you. I can't…"

"Stop, Wilhelmina, we have a ball to attend," she teased in her haughty pretentious voice. Wilhelmina started laughing, just when several ladies entered the room without greeting her but nodding to Lady Henrietta.

The Barclay ballroom's gaiety reached everyone. Colorful flowers were everywhere, though not overwhelming. Crystal chandeliers with hundreds of lighted candles were reflected in full-length mirrors surrounding the room. Wide white cornices designed and exquisitely painted with ivy vines around the massive ballroom with the white walls tinged with ivies color. Sconces, holding eight lighted candles, were on every panel between the mirrored panels. The polished parquet flooring along with glass doors leading out to the wide veranda reflected a warm glow. In the ballroom, the orchestra platform, not relegated back in a corner, was set on one side in the middle of the room surrounded by greenery with the musicians donned in Barclay colors. Crossing into another room through wide entrances were long linen clothed tables teeming with food of every selection and choice. A separate table set for drinks of every variety and footmen everywhere to assist. From there, one could attend the card room with set-up tables ready for play and footmen waiting to serve the finest wines and whiskeys. Nothing was left to chance or forgotten. Comfortable chairs and sofas were set around parts of the perimeter of the dance floor, and in the alcoves with its curtains' ties knotted; there would be no secret rendezvous. The four hundred guests were not crushed as the ballroom's size made everyone move comfortably and as Dowager Countess Julia said, "If our guests are joyful, our ball is a success," though she knew that a Barclay Ball couldn't be anything but triumphant.

Waltzing with the Duke of Baystone gave Wilhelmina instantaneous prestige. Especially when waltzing and both smiling, and both with eyes gleaming and talking, and often, the Duke would beam and laugh and then spin Wilhelmina around several times, keeping her eyes sparkling and wide smiles.

Wilhelmina waltzing came across as happy, but she still kept an eye out for the Earl and spotted him waltzing with the beautiful blonde. She missed a step, and His Grace corrected it immediately. "Not to worry, my dear." She thought it was meant for her missed step, but the Duke meant it for the Earl and his dancing partner.

There was no doubt that because the Duke of Baystone chose Miss Thaylor to waltz that many wanted to dance with her also, perhaps to wonder what it was about her that the Duke preferred. After all, she wasn't part of the *ton,* though discovering that she was the ward of Dowager Countess Edith Marlowe. Still, they crowded and requested to dance.

Half the night passed, and dancing was at its fullest. The Earl of Grenmoor had just returned his dancing partner to her mother when the Duke of Baystone moved to walk with him. Handing a glass of whiskey to Lucien, the Duke said, "She's sailing in two days, Lu. Are you really going to allow that to happen?" The Duke knew he didn't have to say *who.*

Struggling not to tell His Grace as well as his friend to mind his own business, Lucien said, "I believe you are speaking out of turn, *Your Grace.*"

"Of course, I'm not, and you know it, Lu. She loves you even though you treat her like a brat. That young lady has more grace, kindness, integrity and strength than any woman I have ever known."

"Then why don't you keep her?" he uttered though tight lips.

"I'd marry her, but you know why I'll never marry. She's a jewel. Look at her—those rosy cheeks, her hair that won't stay in place, and she lets it be, not worrying, and that gown that she probably thinks hides her body only creates a vision of perfection." The Duke of Baystone took a drink and watched the Earl of Grenmoor's jaw tighten and his mouth pull into a grimace.

His tone low, he asked, "Why do you say she has integrity?"

The Duke laughed. "You mean because she acted as *Willie* and didn't tell you?"

Lucien's head turned quickly to look at the Duke. "You know?"

The Duke nodded and went on to say, "Yes, but I promised not to tell anyone. But since you know, it's not breaking my promise." They stepped back to show they didn't want to be disturbed. "It was at Sheldon's. The funny thing is, I didn't plan on attending, but my sister talked me into it, and seeing those magical green eyes, I recognized her. I just knew they belonged to the lad with bright, dewy, leafy eyes. You see, I'd been traveling and having stopped to rest, this lad had the daring to walk over and tell me what was ailing my horse. I'll never forget those green eyes and the audacity of the lad to address me in a polite yet disrespectful manner and telling *me* what must be done for Samson." Grinning, the Duke's silvery voice added, "The lad was right and..."

"Don't... I know the lad was Miss Thaylor... our *Willie!* She is the most outspoken, nervy busybody of anyone I know." Lucien's smile reached his dark eyes, "And she rode Samson as though she was floating through the air."

"My god... you know? Does anyone else?"

"No, Ger, not to worry... no one even suspects."

"Then how do you—"

"I studied the jockey as I thought I'd like to have him work my horses, and I saw a red curl slip out behind her ear," he laughed. "It escaped but not noticeable, only to me."

"I'll be," the Duke was smiling as he touched Lucien's shoulder and then moved a step back and shook his head. "You do care for her, and yet, you'll let that smart and lovely vision sail away. It's not because she's not of our class, is it?"

Lucien's expression set with cold fury. "You know me better than that."

The Duke's expression stilled and then grew serious, "I do. So, what are you waiting for? Do you think she'll come to you? She has her pride... after she heard you and Restin laughing about her being Willie, she had to get away from Seahurst. She's too proud to allow herself to be held with derision, even when Lady Julia asked her to remain silent, even though she wanted to tell you who she was. But she gave Lady Julia her word, and knowing Miss Thaylor, that's as good as if it was written."

"But we weren't laughing at her… in fact, both Johnny and I think she is more woman than any we know. She rode Zephr," Lucien's tone was impressed, "You know my horse and she floated along, just like with Samson, and then, she looked after me when I had a fever when the doctor told my grandmother there was little hope. I'm astounded that you know her situation, and yet, you're helping her to sail and leave us."

"I have no choice, Lu. I gave her my word. And just like you and me, she treasures one's word just as one can trust hers."

Lucien set his glass of whiskey down. "Excuse me, Your Grace, I hear a waltz starting."

Wilhelmina curtseyed as the Marquis of Bennington came to claim his dance. Lord Barclay stepped in front of them and looked at Bennington. "Baystone asked me to tell you he'd like to speak with you, *now!*"

The Marquis nodded to Wilhelmina. "I apologize as I'm needed elsewhere."

The Earl of Grenmoor swept Miss Thaylor into his arms, not allowing her a minute to think as the waltz began. She felt so good; his heart was pounding, and he hoped she couldn't hear it.

"What are you doing?" She took a deep breath, intense, yet her heart seemed to race. She wanted to be upset with his arrogance at just whisking her into a waltz and not asking. It was impossible, still she said, "You said *no!*"

Lucien Barclay, the Earl of Grenmoor, whom everyone was watching because they saw him rush *un-ton* Miss Thaylor onto the dance floor, said as he leaned and whispered into her ear, causing her chills, "I changed my mind. I want to waltz with the finest winning jockey in all of Richmond."

Wilhelmina missed her step, and Lucien's smile widened as he lifted her and gently twirled, and then they were in step again. He never expected her reaction. He thought for sure she'd try to leave the floor, but she looked up into his eyes, hers mischievously gleaming, and tried to smother her quiet giggle, but soon, tears were hanging on her long lashes; still, she didn't miss a step as she followed and let him twirl her about, paying not one iota attention to her surroundings. She was in *his* arms.

Lucien seemed to be under some spell, as never had the Earl of Grenmoor acted with less decorum than he was doing now.

Lady Henrietta finally made it over to her brother. "I see, Your Grace, you did exactly as you vowed." Her warm smile felt good. "Do you think he'll propose, and will she accept? Our Willie isn't one you can push around, you know."

The Duke of Baystone let out a bark of a laugh that turned heads. "Well, the Earl isn't either." Quietly, he said, "He knew it was Miss Thaylor riding Samson."

Henrietta's mouth dropped open and then curled as she hid her laughter. "Truly?"

"Truly." The Duke suggested they make their leave. "We'll sneak away and make our apologies to Lady Julia and Lord Barclay tomorrow."

And just as they first danced at the Benton party, waltzing together because they were then put into the position that required they dance, it was being repeated, only this time, with the same two people waltzing in each other's arms, completely unaware or not caring that they were the only two on the ballroom floor radiating a current between them that could not be overlooked. The Earl of Grenmoor held his dancing partner closer than society permitted. The ladies of the *ton* were aghast, but men were envious, and one could be heard whispering, "Grenmoor has all the luck."

Dowagers Julia Barclay and Edith Marlowe sat, not saying a word but with the corners of their mouths turned up, and their eyes warm with happiness.

"Lucien," Wilhelmina whispered when she looked around, discovering what had again happened, "no one else is dancing."

Lord Barclay looked into her effervescent eyes that had never left his or blinked, bent his head, not missing a step, his words a caress. "I know." He wanted to kiss her; instead, he put his mouth to her ear, and with his warm breath sending chills through her as his lips were feathering her ear, said, "Marry me?"

She stopped—stunned and yet perplexed. *Did he ask me to marry him?* She couldn't get her feet to move—it was obvious to everyone watching that something occurred, but what? They gasped as Lord Barclay, smiling, took hold of the flashing red-haired ward of Dowager Marlowe and what seemed to force her to move and leave the dance floor with him. All eyes followed them when they didn't stop, and the Earl's hand possessively held her elbow, guiding her toward the door, leading to a secluded patio. But then, he paused when eying a footman. "Please tell Dowager Countess to proceed with the ball and the dancing." But then, he heard the orchestra begin. He reached for Wilhelmina's hand, leading her further back from view. "My lord, we're causing a scandal."

"I know."

"You purposely led me out here?"

"Yes… you haven't answered my question, and now, it will have to be *yes*."

"Why?"

"Because a lady doesn't walk off the dance floor for all to see and disappear into the dark with someone not her husband." Grinning, he added, "If we don't marry, you'll be disgraced."

Very haughty, she accused, "But not you, my lord?"

"That's right… you see, everyone is already envious of me." His voice held a tenor of pride that couldn't be missed. "My most important reason at this moment is that I want to hold you in my arms, and I want to thoroughly kiss you." *Oh, little one, I want to do so much more… I want to devour you while I'm thoroughly ravishing you.* Holding her shoulders, he brushed a gentle kiss on the tip of her nose followed by gently pressing his lips against her warm rosy mouth, and he happily found she was willingly kissing him back, though tight lipped. He was ecstatic as his sassy, bossy know-it-all had never shared a true kiss with anyone. Lucien clasped her in his arms and looked down, her face so close he could feel her short gasps zoom through him and softly said, "When I kiss you, I'd like you to follow and do as I do." He didn't want to shock her, but then, he didn't know if anything could shock this incredible innocent.

"I can do that. But," she teasingly scolded, "If you tell me you are thoroughly going to kiss me, I'd like to try it as Aggie said a real kiss makes one's stomach turn to mush. And I must say, my lord, my stomach is in very fine condition from your kiss."

Lucien couldn't stop feeling his insides turning into butter; she did that to him with only her bantering words. *She doesn't know, thank goodness, what will happen to me when we truly kiss… this firebrand is lethal when I forget control. Let's see if she's as brave as she claims.* Lucien had no compunction about testing the sassy spitfire as he pulled her into his arms with strength that told her he wasn't letting her go, and not surprisingly, she didn't resist him.

His exhilaration at an all-time high, he brushed his lips below her ear, his breath warm—she could smell a trace of whiskey as he uttered, "This, dearest, is the way it's done… are you ready to follow my lead?"

She was already feeling the heat from his body transferred to hers standing so close. She teased, "Perhaps you'll want to follow *my* lead," and reached up on her tip toes.

"Not a chance…" His head bent in a second, and his tongue traced the fullness of her lips, sending shivers up and down her arms; a new sensation zipped through her as he then trailed kisses to the hollow spot on her throat and not letting up, he trailed more kisses up to nip her ear lobe and unexpected coils mushroomed as her body, succumbing to his mastery. His voice having turned raspy and mellow, he whispered, "We've only just begun," as his mouth touched her lips with his tongue leaving a trail of kisses across them, but his tongue was persistent, tracing its seam and surprising him when he felt her response to be part of these heated currents he ignited.

She opened her mouth, and the tip of her tongue traced the contour of his lips as heat raced throughout his body. He'd give away one of his estates to be far away and alone with her. Wilhelmina was unaware of its magnitude when his tongue explored the recess of her mouth, caressing it and touching his tongue to hers. She didn't hesitate to respond when a streak of sizzling heat erupted. She didn't want it to stop, for his kisses set her body aflame. Lucien was devastated, knowing he had to stop when he'd give anything—even Zephr at this moment—*not* to be at this ball.

The music from far away penetrated in the back of his mind, reminding him where they were. *We've been gone too long.* She kissed him like an innocent that knew no boundaries, and it was up to him to extinguish the flames. Wilhelmina clung to him, and on her toes, reached to place kisses on his face and down to his neck that was blocked by his cravat. Catching his breath, he layered kisses on her eyes, her cheeks, her ear, that pulsing spot on her neck. *I want you in my bed as my wife and make love with you for the rest of our lives.* Then, recapturing her mouth his tongue, he invaded the velvet warmth that joined his. Lord Barclay felt like an adolescent unable to curb his desire.

Wilhelmina was stunned at her own eagerness to touch her tongue to his, and when she did, he pulled her tightly against him, and she knew then what Aggie was talking about. She kissed him with a hunger that she didn't know existed—a heady sensation that left her weak, and yet demanded more. It was Lucien who suddenly moved his mouth from hers, his breathing like hers, gasping, his voice gravelly. "We must stop." *Or I'll spend right here, unable to return to the ball.*

"Why?"

He chuckled, "I think you know why. And have you forgotten where we are? Too, because what we are doing is wonderful and makes my heart and body sing, but until we are married… my dearest Willie, these feelings we've created here belong only to us, and" he couldn't resist planting a few more kisses on the corner of her mouth, knowing he must not touch her full lips, "right now, they don't belong here with hundreds of people yards away." Holding her to him, he whispered, "Have you forgotten that I asked you to marry me? You haven't answered," he nipped her neck, "perhaps a better way to say it… is that I want to marry you. Will you say *yes*?"

At this very minute, all Wilhelmina could think to say was yes, yes, yes, especially feeling those kisses swirl through her. They kept swirling, so something was amiss. It seemed like a shock wave waiting to explode, still, she had to be cautious with this mighty charming handsome man she'd dreamed of so often. *I'll marry you, but I can't make it easy, or else, the rest of our married lives, you'll command. I've seen how the aristocrats treat each other. Lucien, I love you more than I thought possible, but I want us to be partners, not only husband and wife, or Earl and Countess just for you to get an heir. I've heard about arranged marriages. I want more. You haven't said you love me, and I won't ask.*

They were standing facing each other, their temperatures having receded as the Earl held her at half arm's length waiting for her answer.

Wilhelmina's heart swelled. *Lucien, the Earl of Grenmoor, has asked me to marry him.*

"Well?" he prodded.

"My lord, I very much like for you to kiss me and I very much like for you to hold me, but as to marrying… well, you see, my plan is to sail in a couple of days, and I don't know how our married lives will be possible with me at sea and you in London. I don't think it will work."

The Earl of Grenmoor broke out with laughter. "Why, you nervy, fiery little imp! The first thing I'm going to do is kiss the devil out of you while I'm holding you so you won't get away to sail out of my arms. And then, after an hour or so, we will seriously talk, and I'll tell you how special you are and you'll tell me that you still think I'm handsome, and you care for me, too." Then, saying not another word, Lucien Barclay scooped Willie Thaylor into his arms and claimed her lips with his strong, firm lips, covering hers hungrily, and slowly, his kiss gentled, sending shivers, racing down to her toes and up into her heart, again. His kiss turned into one of possessiveness. Holding her closer, he could feel the heat between them ignite as his heart swelled having her as his own.

Wilhelmina moved her head so she could speak; he allowed it only because he kept her in his arms and rested his cheek on her luscious head of hair. "My lord…"

"I liked Lucien better," he whispered in her ear as he then moved, using the tip of his tongue to touch her ear.

"It's when you do that to me; I'll not be able to tell you what I think."

Lucien pulled back giving her his attention, his voice husky. "Tell me…"

"My lord… *Lucien*, I want you to know that you kiss so well it makes my senses melt and they reach inside of me that I don't how to handle them… like shock waves." She put her fingers on his mouth as he was about to speak. "And having you hold me is what I've dreamed," she semi-chuckled, "really. You have no idea what a magnificent man you are, and I mean, the way I see you. And as for my leaving," her tone purposely saddened, "To live apart," and then her tone held a tremor as she felt Lucien stiffen and then she said matter-of-factly with a warm smile, "I don't want to do that… live apart from you."

Wilhelmina couldn't say more as Lucien swung her around in his arms, grinning and laughing and kissing her with light kisses. "So, help me, Willie, you're going to turn my hair gray with your tease. My love, you are wonderful. Willie… please do not change."

He took her back into his arms, burying his face below her ear and planting a kiss just so wanting to do so much more but didn't. "One more kiss, and then we must return to the ball and tell Grandy." His smile warmed Wilhelmina down to her fingertips, and returning to stop in the pit of her stomach. "You have agreed to marry me, haven't you?"

"Try and stop me, *my lord*." And this time, she was the aggressor. She stood on her toes to reach his lips as she put her arms around his neck and pulled him to her. Their lips and tongue explored each other until Lucien knew it had to end. He had no room in his trousers.

Both their bodies heated, they hated to let go. Lucien took the initiative, pulled back, and started to walk. Coming upon a bench, they sat, neither talking. Wilhelmina needed his touch as she reached to hold his hand. "Lucien," her voice a clouded whisper, "are *you* certain? I mean, marrying me means *me*… no side interests, you know what I mean?"

The Earl of Grenmoor, never in his life, expected to be this happy with the prospect of marrying; before he had time to answer, he heard footsteps.

Lord Restin appeared. "I wondered where the two of you had disappeared. That waltz must have tired you both," he teased. "In fact, Miss Thaylor, it twisted some of your curls," he reached over to push one off to one side.

"Watch it, Johnny."

Lord Restin chuckled, "I take it, Lu, you're finally going to make the leap?"

"Yes. This lovely lady willingly agrees to be my wife."

Very sincerely, Lord Jonathan Restin, said, "Lu, I'm very happy for you and Miss Thaylor." Jonathan smiled at Wilhelmina and said, "The Earl of Grenmoor is my friend and I hope to be yours, too."

With a bright smile and a soft sincere voice, she said, "Thank you, Lord Restin. I have no doubt."

Lucien stood holding Wilhelmina's hand and started toward the ballroom. "Johnny, will you do me a favor and bring Grandy and Lady Marlowe to my study? We'll go around and enter without going through the ballroom. I'd like to tell them in private about Miss Thaylor and me before announcing our betrothal."

"Happy to—they will be delighted. However, before you let anyone see your bride-to-be, I think it's best to sneak her in so she can straighten those lovely curls that have somehow gotten restyled." Then Lord Restin said, "If you've got a minute, Lu…?"

"What's up, Johnny?"

"Not to worry, I'll see you in your study."

At another entrance, Lucien placed a gentle kiss on Wilhelmina's lips and then hurried out of sight to get to his study.

Lucien entered, finding Johnny there, pacing. "Where's Grandy and Lady Marlowe?"

"I haven't told them yet. I have something to tell you, Lu. Not for any reason other than we're best friends."

"It can't wait?"

"No." He asked Lu to sit down across from him and Lucien did, because it was Johnny and knew something was troubling him.

"Remember when I told you that I have no interest in pursuing Miss Thaylor and that it was a promise that I couldn't tell?"

"I remember, but what?"

"Please listen and don't interrupt. What I am going to tell is a family secret and it involves Miss Thaylor. Lady Karen Marlowe was in love with William Thaylor, the vicar at Marlfordshire. They wanted to marry, but the Earl would not permit his daughter to marry an untitled man. A baby was born to Karen, and rather than have to give her baby away at the persistence of the Earl, Karen promised her father that she would marry whomever he designated if her baby could be left with its father, the vicar. So, Karen went into hiding and Wilhelmina was born, as agreed with the vicar, as an abandoned baby that he would adopt and raise as his own. Karen then wed the Duke of Rainstone as her father arranged and later died… leaving a daughter, baby Agatha. Because the Duke wanted a son, he willingly gave his and Karen's daughter to Lady Edith. Agatha and Wilhelmina are half-sisters."

Lucien was furious, his voice scalding with anger, "You mean to tell me that Miss Thaylor, Wilhelmina has not been told? Why?"

Torment pressed into Lord Restin's words, "Because as a mother, Lady Edith, my aunt, was desperate to keep her daughter valued and respected. She could not allow her only child's name to be branded and besmirched or that of her first baby granddaughter. The vicar agreed, kept his word, never telling his daughter how much he and her mother loved her."

"Because he loved us both," Wilhelmina cried as she closed the door and walked toward both earls. Her composure wobbled with tears rolling down her cheeks. "I always believed that my father knew who abandoned me but having given his word, would not say." Her smile reached the wet tears dusting her lashes, her voice soft and in awe, "My father was protecting my mother as he'd promised. Just think, he made a promise, and having given his word, he couldn't tell me I was really his daughter and that I was with him because he and my mother wanted me there with him." More tears blossomed. "He loved us both very much, that poor man. How his reminiscences must have pained him; living with memories of the woman he loved."

Looking at both men, her throat clogged, but clearly voiced, "My father would tell me to always be the person you are; to remain kind and admire people for themselves and not what or who they are or where they come from." Now learning the clarity of her birth parents gave Wilhelmina an indefinable calm filled with a comfort that was missing that she didn't realize was augured deep inside of her with her need to know. Unspoken questions now had answers. It was as if a door had opened, welcoming her, and she had the right to enter.

Instinctively, she said, "Having heard this truth proves more than ever that my father and mother were honorable, and how they must have loved each other and how they suffered because of this aristocracy with its arranged marriages by heartless snobs." So enraged, Wilhelmina's green eyes flashed, her red hair had fallen like a waterfall down her back and her face a mask of sadness. "My father wasn't good enough for your high-society elite." Her eyes flashed as her tone rang with finality, "Well, he was of a higher caliber and far better in character than many known as the *ton*."

Lucien was on Wilhelmina in seconds and was holding her arms when she tried to pull away with tears splashing down on her golden silk down, spotting it. "Look at me," Lucien ordered, "Do you think for one minute or even one second that being Karen's daughter matters? I know you as the vicar's daughter and that's all that matters. Don't judge me or Johnny or Grandy as prejudice or bias toward what you call *our legacy*." Still trying to pull away from Lucien's grasp that he wouldn't allow it, he went on, "Do you know that when Johnny told me he was going to pursue you and make you his countess, he told me he didn't care that you had a title? You are our *Miss* Thaylor, and we liked *you*." He chuckled, "Yes, Miss Thaylor, I liked you too, but Johnny spoke up first."

Lord Restin walked near and explained, "When Aunt Edith told me why I couldn't consider marriage with you," his voice softened, "We are related and that it had to remain a secret. I only told Lu because he is going to marry you and as his friend… not to try to turn this news against you, but for you both to have a solid marriage. There must not be any secrets." He said with dismay, "It would grieve me if my telling will cause either of you heartache and end what is the best in matchmaking history. Please, Miss Thaylor, *Willie*, accept my apology. I mean no harm."

By this time, Lucien had his arm around Wilhelmina and kept her at his side. "You haven't changed your mind about marrying me, have you? I won't have it." He knew she hated when he demanded or commanded. He teased, "If you agree to still marry me, I'll pledge not to command, but to ask." Lucien took his hankie and gently patted away her tears.

Wilhelmina looked at both earls. Her courage and determination expressed in a bleak forceful strength to impose her will. "Would either of you have told me if I didn't overhear your conversation?"

Lucien said, "I would, but only after we are married. We'll have no secrets from each other."

"As for me," Lord Restin answered, "No, I would not have mentioned it to you, ever."

"I'm glad, my lord, as that is why Lord Barclay has a true friend and I know now that I can also put my trust in you. Thank you."

"You know, Miss Thaylor," he growled, "I expect you to call me *Johnny* with or without the Earl's say." Winking he added, "after all, we are family."

Wilhelmina's silent smile was her reply as she moved away from Lucien and pushed a loose curl behind her ear. Her puffy eyes glistened from the candle's flame. She felt like a volcano about to erupt, but her heart seemed to swell as she gripped the back of a chair. "I'm going to ask a great favor of the two of you lords." She knuckled gripped a chair, looking first at Lord Barclay and then at Lord Restin and then taking a deep breath, said, "I'm asking that neither of you tell Lady Edith or Lady Julia about this conversation that took place in this room. I don't want them to know that I'm aware of the necessary fabrication of my birth and ask, no I'm begging you to leave my birth as it is believed that I was abandoned and adopted by the kindly vicar."

"But why?" Lucien's angry tone countered. "It matters not a smidgeon to me."

"Because it matters to Lady Marlowe; her wish that her daughter… my mother's memory remain intact with its value and distinction she deserves. Why expose my parentage, even within our family setting, so to speak? Surely, it would leak somehow, and then give the gossips this tidbit to gnaw on, and might I add, your *ton* would do it with glee."

"Your future countess doesn't think well of us, Lu. We don't measure up to her standards. The vicar excelled raising his daughter."

"I concur, Johnny. A thousand percent and then some."

"Then are we agreed?" Wilhelmina reiterated.

The three moved together and touched to hold hands—each with pressure, solemnly said in unison. "It is agreed."

The tension vanished, and warm smiles emerged effecting three people to believe and trust in each other.

Lord Restin then spoke, "This evening has turned perfect; never would I have believed the two persons I care about most are going to marry each other. We're family." He walked toward the door. "I best get the dowagers. They will be surprised, as I overheard they were saddened that they couldn't get the two of you together and worse, Willie was sailing away."

Knowing his friend, Lucien said with heartfelt import, "Thanks, Johnny."

"Lord Restin?" He stopped and looked at Wilhelmina as she said, "Please accept my sincerest gratitude for your goodness."

"Of course, my lady," and nodding to them both, left.

Lucien stood, amazed at the woman he wanted to be his countess. His eyes were aimed directly at her, and Wilhelmina not only saw tenderness in them but the depth of this shared moment. With intense composure yet with smug animation, she winked, "You know, my lord, if you meet me halfway, I'd like very much to have you in my arms to that I may ravish you with my kisses." Her green eyes flashed like lighting, and she moved quickly toward the man she loved. Lucien didn't have to be encouraged; his heart double beat knowing her warmth for him was genuine.

Lucien reached Wilhelmina, holding her while his heart swelled now, knowing he didn't want to survive without her. Holding her close and feeling the warmth of her body as she without thought clung to him—her hands on his solid chest as her fingers moved to feel him through his clothing while his body reacted, he knew he had no power to control these feelings.

Wilhelmina tried to nestle her face under his chin and found his cravat in the way, wanting to tug at it, but she didn't have time as Lucien captured her lips, sending a delicious sensation racing through them. She slowly raised her hands and put them around the back of his head and held him tightly as their parted lips seared with hunger, exploring their need.

So lost in each other were they that they hadn't realized the two dowagers and Lord Restin had entered.

Lady Julia was beyond herself—not an iota of thought came to mind, and Lady Edith seemed frozen in place as they both stopped and stared at two people literally tightly wrapped in each other's arms. Lord Restin choked back laughter that pushed to explode and called out, "Lu, you have company."

Wilhelmina, lost with tremors running through her, heard nothing, but it was the Earl that caught the last of Johnny's voice… *company.* He lifted his head and moved to put Wilhelmina behind him, but it wouldn't have done any good as she wasn't going to comply, probably because she didn't know why he suddenly stopped.

"No," she gasped, "Don't stop…" She looked and saw three people astonishingly gaping, and then she knew she had to brazen it out and not allow them to think that Lucien had taken advantage of her. Giving her best open smile and straightening her gown back to its right position and then pushing her hair away from her face, she said, "I was just teaching Lord Barclay how I expected to be kissed. So far, he's doing it right." The ladies stared, unable to know if she was jesting or what exactly occurred. But Lord Restin released the laughter he had swallowed.

Lucien moved, taking Wilhelmina with him with his arm around her waist, and said with calm assurance, "Wilhelmina… Miss Thaylor has accepted my proposal, and we will be married as soon as I can obtain a license." He looked at his impending countess, "If that meets with your approval?"

Wilhelmina nodded and then said, "It does, my lord." She looked at him and winked.

Lucien tightened his hold. Never had he felt as euphoric as he did that second. He wanted to roar with laughter over her unabashed reply.

Lady Edith gasped. Lady Julia began shaking her head—no! Lord Restin blinked, for here was his friend that had always been referred to as cold-hearted and arrogant and would take no backtalk, and had just asked his future countess for her input; offering to have her make their decision. *If I were not here to hear and see this, I would not believe it of Lu. My friend is definitely hooked, and that lovely redhead has made quite a catch.*

It seemed that his bride-to-be took it all in stride, as though that was the norm. Looking at Lucien with her dreamy, shiny, dewy green eyes, said, and it astounded the two grandmothers, "The soonest… tomorrow? Two days… three… is that acceptable, my lord?"

Lucien picked her up and swung her around, turning something over, but neither cared as they were laughing. She whispered into his ear, "I better go set my gown and hair right again." She looked at three astounded people. "If you all will please excuse me."

He obviously reluctantly let her go but not before brushing a kiss over her rosy lips.

With Wilhelmina out of the room, Lady Julia spoke, "Grandson, I'm pleased, but you must have a wedding… a proper wedding. You must not carry on as you have just now been doing. There are rules."

Happy, his tone joyful, he said, laughing, "Of course, Grandy, if that is what my lady chooses. But don't count on it."

"But, Lucien, you said a special license."

"Yes, I know. Worry not, all will be well."

"NO!" Both grandmothers' spoke in unison. Then Lady Edith added, "Impossible!"

The Earl of Grenmoor's demeanor changed in that second. "I beg your pardon?" His tone sparked, "It will be with Wilhelmina's approval as to the sort of wedding she prefers. And know this, whatever she decides is the way it will be."

When Wilhelmina returned, it was decided their engagement would be announced but there would be no other details. All agreed and returned to the ball.

Chapter Twenty-Six

Five Days After Barclay Ball

Lord Restin sat across from Lord Barclay in Lucien's study—the same seat when not long ago, where he had sat glum and unhappy, being unable to court Miss Thaylor. Today, Jonathan was a total reverse, and he had trouble holding back laughter. "I'm telling you because you're my friend, so don't kill the messenger."

Lucien snapped the pencil he was holding and threw the two pieces on his desk. His eyes narrowed while gritting his teeth. "I swear that old lady has gone too far."

Lord Restin had to bury his laughter; he recognized Lu saw this humorless. "It's just, Lu, I think Aunt Edith and Grandy plan to *run the show*, so to speak. They both have taken the reins for your forthcoming wedding. I suspect Willie doesn't want to hurt their feelings and has gone along with them."

"So, what brought on all this other nonsense about you trailing me? I'm telling you, Johnny, I'll not stand for it."

"Think, Lu. They're both thrilled that you proposed, but when they walked in on the two of you smothering each other that it would have been impossible to place even a feather between the two of you, they concluded that keeping you from being *alone* together is an absolute for any scandal to be averted. They have made Lady Henrietta and me their ally."

"What has Lady Henrietta to do with any of this?"

"They've somehow inveigled a promise from Lady Henrietta covertly to watch over your intended and assist me in keeping the both of you occupied and never alone. In other words, you are *never* to be alone together." Laughing, Lord Restin added, "That is, until Willie walks down the aisle and you put that ring on her finger."

Lucien's anger flared. "They have gone too far. How they have coerced widowed Lady Henrietta to agree to this nonsense is beyond me. Did she actually agree?"

"Oh yes. I received a message from her, and I visited with her at the Duke's London home. She wouldn't say why; only that she had no choice. Her exact words to me were, '*We must favor those two old warhorses*'."

Lucien sat with his fingers dancing atop the papers on his desk, not saying a word, having listened to Johnny. He wanted to pound his fist on his desk, but knowing it would do no good, he sarcastically voiced, "What the devil do they think I would do if we were alone? They are acting like neither of us have any common sense."

"It's to avoid scandal and Willie's reputation. Face it, Lu, the way you two were going at it at the ball, I swear the room was so hot it would have taken six winters to cool it."

Lucien broke out with a grin. "You think so?"

"I'm afraid I might just see the grandparents' point of view."

It then came to Lucien's mind that when he last stopped to see Wilhelmina, either Lady Edith or both dowagers were present. He and Wilhelmina were never alone except when she walked him to the door, and then the butler was there. She'd lean forward and whisper to him in her mischievous voice, telling him she had every intention of being in his arms soon and continuing whatever they wanted to do without being interrupted or guarded. Lucien unclenched his fisted hand and the corner of his mouth turned up and then broke into a wide smile.

"What's up?" Lord Restin saw Lucien's demeanor change. *Oh, oh.*

Lucien cheerfully exclaimed, "Let's take on those two old grandmothers' plan on the four of us going on an outing… say, a picnic?"

"Hold on, my friend. Henrietta and I have to hold to our promise that you two not be alone; that one of us must always be with you or your future bride."

"That's absolutely idiotic," his tone hardened. "and you agreed? Why?"

"Would you believe those two old biddies said that they'd tell Mary Louise's mama that I have eyes only for Lady Mary Louise but I'm too cautious about saying so? And they meant it to the degree they would also spread that tidbit at parties."

"You can't mean *Mary Louise* Caruthers? Why, she's bedded anyone that will have her, and she smells." Smirking, he went on, "Really? You and Lady Mary Louise?"

"Not funny. This is serious, and my neck is in a possible noose, Lu. How those dowagers know about Mary Louise, I've no notion, but I do know about her mama, and may I remind you… if Duchess Caruthers decides to pursue me for her daughter, there will be no stopping her. If the Duke persists, I'll have to leave town for at least three years. Now you see why I had to agree to guard you. I'm not supposed to tell you what they're up to."

Lord Barclay's velvet black eyes darkened, and his jaw tightened as he stood and leaned down to gather papers scattered on his desk and pushed the broken pencils aside. Without explanation, he said, "Will you agree to the picnic or not?"

"Lady Henrietta and I will enjoy a picnic, so consider us to make it a foursome."

"So you say."

"What are you up to?"

"Just that I'm not waiting *months* to be alone with Willie, and she deserves my respect to do no more than kissing until we are married."

Lord Jonathan Restin grinned, "I'm going to dog you, my friend… no hard feelings."

"Agreed, Johnny. However, remember your words… no hard feelings."

* * *

Two days later, Picnic Day, Richmond

Enjoying the warm sunshine on this glorious day were four people in Lord Barclay's open carriage. Two footmen brought along to assist and Lucien's regular driver, Hudson, were also enjoying the Earl's outing.

Hudson stopped near a stream, as having been directed by His Lordship before departing. The footmen hurried to unload the overstuffed food hamper along with bottles of wine and lawn blankets.

"This looks like the right spot for our picnic," Lord Barclay exclaimed. Dressed in brown breeches, leather vest and fine tweed jacket, his white shirt with its loose cravat, he appeared a man of quality, but it was his broad shoulders, long legs encased in shiny leather boots that turned Wilhelmina

Thaylor into a gloating damsel in distress for wanting his arms around her and tasting his kisses. Lucien brushed her shoulder and winked.

She boldly winked right back at him. Her sunflower day gown clashed with her red hair as she removed her gloves and pushed a loose curl back in place.

Lord Restin always appeared in fine clothing, and only at balls did he and Lord Barclay dress alike in their dark clothes. Today, his brown breeches fit snugly with his light tan jacket and cream shirt blending with his blond hair and brown eyes.

Lady Henrietta's golden hair was pulled back and tidy as usual, along with her day gown of light green and cream stripes with its low square neckline. Though she didn't care to be fussy about her appearance, she was unquestionably a refined lady as she eyed the picnic setting.

The couples stretched their legs while their luncheon was put in place. Lucien glared at Lord Restin and said with a touch of sarcasm, "I don't suppose you're going to allow us to walk a way down *alone* so we may *talk* privately?"

"Not a chance... we will all converse together. Agree, Lady Henrietta?"

"Yes, my lord."

Wilhelmina put her hands on her hips and brazenly attacked, "Henrietta, how can you do this to me?"

A serene smile broke across the lady's face. "Because I gave my word."

"Well, I for one don't understand any of this. Lord Restin, as a special friend to Lord Barclay, I would presume you would take that into consideration."

Lucien, without thought, put his arm around Wilhelmina's waist and drew her to him, whispering, purposely wanting their chaperones to hear, "We'll get over this, my sweet."

Wilhelmina turned to him, her eyes blazing, "Not soon enough, my lord."

They all leisurely sat on the blankets, enjoying foods deliciously set out for them, including wine, lemonade and Lord Barclay's favorite tarts. Though they tried to make this outing congenial—it wasn't working.

Lord Barclay's arrogance being at an all-time high as Wilhelmina's temper flashed while Lord Restin sat grinning, and Lady Henrietta seemed to take it all in stride—composed.

When Lady Henrietta offered Lord Barclay the plate of tarts, he refused, claiming he didn't feel all that well.

Wilhelmina quickly reached for his hand. "Is there something I can do?"

Still grinning, Lord Restin said, "Oh I'm sure there is, Miss Thaylor."

At that moment, Lord Barclay moved with alacrity and headed for the bushes where he vomited his food. Lord Restin was right there as the Earl dragged a cloth over his mouth. "You are ill, Lu… I'm sorry. We'll get you back as quickly as possible."

By now, Wilhelmina was meeting them coming from the bushes and went to Lucien and put her arm around his waist to help lead him. He looked down at his charming wife-to-be and said, "I'm alright, my sweet, can't imagine what it is." And then he stumbled, and Lord Restin grabbed him with Wilhelmina, and they moved toward the carriage.

Lady Henrietta had their personal belongings together as Lucien faltered, and they almost didn't make it to the carriage.

A man on horseback was riding by and Wilhelmina called to him.

Lord Restin scolded, "What are you doing?"

Ignoring the Earl of Ventry, she waved to the strange man who rode closer. "Please Sir," Wilhelmina pleaded, "Is there a doctor nearby? We need one immediately?"

"Quite," the man spoke, "there's a surgery about twelve-fifteen minutes that way," he pointed in the opposite direction of from London.

"Thank you." Wilhelmina said to their driver, "You heard what the man said, go!"

"Wait," Lord Restin spouted, he was suspicious as his friend never had an attack in all the years he's known him, "I think we should return to Barclay Square."

"Don't be ridiculous," Wilhelmina blurted, "Lucien is ill, and we're going to find that doctor, now. Go, Hudson, or I'll have the Dowager Countess hang you."

Just mentioning the Dowager Countess Lady Julia, he needed no more prodding, and they were off.

Wilhelmina sat beside Lucien, holding his hand her with gloveless hands, not caring one iota for propriety. He sat with his head back and his eyes closed.

Lady Henrietta, seemingly only a trifle concerned, remained calm while Lord Restin sat with his eyes narrowed and his mouth set in a grim line. *Something is up, I just know it. But Miss Thaylor isn't aware… oh, Lu, I just know you're up to something.*

They reached the surgery hall, and with the help of an orderly, Lord Restin guided his friend into the unit where a doctor appeared and ordered they were to put the ailing man in a separate room until he could diagnose his illness. The only room available was small at the end of a long hall. If one gave it thought, the room appeared to be someone's private area.

Wilhelmina took over. "Whatever Lord Barclay has to have you are to take care of him… fully. What can I do for him?"

Lord Restin stood by and said, "Lu, open your eyes. I want you to look at me."

"What's wrong with you, Lord Restin?" Wilhelmina exclaimed. "Can't you see there's something radically ailing Lucien?"

"Oh, I don't know…" his tone teasing, "I think perhaps our friend isn't all that sick."

It was then the doctor, at Lucien's bedside shook his head. "His heartbeat is too slow. He shouldn't be moved until he's thoroughly rested. I can give him something to ease any pain he has, and it will also put him to sleep for a few hours."

"Do it," ordered Wilhelmina.

"I don't have the authority, Miss. Who can make that decision now?" Looking at Lord Restin, "Can you take responsibility for him?"

"I can," Wilhelmina's temper exploded. "We are to be married and I want what is best to be done for His Lordship, now!"

Lord Restin became concerned. *Maybe Lu is ill.* He studied his friend who hadn't moved an inch. His eyes remained closed; he lay wilted. He looked at the doctor, "Do as the lady says, but be sure no damage will come to him." Lord Restin asked the orderly to remove Lucien's boots and when he did, Lord Restin picked them up to leave the room taking Lucien's boots with him.

Wilhelmina noticed, but she was more concerned over Lucien's weak heart. "I'm staying right here with him."

Lord Restin nodded, "Of course. Lady Henrietta and I will gather our things from the carriage and be in one of the other rooms. Please call us if you need us." He still wasn't sure Lu wasn't trying to pull a fast one. *I do have his boots.*

An hour passed as Wilhelmina sat holding Lucien's hand, staring at his handsome face. Tears rolled down her cheeks. "I love you so much—won't you open your eyes and be well?"

She felt the slight pressure squeeze her fingers as Lucien's other hand reached and covered her mouth so she wouldn't call out and then he softly said, "Shh."

Her eyes lighted.

He motioned for her to come closer and whispered, "We are going to break away and be married while on the run… agree with me?"

She was so happy she was nodding her head like a rubber doll with her hair falling loose covering half his face.

Lucien, aflame over her exuberance, was euphoric that he would be spending the rest of his life with this daring, passionate woman.

She whispered in his ear, giving him the urge to pull her onto him when she said, "How soon?" and then kissed his ear with her tongue tracing its curve.

Lucien's private part did exactly what it wanted; it enlarged, and he had no control. "Stop that," he very softly threatened.

Wilhelmina smothered her giggles.

Then Lucien became sober. "We've got to get rid of Johnny and Lady Henrietta. I haven't figured that one out, but as soon as they're gone, so will we be."

"Let me work on them… I love you, Lucien."

Elation swept through him hearing his name on those rosy lips; this bold little lady was his… *forever.*

"Close your eyes… you're supposed to be sleeping for a few hours."

His heartbeat quickened. *She is so bossy.* He did as she ordered.

Unexpectedly, he heard her sobbing as she held his hand with her cheek in his palm. It was all that he could do not to allow it to affect him… *think of something horrid.*

Lord Restin hurried into the room with Lady Henrietta right behind him. "What happened, Miss Thaylor?"

Wilhelmina picked up her head, her eyes red from rubbing them with her tears. "He isn't getting any better, Lord Restin. His head is warm, and he hasn't moved." Tears plowed down her face, and her voice cracked. "I don't think this doctor knows what he's doing… maybe we should take him to London so he can be in his own bed." Choking back a sob, she said, "I'm sure Lady Julia will want him home."

Lord Restin became less sure of his original thoughts; maybe Lu did come in contact with something. He studied his friend and noticed he hadn't moved. "I'm going to talk with the doctor, and then I'll decide."

"Oh please, we've got to get him home where he belongs." She felt the pressure of Lucien's hand and returned it. "We can't take him in the carriage it isn't large enough to allow him to lie down."

The doctor entered and went to Lucien's side. "I see there is no change."

Lord Restin said, "I think we will make ready to take him home to London."

"If you do," the doctor measuring his words, said, "I will not be responsible for what may occur."

"What do you mean?" Wilhelmina cried out.

"Until it can be diagnosed what has caused him to spill his food and make this strong man weak, it would be wise to let him rest here for another day, at least."

Lady Henrietta gasped, "Lord Restin, I cannot stay. It's impossible."

"I know, Lady Henrietta."

Wilhelmina wasn't shy. "Why ever not? What can be more important than caring for the Earl? Surely, you can see that he must stay the night?"

"Willie," Lady Henrietta's voiced in her soft calm, "the Duke is expecting guests, and I must be there… I must. You know how generous he is, and I will not let him down."

Wilhelmina reached for her friend's hand and apologized. "Of course. I'll stay, and by morning, I'm sure the Earl will be ready to travel."

Lady Henrietta offered a half-smile. "Lord Restin will escort me home and can return with a larger conveyance to assist Lord Barclay." She turned to Lord Restin. "Is that agreeable?"

Lord Restin didn't like being maneuvered, but he had no choice. "I don't like leaving Miss Thaylor here; I'll leave one of the footmen and return as soon as possible." His tone hardened. "I am taking Lord Barclay's boots with me." He nodded to Miss Thaylor.

"Thank you, Lord Restin. But why take His Lordship's boots?"

"Because I want to be sure he's here when I return, and I prefer to be assured the Earl has cold feet. Take care, Miss Thaylor. I'll return as soon as possible."

Wilhelmina maintained a stricken façade. "That doesn't make sense."

He studied her demeanor with red puffy eyes and believed her concern with Lu's health. *I know you, Lu, but I have no choice. I must escort Miss Henrietta home, or the Duke will call me out. This is your doing... I just know it. But you'll have to go barefoot and without transportation.* "I asked the doctor, and he said the town is too small to have mail coach service." Lord Restin empathized. "I'll be back, and we'll take Lu home today."

Lucien didn't move, and Wilhelmina wisely kept up the deception. The footman was outside the door as ordered by Lord Restin. "Please hurry as fast as you can," Wilhelmina pleaded.

Thirty minutes passed, and Wilhelmina stood and purposely yawned for the footman to notice. "You must be tired," she spoke quietly to the footman. "What is your name?"

"Shipply, my lady."

She walked out into the hall, looking back at Lucien's still form. "The Earl is sleeping, Shipply. Why don't you see if you can find yourself something to eat?" She reached into her reticule and offered him a coin.

Shipply's eyes stared at her open hand at the pound as no one had ever offered him money to feed himself. "I don't know... His Lordship said I was to stay and guard you and the Earl."

Wilhelmina smiled, but her insides were in turmoil as she knew she was going to get the young man in trouble. "Still... As you can see," she said, her voice gentle, "the Earl is in safe hands here, and so am I. There must be an eatery in the village, so you can buy a pie or something you'd like. Go," she nudged with her head as a curl loosened, "take rest and have a supper."

Excited and having no thought that he was being blindsided, he accepted the coin, bowed with a smile and was off.

Lucien sat up, grinning. "You're a wise one. Remind me to say thank you later." He whistled and the doctor and orderly showed.

Wilhelmina staggered. She thought they'd been caught, but Lucien was all business. "Is everything as I have left it? No one knows?"

They both nodded, and one said, "We did it. But you better go before Doctor Bloster returns. We all have to get out of here."

Lucien eyed Wilhelmina, who was standing there with her mouth open. "These two young chaps and I have an agreement." Lucien reached into his jacket and gave each a sovereign. They led them out a back door that took them to the stable, and there were Zephr and Zairian waiting. "That's all," Lucien said, and they took off.

Wilhelmina threw herself at Lucien and he grabbed her too and they twirled, laughing. "You set this up," giving him a quick kiss, "How?"

"My sweet, surely you didn't think I'd let Johnny get the best of me or Grandy get the best of us? By the way, the man on the horse that gave directions did his part well, too."

"But how did you know I'd insist?"

"Because, my Mina, you are bold and bossy, and you have heart."

"Yes, but what if I…?"

He interrupted her, "Then the ten pounds I paid him would have caused him to become nosey and insist I needed a doctor. Come," he said leading her to an empty stall.

"I'm all yours, my lordship."

Lucien couldn't help being ecstatic to have this lovely lady become an important part in his life; this hot-tempered, bold and sweet, thoughtful young lady. "Without question, you are and always will be. Come and see what I have for you."

When Wilhelmina walked out of the stall she was dressed in superfine navy breeches with a white silk shirt, a silver vest, and matching navy coat. Her boots were as shiny as the ones Lucien was wearing. He also had a change of clothes; his were black breeches, white shirt, silver vest with dark gray jacket. He stood admiring Wilhelmina, his eyes telling her all she needed to know. "I haven't anything to hide my hair," and she stepped toward him as he gently put his closed fist under her chin and feathered a kiss on her rosy lips—she wanted more, but he pulled away laughing, "Oh, no," he said, handing her a well-formed navy cap to stuff her red curls. "My dear Miss Thaylor, if I do what I wish more than anything at his moment to take you in my arms… I know I will not stop, and we must be away," he empathized again, "we must. Johnny is no fool." One last feathered kiss across her rosy lips, he gave her the cap, cross stitched with a bill to match her coat. "Put that on and let's be on our way."

"Where are we going?"

He chuckled, "Now, you ask… do you care?"

"No, my lord, as long as it's with you and we don't head toward London."

"You're in luck, as we're going in the opposite direction, and when we get to Dropshire's little church, we will be married. Are you willing to marry me now or wait and have a proper aristocracy wedding? It's up to you." Lucien held his breath as uncertain what her answer may be.

Her hands on her hips, her green eyes warm and gleaming, she scolded, "You have the temerity to even think to ask… we can have a big wedding later if we must."

Lucien, with his big gray eyes darkening, unable to hide his grin after being chastised, "That's my girl."

"Yes, yes, yes." She hurled out yeses at him and hurried to ride Zephr, but Lucien stopped her.

"Oh no, you don't. You, my lady, will ride Zairian."

Smirking, said, "Just thought I'd give it a go."

Laughing, they both sneaked out the back way. She looked over at him and, without a word, gave Zairian his head, and side by side, they were off to be married.

Two hours later, they stopped in a small churchyard. Before Lucien could help Wilhelmina down, she was off Zairian's saddle and meeting him halfway. "I love riding; especially with you beside me."

"Keep that thought." Lucien draped a navy cape over her shoulders, covering her fully from top to bottom. He lifted her cap, and her curls fell every which way. She reached to straighten them, but he held her hand. "Don't, please… they're lovely."

So filled with emotion from his thoughtfulness in having her dressed in comfort and not minding her riding astride and then saying he thought her messy hair was lovely, she thought she ought to pinch herself for she must be dreaming. She took a deep breath. "Lord Barclay," her heart thudded as her knees weakened and her voice was clogged with emotion, "I must tell you I think you are wonderful," and then teasing to relieve the pressure within her, she added, "but at our first meeting, I didn't think so."

His laughter carried out into the cool invigorating air, as he teased back, "I know you didn't like me, and I couldn't figure out why… I am so amiable."

Wilhelmina was looking up at him with love visible in her eyes—before she could retort, the reverend appeared, carrying a black book; its cover ragged around the edges from long use, matching the cloak he was wearing. "May I help you?"

"Yes, Reverend," Lord Barclay's tone was authoritative; "this lady and I wish to marry."

"I see, however…"

"There is no worry, Reverend, I have the license required." Lucien's aristocratic tone brooking no refusal as he continued, "If you would bring two witnesses, we may begin."

And so, in the little country church in Dropshire, Lucien William Barclay and Wilhelmina Katherine Thaylor were wed.

Upon leaving, the Earl tucked a ten-pound note in each witness's hand and a sovereign for the reverend.

The Earl and his countess were on their way, Zephr and Zairian traveling at a good gallop when Wilhelmina called over to her husband, "There's a stream up there; let's stop."

So bossy… I'll just have to get used to it. "Agree and I will properly kiss my bride… my wife."

"That is my exact thinking. More so that I may kiss my husband."

His glory knew no bounds. He pulled back. Both were breathless, and holding her in his arms, their body heat matched, and it was difficult to think of separating.

Lucien's voice deep and resonant, he said, "Galesford, one of my estates, is less than two hours from here." His mouth grazed her ear lobe sending shivers over her entire being, "I've sent word to expect us. We will begin our lives with privacy and with no interruptions," his voice husky, "To love and learn about each other from head to toe." They stared into each other's eyes— hers glowing as emeralds, and his like a bright silver moon. "You're special, my countess, and know that you will always have my love and respect."

"Lucien, I do love you so." She made an outrageous bow, "My lord, and I mean that *my lord*, let us not waste any more of this day." She looked at him with love, knowing the feel of his arms holding her and his body meshing with hers. "I am indeed fortunate. My father would be happy for me."

"Don't ever question my love," he nipped her ear lobe, "and after I get you in bed, you'll know how rock-solid," he chuckled, "I am about loving you… forever."

The Earl's countess couldn't hold back offering him her warmest smile, and whispered, "To think the first time we met… who knew?"

He planted a swift kiss on her lips and lifted her up on Zairian and quickly mounted Zephr, and they were off to Galesford. *I hope Johnny hasn't a memory of Galesford being so near.*

Reaching Galesford, his new countess had no idea of the surprise awaiting her.

Now, she sat bathed before a warm crackling fire, well-fed and suddenly became shy as she looked over at the virulent man, her husband, and couldn't look away. *We are truly married!*

Lucien, robed, sat across from his wife, taking in her loveliness and also her unexpected shyness. *Her bold aggressive manner is now apprehensive.* He wanted her so but this being their wedding night, he wanted it to be memorable with tenderness as well as joy.

Wilhelmina seemed to be delaying their bedding. She reached for her wine, sipped and said, "You really planned our escape well, my lord. You not only have Crooks here, but he's also sneaked Tess from Marlowe House with some of my clothes."

Lucien swallowed some wine. *I want to lift her from that chair and take every bit of that silk gown off of her, but she's stalling. I'll soon know why.*

Wilhelmina gripped the stem of her glass. *Up until now, I thought I'd know what to do and not think if it would please Lucien, but now what happens if I disappoint him, and we're married and he's stuck with me? I wish I knew what to do… he seems to like my kisses as I do his. Should I just be honest and tell him? I don't know.*

"I wonder what has made my countess turn silent." Lucien's tone was a soft caress. "You aren't having second thoughts about having married, are you?"

Restlessly, unconsciously, a blush appeared, almost matching her mahogany well brushed hair, the firelight adding to its magnificence adding to her rosy complexion. "No, no, Lucien, it's just…" her fingers working tightly together, yet her voice soft and sensuous, she confessed, "I love your kisses, and when we arrived here at Galesford, you had a bath set for me with Tess helping me with this lovely, filmy gown, and then we kissed and I thought everything was well, but then you insisted we must eat and we're here in your bedroom and then Crooks removed our trays, but…" She murmured while an uncontrolled blush, seemingly embarrassing, added to her shakiness. "You don't seem to want me… you haven't even tried to kiss me again or even touched me a little, and you know how I love being in your arms.…"

Before she could finish saying another word, Lucien was out of his chair and taking Wilhelmina into his arms. "My little innocent, I didn't want to jump on you the minute I had you alone." She felt the heat of his body course into hers, as his voice turned deep. He took a breath as he pressured her in his arms, bringing her closer until their bodies merged. "I want you so very much. I've been struggling to hold back." He began dropping kisses over and over—everywhere; her lips, her neck, her ears, her eyes, her cheeks, her chin, while his hands were removing the flimsy gown, letting it slide silently to the floor. The Earl picked up his bride and, in a few steps, gently laid her on his bed, eyeing her with obvious desire while her hands were tightening at his nape refusing to let him go. She was smiling; her leafy green eyes were misty. *Let me do this right for him. I so want to make Lucien happy.*

Lucien believed at that very moment he could walk on water—*she is mine.* "If you release me, my sweet," his body electrified, "I'd like to join you on our bed."

She didn't, instead lifted her head to kiss his mouth, forcing her tongue seeking entrance.

I've died, and this is heaven. It was no problem for the Earl to allow his countess take from him whatever pleased her. Still wearing his robe, and she with nothing on, pressured him with kisses to lay with her as they both justifiably began smothering each other with kisses as Lucien's hands caressed her body. By now, Wilhelmina had released her hold and was touching his face as though it was glass, her fingers lightly followed every contour and then kissed every spot she had touched. Her tongue traced the scar above his eye. Her voice sultry, she asked, "What happened?"

He chuckled through kisses, mumbling, "Johnny… playing." His mouth met hers, and their tongues touched, igniting more sparks.

She in turn pushed the front of his robe aside and her fingers moving until they found his nipple and she gentled two fingers, stroking it and heard him gasp. "Am I hurting you?"

Lucien wanted to shout, *don't stop!* Instead, he said to his innocent bride on their wedding night, "You set me afire with your touch, my love. You have no idea." He pulled away to remove his robe and purposely stood beside the bed, wanting his bride to see him, and to know that the part of him that had risen and hardened was because of his need for her.

Wilhelmina couldn't help but blush, but there wasn't an iota of fear, her voice throaty and just a shade shaky. "Is that the part of you that is forcing hot currents to coarse through me and making my insides twist about with no control and causing me to have a mysterious tightening… something like knots that I've been carrying around with me," she sighed, "that won't go away and especially intensify when you hold me, and we kiss?" She actually grinned, "Truthfully, my lord, it is all very disconcerting."

Lucien actually giggled, "It does all that?" Lucien lay down on his side, pulling her against his body. "It's the part that I hope pleases you and does away with all those knots." He nipped her ear and said, his tone raspy, "I'm doing all that I can not to hurry our first time together. I want it to be perfect just as you are. You are *mine, my* countess."

"I definitely am, my lord." Pleased, she fluttered a kiss on his chest. "You are very warm. I like it."

He laughed and then began kissing her, and he didn't stop this time. When his lips left her lips and reached for the spot below her ear, feeling its beat, Wilhelmina couldn't help but feel anxious. *But this time, there are no clothes between us,* and she danced her fingers down his bare back—it excited her, feeling his muscles seemed to bounce, but when Lucien moved down and put his mouth on her breast, she erupted with unexpected bliss. "Oh, my," she breathed her words in wonder as he continued on to the other breast, and his palm lay upon the other, gently kneading it as her hands automatically touched each side of his head wanting to hold him to her. *I never knew…*

She discovered her husband's hands were magic as well as his mouth and finally they became one—joined as nature planned, but to them, it was magical. All that mattered was being together as husband and wife.

"Never," breathing into her husband's ear, "did I have any idea being married is like this." Her voice took on a fiery ecstasy. "Our joining… our bodies make us into one. Oh, Lucien, thank you for our beautiful wedding."

The Earl of Grenmoor had feelings he had never contemplated… this bold, beautifully wise seductress had turned him into a giant of a man, and he vowed silently to never let her down. He cleared his throat, snugly holding his wife, and said, "Our wedding day is beautiful, because of the way we feel for each other this glorious day. It will stay with us forever." He couldn't help but think how all other sexual encounters were just fulfilling a man's need. *This* overwhelming sense of right and want and need was because of his totally pure feelings for his wife. He was amazed as well as astounded about it being possible. He held his wife to him; their bodies damp, the air seemed cool, and Lucien pulled the cover over them as Wilhelmina clearly pasted herself to her husband's side, leaning on her elbow to look at the man she loved. "My lord, if this is ravishment, I heartily approve." She raised her head and feathered a kiss at the corner of his mouth, "You've made me feel as though I could conquer whatever trial is set before me." Then she giggled, "because we're going to need it when we meet up with our grandmothers." She nipped his ear and feathered it with a kiss. "How wonderful you are. I promise you, from this minute on, I could possibly be your slave if you will promise to do to me what is the most exhilarating… invigorating… amorous experience in my life— promise me, it will be repeated again and again." Then her tongue traced his lips, and she nipped the bottom lip as Lucien had done to her and whispered, "That is possible, isn't it?"

Lucien William Barclay, Earl of Grenmoor, known to be stoic, heartless and often mundane, burst with joyful laughter swinging his countess on top of his body, plying her with kisses and said, "Oh, yes, and there is so much more to come. I love you, *wife*. Thank you for marrying me, and after this secluded honeymoon of ours ends, I'm going to allow Grandy and Lady Edith to plan the grandest wedding reception London has ever known. I want everyone to meet my beautiful countess and observe how positively well-suited we are together."

Wanting to tease her husband, she said, "Admit it, my lord, you didn't like me and wished to see gone from Seahurst." She actually bit his bottom lip, "And here, we are delightfully loving each other and yet…"

His voice husky yet soft as his eyes illuminated a look of amusement, "Go on… something's on your mind. Tell me—remember no secrets between us." And then he claimed her lips by softly brushing his over hers again and again.

"Lucien, are you trying to distract me? Because you are, but I will still have something special to ask for."

"Tell me. If it's possible, I'll make it happen. Anything your heart desires, it's yours." He couldn't imagine what suddenly made her shy. This wasn't his Mina.

"If you really mean that." It was the first time he heard her voice take on a tremulous tone as her eyes caught his and held.

Jewels. Come to think of it she has never displayed wearing any but that rose brooch. Oh, my love, I'll smoother you in jewels.

His countess tried clearing her throat and softly said, "I want to waltz with you again."

Lucien was astounded. His wife asked not for jewels or travel or balls, but the memory of their first meeting. The genuineness of her words reached into his being as no one ever had. "I'll hire us our own orchestra and we'll waltz, my love, for as long as you wish. I never told you or anyone, but our first waltz never left my mind. You were splendid." Then, purposely flaunting his arrogance, he teased, "You do know how to waltz, do you not?"

"I… I think so."

End